TWICE THE GUNS, TWICE THE GRIT— TWO RIP-ROARING WESTERNS FOR ONE LOW PRICE!

RIM OF THE RANGE

"You're a fool, Leavitt," Johnny said. "And I'm going to kill you."

Johnny sidestepped, then evaded a murderous twisting kick. He had never seen so sharp-toothed a spur, and there was blood on the wheel.

The raking kick came close. Before Johnny could recover, Leavitt threw him to the ground and came down on top of him. The shock of the fall almost knocked the breath from Johnny's body. But the memory of Myra and the appeal she had made gave him strength. If he failed, he wouldn't be the only one to die....

THUNDER TO THE WEST

Gordon jabbed the muzzle of his gun into the ribs of Lomax, countering the foreman's move for his own gun.

"If anybody gets roughed up, Lomax, you top the list!" he warned.

Everyone in the restaurant was on his feet, half the men with hands on guns. Not until that moment had Gordon taken account of the fact all of them were armed.

"Make your choice, Lomax. Should I have to pull the trigger, it would mean your death!"

RIM OF THE RANGE/
THUNDER TO THE WEST
AL CODY

LEISURE BOOKS NEW YORK CITY

For Ruby and Gordon Montgomery
In memory of many kindnesses

A LEISURE BOOK®

June 1993

Published by

Dorchester Publishing Co., Inc.
276 Fifth Avenue
New York, NY 10001

The name ''Leisure Books'' and the stylized ''L'' with design are trademarks of Dorchester Publishing Co., Inc.

Printed in the United States of America.

RIM OF THE RANGE

1.

Rain swept in gusts out of a sagebrush-tinted sky, driven by a prankish wind. John Malcolm's long jaws were coldly bedewed, his lean frame shivering, despite his slicker. May was a spring month, but in Wyoming it could be rawly dank. In a larger sense, the weather was like that part of the country—beguiling, full of promise. But somehow the promise was never quite fulfilled.

For the past ten days, the crew of Wagon Wheel had been busy with roundup. During all that period the clouds had lowered, promising rain.

Rainfall had been insufficient every year since Malcolm had come to that range a decade before. He had grown from scraggly youth to lean-fleshed manhood, but the land's promise remained unfulfilled. Instead of springing rich and full-bodied, the grass curled thin and sparse, and the rains which might have made the difference between leanness and prosperity stopped short at the Big Horn, a day's ride to the west.

If additional proof was needed, the roundup had furnished it. Howard Denning, turning as grizzled as summer grass, was a cattleman by instinct as well as by training; with all the range which was at his disposal, the Wagon Wheel should have been rolling as on a downhill grade. Instead, it was a hard scrabble, and its groanings and squealings could almost be heard. The calf crop of the ranch was always short, the winter loss heavier than could be borne. It was demanding country, giving little in return. It was necessary to run at full speed to make sure merely of standing still; even with prodigious effort, there was always danger of losing ground.

After ten rainy days, the top soil was scarcely wet enough to look muddy. It was drizzle, Oregon mist; never a soaker. And this year, the lack of good spring rains could spell the difference between the Wheel keeping turning and being broken and discarded.

Smoke lifted in a discouraged twist from the chimney of the cook house, whipped back upon itself by the blustering wind. He was late for the first under-cover meal in nearly two weeks. As Malcolm stabled his horse, the disconsolate lowing of the herd drifted from the corrals. On Denning's order, they had held all the gather—calves, cows, yearlings, prime beef. The herd was behind bars, instead of being permitted to race back to the range, as was customary, once the branding was finished. Their voices mourned in never-ending protest.

Denning had not explained the order, even to his foreman. He had always made his own decisions and kept his own counsel. Johnny pushed open the door, shaking his sliker. The crew were at the table, most of them looking as rough as a steer in March. Three or four who had found the opportunity to shave looked out of place. The savory odors of food wafted from the stove. Bowls of stew were along the big table, while a pudding cooled on the stove's high oven.

The men looked up at the foreman's approach and went on eating. Howard Denning nodded. It struck Johnny anew how grizzled he had become, the rawhiding effect of a year of strain. Denning was big, troubled by an old injury to his left leg which gave a list to his walk. Once in the saddle, he was as good as ever, but getting on and off a horse was a painful chore. For the past year, he'd done less and less riding, leaving the responsibility in Johnny's hands.

Johnny slid into his own place, accepted the bowl of stew which Cy Robbins shoved toward him, helped himself from a heaped platter of biscuits, and downed a scalding cup of coffee. He could feel its bite all the way down. It helped dispel the numbness, and he ate silently, catching up with the others. Hungry men had no time for talk. Only when Dinty Toole, his red face matching his stubble of beard, started to scrape back from the table did Denning's heavy bass check him.

"I'd like for everybody to stay," he requested. "I've a word for the ears of every man."

Dinty looked surprised, a quick glint coming and going in his eyes. Johnny had seen the same sort of look in the eyes of a trapped coyote, watching a rifle muzzle center on it. It lasted only an instant; then Dinty reached for another biscuit.

Howard Denning placed both hands on the table, shoving his bulk partially back but not rising. This was the second time in ten years that he'd made any general announcement to the whole crew. The last previous occasion had been seven years before, when he'd informed them that twenty-year-old Johnny Malcolm was their new foreman.

"I've something to say that you may not like," Denning began, and the muscles of his face knotted. "And the devil of it is, I don't much like it myself. But hear me out, and afterward each of you can make up your minds as to what you wish to do. Whatever you decide, there should be no hard feelings."

They eyed him expectantly, intrigued. His face again twisted in what might have been a rueful smile. Then, blunt as always, he gave it to them without preamble.

"I'm going into the sheep business."

They stared, doubting the evidence of their ears, looking at one another and back at him. Had he suggested that he'd found a trail to purgatory, with good grass somewhere along the way, and wanted them to take the herd there, they would have accepted the statement and the request without question. But this was beyond belief.

"You heard me right," Denning grunted. "I'm quitting cattle and going into the business of raising sheep. I know how you feel," he went on. "So do I. I've been born and raised a cattleman, and cattlemen hate sheep and sheepmen. I know all the arguments: the stink of sheep, their eternal bleating that can drive a man crazy, the way they eat grass into the roots and destroy a range, the fact that cattle won't graze where sheep have run. If anyone had suggested to me, even half a year ago, that I'd ever turn sheepman myself, I'd have called him crazy—and probably worse.

"But lately I've been doing a lot of thinking, and I've made up my mind that hanging onto pride and cattle and going deeper broke each year is the way of a fool, especially when there's a good chance that with sheep I can make the sort of money I've got to have. So I'm choosing sheep."

He looked about, half-challengingly, half-hopefully. The first shock vanished from most faces, leaving only a careful blankness. Johnny swallowed his last spoonful of pudding, realizing that though it was his favorite, he hadn't tasted the other mouthfuls. He was beginning to understand. Money. It sounded crass and material- istic, but Howard had an excellent reason for wanting to make money.

A year before, Ma Denning had been hurt when a team had run away, spilling Ma onto the icy ground. At first, turning a grimace into a grin as they lifted her, she'd kidded them if not herself. Her injury hadn't seemed to amount to much. They'd gotten her to town and the doctor, making her as comfortable as possible, padding the wagon box with hay and blankets. Everyone, including the doctor, had figured that she'd be back in her own kitchen within a matter of ten days or two weeks, as good as ever.

Instead, six weeks later, she had made the hundred-mile journey to the railroad, thence to St. Paul and a bevy of specialists. She had written back that they clustered around her like chicks around an old hen. Something was wrong, a twist and a hidden injury.

Now, a year later, Ma was still in St. Paul, still undergoing treatment and operations, with the result still in doubt.

The one thing about which there was no doubt was the cost. The next operation which was to be tried would be very costly. Howard Denning had told the doctors to go ahead, but Johnny had wondered privately where the money was coming from. This time, Howard couldn't afford to go to St. Paul. He'd made the trip twice. He went on, his voice flat.

"I made the same mistake, coming in here, a lot of others have—I supposed this was cattle country. It's not. What do we have? Broken range, gullies and a few small hills. A lot of brush and sagebrush, a scattering of scrub trees. The hills to the west of us are too far away to do us any good as winter shelter. The rains stop at those same hills. Here they keep tantalizing us with the promise of plenty of rain, but what do we get? In ten days of riding, we've been damp all the while but never once wet!"

That was true. This was the rim of good rangeland.

"With plenty of range, I figured to make it, but other factors are against cattle. The grass grows scant and thin, so that the cows are never quite in condition. The calf crop is always short, and those who live out the summer are never in good shape to stand the winter. Our losses run too high. Our beef, when we market it, is far from prime—it's a long drive to the railroad, and shrinkage all the way to Chicago. In short, it's a losing game, because this is not cattle country.

"With sheep, it should be a different story. They can graze and grow fat where cattle will all but starve. They spend the nights in corrals, because of coyotes and wolves, and those corrals can be roofed, as they often are for sheep. So in the cold of winter sheep lie snug. And when a crop of wool is harvested, there's no shrinkage in a long drive to market.

"So I figure this is sheep range, and I am driving every last head of stock to the railroad, shipping east to Chicago, and selling. Most of the money will pay for nine thousand head of sheep, for which I have already more or less contracted. They will be shipped back by the railroad, then driven here. Since there is a bridge across the Termagent, it should work fine."

The Termagent was a tributary of the Big Horn River, lying a third of the way to the railroad, athwart their path. In bygone years its high banks and swift waters had posed an ugly problem, only partially solved by a ferry. Now it had been bridged.

Howard's glance roved questioningly. There was no comment, and he went on.

"I may lose my shirt, but it's too ragged to matter much. Of course, my neighbors will hate me for bringing sheep to this range. There will be trouble. But it is my land, and I have made up my mind. If you prefer not to work for a sheepman, there will be no hard feelings on my part. If some of you decide to stay, I'll like that. Think it over and let me know."

2.

This time, Denning shoved clear back from the table, balancing himself heavily as he stood up. His glance fixed on Malcolm, as did the others' eyes. He knew, as did Johnny, that most if not all of the crew would follow his lead.

That was not entirely because he was the foreman, the man from whom they were accustomed to take orders. They respected the boss, and they loved Ma Denning and wished her well. But Howard Denning was a hard man, taciturn and aloof, though a good employer. It was to the foreman that they instinctively turned. He'd been Johnny to everyone before becoming foreman, and while they still called him that, it was with respect.

He had an easy smile and a competence which seemed equally unforced. He had been a natural choice for foreman, even though most of the crew had been his seniors. Not only did he know cattle and how to handle them, but he possessed qualities of leadership. In war he would have been a general. Where he led, others followed unquestioningly, even gladly.

He drew a deep breath and gave a partial answer.

"What you say makes sense, Howard. One thing sure: this ain't cattle country. I hadn't considered the other, but it might be good range for sheep. As you say, that's a gamble. As for the other part—well, this is sort of sudden. I'll want to think it over before deciding."

"That's what I want you to do, all of you," Denning agreed. "I wouldn't want anyone to stay who didn't feel right about it. On the other hand—" He drew a deep breath and made a surprising confession. "I reckon Ma would like it better, when she gets home, to find the boys she knows still underfoot."

Johnny doubted if that was what he had started to say, but it was hard for Howard to express himself, particularly on emotional or personal matters. In any case, he had hit the right note. They'd do more for Ma than for anyone else on earth. And that was as it should be.

On the other hand, there was a deep, virtually unbridgeable gulf between sheepmen and cattlemen. Cowboys, raised in the tradition, found even the suggestion of sheep shocking. This had been cattle country, with no sheep anywhere. Whoever broke the unwritten law and was the first to deviate from the standard, bringing sheep to the range, would find himself ostracized, hated, bitterly opposed by former friends and neighbors.

Few, if any, could be expected to understand. Even if they did, they probably would not accept or forgive. If Denning's crew stuck with him, they could count on suffering from the same hatred, which would almost certainly erupt into violence. Sheep would never be permitted on the range without a fight.

"I think maybe a few head of cows are still ranging back toward Lampases Spring," Johnny observed. "I've been aiming to ride and have a look."

"Sure," Denning agreed understandingly. Johnny could just as well have sent a man, but he wanted time to think.

Selecting a fresh horse, Johnny saddled it, then made

a small pack, since he might well be gone overnight. There was still a tantalizing beat of rain in his face as he headed west by north. The lowering clouds looked as though they might spill a deluge at any moment, but they had had that look for weeks.

He pondered as he rode, not at all certain what his decision would be. Had it not been for Ma Denning, there would have been no question. As a cowboy, fore-man for a big outfit, thereby virtually on a footing with the cattlemen, he would have remained loyal to the tra-dition, riding to hunt a new job, doing so without qualms. Howard Denning was a tough man, giving few favors and asking less. He'd make out.

But Ma was different. She had been Ma to every one of them. And now she was flat on her back, among strangers, with less than a fifty-fifty chance that she'd ever walk again, or even return to the land she loved so well.

Johnny pushed steadily but without hurry. He saw no fresh sign of the cattle he'd believed might be hiding off that way.

He saw something else which caused him to wonder: a wheel trace, showing at intervals where conditions were right, lost again where the ground had been hard or the grass had grown well.

That was odd. As foreman, he knew pretty well what occurred on Wagon Wheel range, as well as in the surrounding country. But he, like others of the crew, didn't venture that far back very often, and he'd had no word from anyone of such a wagon. Certainly it didn't belong to the ranch. And who else would come there with a wagon, or why?

Probably it wasn't important, but he was intrigued.

In late afternoon the clouds broke, allowing the sun to pour through in brief glory. This was his first glimpse of the sun in three days, and welcome.

It was as the sun came out that he saw the other track—this the hoofprints of a shod horse, much fresher than the wagon wheel trace. The hoofmark was only days old, and something about it intrigued him. It might have been made by one of his own crew on round-up, but he doubted that. Just over a low hill he found it again, and his hunch was confirmed.

Here the rider had halted, dismounting to rest and look about, to build and smoke a quirly. Part of the sodden remains of the cigarette attested to that. His horse had cropped the grass, making a small, hungry circle, as though held by an impatient rein and forced to eat around the bit.

There was something else. The ground had been fairly soft from the rain, but on that part of the knoll it was normally quite solid, and where the man had stood, little grass ever grew. The marks of high heels were deep, clearly imprinted, as though he had moved impatiently.

There was nothing unusual about that. Cowboys all wore high-heeled boots. But few cowboys wore boots as distinctive as these. In three separate imprints, Johnny found the insignia which subsequent rain had not quite dissolved. A sign like a brand—which was, in fact, a brand. The Axe.

Barney Vascom's Broken Axe was the other big outfit in that part of the country. A proud, arrogant man, Barney Vascom carried his personal foibles to the point of special footwear for himself and his relatives. His boots, and the boots of his son, his nephew and his daughter were hand-made. And in the bottom of the high heels was a replica of the brand of his outfit, the broken shaft of the axe handle, with the axe head attached.

One of those four had ridden there only a few days before on Wagon Wheel range. It was not a woman's boot, so it must have been one of the three men.

There was another oddity. Despite the shoe being hand-made, the brand being cut deep into the heel, the boot was beginning to be run down at heel and toe.

The sign was days old; certainly there was no reason for apprehension, but he looked about sharply before riding on. Some things were sure in an uncertain world. And the surest was that Barney Vascom and the Broken Axe would most violently oppose Howard Denning bringing sheep to the range.

There had always been bad blood between the two outfits, and though a sort of truce had existed for some time, the mere mention of sheep would be enough to break it. But the news of Denning's intention was still a secret from all save his own crew.

Johnny had found no sign of the cattle he sought, nor was he likely to now. There was a small spring bubbling from under a mossy boulder at the edge of a clump of cottonwoods. This was Lampases Spring, the only one which did not go dry by midsummer. Johnny unsaddled, picketed his horse and built a small fire, finding dry wood without much difficulty, further proof of how scanty the rain had been.

He delved among his provisions, bringing out some cold biscuits, preparing to fry bacon and boil coffee. He was tired from the long strain of roundup, looking forward to relaxing and a long lazy evening. With that in mind he'd brought along a special treat: a can of condensed milk for his coffee—ninety-nine times in a hundred he drank it black—and cans of tomatoes. He had hoped for peaches, but the cook had grumpily informed him that none were in the larder.

The sun was gone now, the last of its glory painting the west. The coffee started to boil over. He leaned, reaching quickly to grab and move it back, and the movement saved his life. A bullet tore a small hole in the near side of the coffeepot, a gaping tear in the far side as it exploded through the liquid, scattering it over the blaze. The shock almost jerked the pot from his hand, and an instant later, as he threw himself flat, he heard the jarring note of a rifle from some distance off at one side.

3.

Johnny's action, in jerking back and flattening himself was instinctive. He lay without moving. The spilled coffee had put out the fire, leaving sudden darkness where before had been a revealing patch of light.

The bullet would certainly have buried itself near his heart but for his sudden movement. Now his action, as though he had jerked at the impact of a bullet and fallen, might deceive the rifleman into believing that his aim had been good. It was a hunch worth playing.

The shot had come from a considerable distance. There was nothing to see. Johnny reached for his revolver, then waited, ears alert, since eyes were of scant use.

Nothing happened. Either the gunman was satisfied

that his shot had accomplished the desired result, or else he was too canny to investigate and perhaps stop a bullet in turn. When it became reasonably certain that no one was coming, Johnny quietly gathered up his duffel and rode a mile to the side before camping again. He did not risk another fire.

The clouds thickened again, and there were more spatters of rain. Sometime after midnight the sky cleared. He awoke to bright sunshine and a sharp chill, with frost everywhere.

He was reasonably certain that the killer would not have remained close at hand. A man who shot in such fashion, without warning, then exhibited such caution, would be discreet enough to remove well away during the hours of darkness.

Nonetheless, Johnny chose a likely spot, where it was possible to watch on all sides, before cooking breakfast. He opened a tin of tomatoes, eating them, then used the can to boil coffee in. He did not bother with the frills which he had originally planned. Afterward, he rode to where he estimated the shot might have come from, and the slight rain was his ally. He found the tracks of the same horse which he had encountered earlier. Nearby, the gunman had stretched in the grass and taken careful aim; only the sudden boiling over of the coffee had spoiled the shot. A heel print, with the blurred brand of the Axe, was a final confirmation.

The killer might still be prowling, with no compunctions against further attacks from ambush. The word concerning sheep had not yet been spread abroad, so it must be something else which had caused one of the members of the Vascom clan to have a try at murder. It might have been no more than long-smoldering animosity and a perfect opportunity. But it would bear looking into.

The sun was beginning to wipe off the frost, but enough remained to show that no horseman had ridden thereabouts since before dawn. Half a mile farther on, Johnny found another trace of the wagon, the sign as old as before. Then, among a small jumble of gullies and low hills, he came upon the wagon itself.

It was an ancient vehicle, its paint long since peeled—almost as though it had been retrieved from the discard. It was almost hidden behind a clump of brush. A stone's throw from it was a cabin, almost equally weathered, so well concealed by its surroundings that Johnny had never suspected its existence. It must have stood deserted and forgotten for many years.

He rode cautiously nearer, maintaining a sharp lookout. A magpie squawked from a tree and flapped away at his approach, and that seemed a fair indication that no one else was lurking. Nonetheless, remembering the closeness of that rifle bullet, the venom behind it, he left his horse among trees and brush and proceeded on foot.

He could see no fresh sign since the rain, but there was older evidence of occupancy. Someone had gone in and out of the door several times. There was the beginning of a path, leading to a spring at the edge of the gulch. Slop water had been thrown out from the door, enough to leave its own sign.

A rusty length of stovepipe protruded from the roof. He was about to hail when a noise startled him—the last sound he had ever expected to hear, under such conditions or in such a place.

It was the hungry, fretful wailing of a baby.

The complaint was not loud. It was as though the child were too weak or tired to put much effort even into crying, a despairing, lonely plaint.

Johnny listened, incredulous, but there could be no mistake. The wail came from inside the house. There was no other sound. He went to the door, hesitated briefly and knocked.

The wailing stopped. There was no answer. Half-consciously he noted that the door was still solid and substantial. It dragged a little as he pushed, but it had recently been rehung on rusty iron hinges, replacing leather ones, the remnants of which still showed.

Even with such a warning he was not prepared for what he saw. The old shack had been erected long years before and had apparently stood abandoned for most of them. It had never amounted to much, nor had its furnishings.

There was an ancient rickety table, made of boards, perched on uncertain legs. A couple of bunks were on one wall. There was an old stool, a box nailed up to serve as a cupboard, a combined cooking and heating stove. It stood in a corner, one side propped up with a stone, barely usable.

There was one extra piece of furniture. It was a small trunk, brass-bound, the lid standing open. Inside, upon a mattress of blankets, covered by others, lay the baby.

A woman was in the lower bunk, looking at him with great, hopefully expectant eyes. Her face looked doubly pale in contrast with the rich, almost scarlet red of her hair, now in disarry about her head.

Johnny crossed the room, staring down with a sense of shock. It was half a year since he'd seen the girl, perhaps more. He remembered her as a bright-eyed, laughing person, shy, with a wild, strange beauty, enhanced by the richness of her hair, a witchery which lurked in her eyes. It was Myra, the daughter of Old Man M'Ginnis, who had a small spread of his own just out of town. At least he'd had it until a short time ago, when he'd died—some said of a broken heart.

That was hard to believe of so hard-shelled a man, but it might be true. He'd been harsh and overly protective of his daughter, perhaps because he loved her but hardly knew how to care for a girl-child. Nearly a year before, she had run away to town and had taken a job in the Mercantile, clerking, against her father's wishes. Report had it that he'd ordered her to return home, then, strangely humble, had begged her to come back.

She did not have red hair for nothing. She had refused to return. Like most of the men on the range, Johnny had found excuses to drop into the Mercantile oftener than business really required, more frequently than in the days before Myra had gone to work there. She had been friendly with him, as with others, but never more than that. It hadn't taken long to understand why.

She was deeply infatuated with Leavitt Vascom, the worthless nephew of Old Barney.

Johnny had liked her, even as he'd felt sorry for her. Old Man M'Ginnis had warned the Vascoms that he'd empty a double-barreled shotgun, loaded with buckshot, into any one of them who dared set foot on his land. That, probably, had been the reason Myra had left home and refused to return. A woman in love could see no evil in the object of her affections.

Later, both she and Leavitt Vascom had disappeared. It had been rumored that they had eloped. And M'Ginnis had died—perhaps of a broken heart.

And it was to this that Leavitt had brought her! Johnny saw her lips move and bent lower. Her voice was hardly more than a whisper.

"John! Thank heaven you've come!"

He dropped on his knees, filled with a sense of outrage, also a feeling of helplessness.

"Myra! What's happened?"

"Could you get me a drink?" she asked. "And the baby—it's starving. If somehow you could feed it—the poor little thing—"

"I'll get you some water," he promised. "And I'll try to do something for the baby," he added desperately. There was an old battered bucket under the table. Questions could wait. He snatched up the pail and hurried to the spring, filled the bucket and returned. He found a cup in the cupboard and held the water to her lips, raising her gently with one hand behind her back, shocked anew at how very thin and wasted she was. She drank slowly, swallowing with difficulty, but her eyes expressed her gratitude as she sank back.

"Thanks, John," she breathed. "That was good. You were always good—always kind—"

She broke off, coughing, and if he had not already known it, he would have been sure that she was desperately ill. "How long since you've had anything to eat?" he demanded.

"I don't know." She seemed to consider. "I can't remember. That doesn't matter now. I'm not even hungry any more. But the baby—she must be starving."

He nodded and went out again. For the next few minutes he worked with a sort of repressed desperation, gathering wood, building a fire in the stove. The baby had stopped crying, settling down to a sort of discouraged murmuring and muttering, and as he drew back a corner of the blanket he saw that she was trying to suck her own fist. She was tiny and red, somewhat like a kitten, and he was appalled but determined.

He heated water in a battered kettle, emptying another can of tomatoes into it, along with chunks of bacon. It would make a soup in the least possible time, not too strong, yet reasonably nourishing. He found the can of condensed milk, thankful now that it had gone unopened. After rinsing the tomato can, he poured some milk into it, diluting it with water, and warmed it. That would be the best he could contrive for the baby.

But how should he feed it to her? He saw a small, empty bottle among the few articles which passed for dishes and household utensils in the makeshift cupboard. He washed it with hot water, pondering, then hurried to his duffel bag again. He brought out a new, unused pair of fancy riding gloves, sliced off one finger, cut a small hole in the end, and pulled it over the neck of the bottle. It was makeshift, but the best he could manage.

The baby was fretting again, crying, a wail of hunger and despair. He picked her up, blanket and all. He noted how wet it was, but for the moment there was no time to think of that. Clumsily he cradled her in one arm, holding the bottle with the other, thrusting the nipple into her mouth.

Her wail rose louder, then subsided, and all at once, as some of the warm milk ran into her mouth, she began eating hungrily. She choked a few times, by which he guessed that it flowed too freely, but by tipping it back, drawing fresh wails of outrage, he managed fairly well. She ate with a sort of starving desperation, and her eyes, very blue, came open and fixed on his face. She seemed to be considering him, deciding that perhaps he was not too bad, after all. He caught a glimpse of Myra's face and saw that she was watching, tender approval in her eyes.

The baby choked; then he saw that the bottle was

empty. It didn't seem much, but perhaps it was enough for so small a person, especially when she had been without food. He saw her eyes close and placed her gently back in the trunk. At least she would be in somewhat better shape for a while, and he felt a strange glow of pride that he had been able to cope with so unexpected a situation.

"I'll fix some soup for you now," he promised, turning to Myra. "Then you'll feel better, too."

To his surprise, she shook her head.

"Thanks, but don't bother," she whispered. "It's too late—for that. And I want to talk—while there's time. Sit down, please."

He hesitated, then obeyed mutely, suddenly afraid of what he saw in her face. He took one thin hand in both of his.

"Myra, Myra, what has happened to you?" he asked. "Is Leavitt responsible for this?"

She nodded, her eyes dark and tragic.

"I should have listened to you—or to Papa," she said wanly. "I didn't understand then that you both wanted what was best for me. I thought Leavitt loved me. I loved him."

"You poor kid."

"I guess you can't help such things." She sighed. "I only found out—after it was too late—that he thought Pa had a lot of money, and that he'd get hold of it. When Pa died, and he found that all he had was a mortgage, he—he came back here, and he was terrible!"

"And you—with the baby?" Johnny asked sternly.

"Not then. That was two or three weeks ago, at least as nearly as I can tell. The baby was born a few days ago—two or three, I think. I don't remember very well."

"You mean that you were all alone?" he asked incredulously.

"I managed—somehow," she said. "But I'm dying, Johnny. I've been sick—awfully sick—for weeks. It doesn't matter—I guess it's better this way. But the baby deserves a chance. She isn't responsible for any of what I did, or him."

"No," he agreed, "she isn't. I'll try and see that she gets a chance. But—do you mean that he went off and left you—knowing what was going to happen—went away when you were so ill?"

"I think he only came back to see if I was dead already," she said resignedly. "When he found out that there was no money and would be none, he was furious, and I was only in the way. He taunted me that I wasn't even his wife—that the marriage ceremony had been a mockery, a fake. But I thought it was real, Johnny. I'd never have gone with him if I hadn't!"

"I'm sure you wouldn't," Johnny agreed. "The striped cousin to a civet!" he added under his breath. "The low-down crawlin' sidewinder!"

He checked and started, realizing suddenly that she was no longer listening. Bending closer, he felt cold. Somehow, in the face of sickness, weakness and starvation, she had willed to keep alive until someone should come. She had done it for love of her baby, enduring until she had whispered her story in a few stark words, making sure that he would look after the child. Now there had been nothing more to keep her.

From where he had left it, partially hidden, his horse neighed, which probably meant that it had heard or scented another horse approaching. Under the circumstances, that would almost certainly be Leavitt Vascom, prowling with uneasy fear as a spur. The bullet, fired to stop him short of the cabin the evening before, was now understandable.

4.

As Johnny stepped to the door, the horseman came into sight, riding not up but down the gulch, appearing around the screening leaves of a clump of chokecherries, white with bloom. Like all the Vascoms, he rode a high-stepping horse, a blooded animal imported from Kentucky. Not for the Vascoms were the half-wild descendants of the Indian ponies, the tireless cayuses such as the one Johnny had ridden. Old Barney Vascom had a high and bitter pride, astringent as iodine. In everything he had to have the best.

Leavitt Vascom had fared better than he deserved because of that pride of his uncle's. Half a dozen times in as many years he had strayed from the home range, a fiddle-footed man intent on making his own way with the power of his fists and his gun. Each time he had returned, sometimes no more than a jump ahead of the law, seeking sanctuary and finding it. Barney's anger had been bitter and raw, his disgust vented in fleering

40

words, but because Leavitt was his brother's son, Barney had stood with him against all outsiders.

Some men learn their lesson from adversity, but Leavitt was not one of those. The same high arrogance was in his darkly handsome face, untempered by contrition or remorse or any doubt of himself. He was solid as well as tall, as powerfully built as Old Barney, lacking only the ruggedness in the face of adversity. His horse had been coming at a trot, as though eagerness were tempered by caution. Now, seeing Johnny, rage seemed to explode in Vascom's face, and he struck savagely with the spurs, sending the blooded animal into a wild gallop.

He pulled it up with a vicious bit, just abreast of Johnny, and sat staring down, his dark eyes almost opaque, his too heavy chin jutting beneath the trimmed elegance of a brown mustache.

"What the devil are you doing here, you stinkin' sheepherder?" he challenged.

Johnny heard the epithet with a sense of shock. Sheepherder!

It was only the day before that Howard Denning had revealed his plans and intention to his own crew. Yet already the word had spread, and that indicated more than a loose tongue in a blabbermouth. For the news to have reached this scion of the Vascoms so swiftly, there must be a traitor in Wagon Wheel's crew, one who also drew pay from the rival Axe.

Johnny returned the stare. His lip twisted in contempt.

"What do you think?" he asked. "This is Wagon Wheel range. Who invited *you* here?"

A flicker of Vascom's eyes suggested that he had forgotten that it was he who was trespassing, but to him that meant little. His voice was a snarl.

"You would have to come sneaking, spying—sticking your snout in where it doesn't belong—"

"Meaning Myra?" Johnny demanded. "I suppose you came back to bury her, figuring she'd surely be dead by now, wanting to cover all trace of your own treachery! Oh, I know how you pretended to marry her, but cheated even on that, then had to hide it, for you knew that your uncle wouldn't stand for the double-crossing deal you had in mind. Even he can't stomach some of your actions. So you got her off here and kept her out of sight, and when you found that old M'Ginnis didn't have any money, you told her she wasn't really your wife, and left her when you knew she was dying!"

Leavitt grew quiet as he spoke, listening, his face momentarily like the grass at dawn. Abruptly he dropped the reins and swung down from the saddle, and Johnny recognized the signs. Report had it that Leavitt had killed three or four men, not always in fair fight. With the bluster gone, he was dangerous.

"Dead, is she?" he asked. "It's about time. She's been long enough doing it." The callousness of his words was even more shocking than what Johnny had seen. "I'll admit I was fooled. I thought M'Ginnis had a lot of loot stashed away, and money is for spending. But I guess I got even with him—taking his chick away. They say it killed him, and good riddance. As for her—she was in my way. I've other and bigger plans, and couldn't be bothered."

Deliberately, he unbuckled his gun belt and tossed it to one side. His smile was mocking.

"I'm just as bad as you figured, ain't I—all the bad Vascom blood, along with the Slade, coming to a head! But I make no bones about it. Your sort are mealy-mouthed hypocrites, who pretend in public and are devils in private. I never could stomach that sort of double-dealing. I could beat you with a gun, but I prefer to kill you with my hands. *If* you've got the guts to fight back! If not—" His shrug was eloquent.

The monstrous conceit of the man was amazing. He could convince himself that what he wanted was right, that what he said was true, even while knowing that with guns he would be helpless before the greater speed and accuracy of John Malcolm's Colts. So he tossed aside the gun, to compel Johnny to meet him on his own terms, where he expected to possess the advantage. He was fully as tall, his reach as long. And in weight, Johnny would have to give him a full forty pounds.

It was foolish to accept such a taunt, to allow a man who boasted that he had no scruples to dictate the terms. But pride was in Malcolm, as high a pride as a Vascom might boast, and his anger was at the bursting point. He unbuckled his own gun belt and tossed it to the side while Leavitt waited, a smile twisting his mouth unpleasantly.

"You're a fool," he said. "And I'm going to kill you."

He rushed, not hitting, his long arms reaching out.

Johnny side-stepped, then evaded a murderous twisting kick, in which the long-shanked spur at boot's end was set to slash down his belly. He had never seen so sharp-toothed a spur, and there was blood on the wheel.

The raking kick came close. It spoiled his own timing, so that his plan to catch Vascom's jaw with his own fist nearly failed. His knuckles slid along the bulge of the chin. Before he could recover, Leavitt attained his objective. His arms closed around Johnny, jerking Johnny against him savagely, while at the same time, exerting all his strength, Leavitt threw him to the ground and came down on top.

The shock of the fall, with two hundred and ten pounds crashing above him, almost knocked the breath from Malcolm's body. But Johnny had the stamina of the longhorn which had battled a variety of enemies and survived heavy odds. The memory of Myra, of the appeal she had made, and the baby, asleep now inside the cabin, gave him strength. If he failed, more than himself would die.

Then, for the first time, he felt a pang of fear and grabbed desperately, forcing a half-numbed arm to do his will. The full, calculated treachery of Leavitt was apparent in that moment.

It had seemed on the surface almost a magnanimous gesture to rid himself of his gun, toss it away, offer a fair fight, first to fists, man to man. But that had been no part of Vascom's plan. The odds might favor Leavitt in such a contest, but they were not sure enough. He'd had more in mind, and now it gleamed in his hand—a long-bladed bowie, produced from a hidden sheath, the glittering, needle-pointed dagger only inches above Johnny's throat.

Vascom's weight pinned him down. It was impossible to throw him off or to twist out from under. Vascom's left hand was on his right wrist, pinning it to the ground. Only with his left hand could Johnny fight the right arm which held the blade, and again the contest was unequal, all the odds in favor of the dagger.

Leavitt was panting, as much from rage as from exertion. Johnny felt his muscles crack and buckle with strain. The eyes above glared into his, hot with triumph. The point of the blade was reaching, descending, despite Johnny's desperate efforts to hold it back. Somewhere at the side, Vascom's horse snorted, as though it sniffed the odor of death.

Johnny knew how it would be, and in one way it would be good. When death came, it would be mercifully swift. He couldn't hold the knife away much longer. His muscles would give way eventually, for the greater weight was overwhelming. Right arm against left, when both men were right-handed, was in itself a tremendous advantage for Vascom.

Leavitt was triumphant, completely sure of himself and the outcome. As nearly as Johnny had been able to gather, Myra had lived, hidden away in there, for more than half a year, and in all that time, he was the first outsider to venture close or find the cabin. Vascom had no fear that anyone else would happen along to interfere or offer help, or to discover his crime, once it was covered with several feet of earth.

A sound startled both of them—the cry of the baby, from inside the cabin. Johnny saw the look in Vascom's eyes, surprised, uncertain for just an instant, and nerved himself to a final desperate effort.

It was not enough. Vascom's reaction was a wild burst of savagery which seemed to give him added strength. And then his weight was even heavier, the knife twisting murderously.

47

5.

Blood spilled across him, and for an instant the world took on a nightmare quality. Johnny threshed violently and threw the oppressive weight off, then sat up, gasping, gazing into a face as white as his own. In its way it was as beautiful as Leavitt Vascom's was handsome, the dark eyes seething with a blend of emotions. They ranged the whole gamut from disgust and rage to revulsion and pity.

Johnny struggled to his feet, looking down at the man who a moment before had been so intent on murdering him. He bent and touched Leavitt, then took a firmer grip on that right arm which had been so menacing, using it as a lever to turn him. The knife had twisted as Vascom collapsed, and now it was buried almost to the hilt in his own chest.

He fell back as Johnny released his grip. Malcolm's mind still boggled at the evidence of his senses. He had seen Vivian Vascom a few times in the past, though not often. She had grown into an aloof, disdainful beauty, reserved, proud, with the arrogance of the Vascoms. Now he regarded her doubtfully, seeing horror in her eyes. She had been away from the country for nearly a year, attending a school in the East. Barney was fiercely determined that his motherless daughter should have the training that befitted a lady.

It came to Johnny that what he had taken for arrogance might be shyness. Her hair was thick and soft and had the sheen and blackness of a crow's wing. Her eyes were stormy as she looked from her dead cousin to him, and she shivered. Her fingers were white from the intensity with which they clasped the butt of a revolver—his own gun, Johnny observed, and understood. She had snatched it up, clubbing Leavitt with the barrel, taking him by surprise. He'd twisted, falling, and the knife had been pointed upward.

Again Vivian shivered, allowing the gun to drop. Her voice was curiously flat.

"He is dead?"

Johnny nodded, sucking air like a swimmer breaking water. His own demise had been so near that his reprieve was still hard to understand.

"He's dead. No fault of yours. It was an accident."

She looked down again; then she ceased to frown.

"I'm glad," she announced calmly. "The insufferable beast! I overheard what you said to him—and what he answered. He was always murderous."

Johnny could only agree. From his own experience and the many tales he'd heard, the term was accurate.

"You saved me," Johnny added, and shivered in his turn. "I'd about given myself up. It was lucky that you happened along."

"It wasn't entirely by chance." Her tone was dispassionate, though a fierce undercurrent vibrated through the words. "That was one time he overreached himself. I got a letter from him, asking me to meet him at the Lampases Spring today. He said that there was something very important that he had to talk over with me, that he had to explain certain things before I talked with anyone else in the family. I've been away, and he sounded quite convincing. So I came. And now I understand what he really had in mind!"

She went on, as though it were necessary to explain, not only for Johnny's benefit, but for her own.

"He was my cousin, of course—but he was always trying to make love to me—oh, for years now. I never took him seriously—I thought it was sort of a game—but apparently he didn't! He wrote me several letters while I was gone. You see—he thought M'Ginnis had money, which he could get through Myra. When it turned out that there was no money, Myra was an encumbrance—to be gotten rid of! By then, Dad had cut him off from any share in Axe, because of all the things he'd done. So he figured still to share in Broken Axe—by getting my share!"

Taken with what Leavitt had said, there could be no doubt that she was right.

"I'm grateful for your help," Johnny said. "More than my life was at stake. There's a baby in the house—"

As though on signal, the baby wailed again. Vivian's face had been set and cold. Now it changed, was transformed. She turned abruptly and went inside. Johnny followed.

She stood in the doorway a moment, as he had done, looking about, and he could see reflected in her face the same shock which he had felt. Then she crossed and picked up the baby, blankets and all. The troubled bewilderment was deeper in her eyes as she turned back to him.

"But this—oh, it's awful! I didn't really understand—"

"The baby is probably two or three days old," Johnny explained. "Myra said she was starving. I had a can of milk, and I fixed some in that bottle, warmed and diluted. But maybe she's still hungry—"

He turned at a slight sound, then, almost past being surprised, crossed to the bunk. Myra's eyes were open, looking at them. He'd thought that she was gone a while back, but apparently, out of sheer weakness, she had merely been on the verge of unconsciousness. Now she had rallied.

"Now this is better," he exclaimed. "You're going to live, Myra, and things will be better. And I reckon the first thing is to give you something to eat, too."

The soup was warm, and it had simmered to a savory consistency. He found a tin bowl and spoon, and set to work to feed it, a sip at a time, to Myra. Vivian was caring for the baby, working with something of the frantic desperation which had assailed him earlier.

She looked about for some sort of clean cloths which might be used for the baby, and found nothing. Johnny heard its fresh wail of protest as she placed it back in the trunk which served as a crib and went outside.

She was gone only a minute. When she returned, she carried a white garment which he guessed must be one of her own underskirts. Quickly she ripped it into several smaller pieces, then, finding a suitable basin, set to work to bathe the baby. From her manner he surmised that such a task must be as new to her as to him, but she proceeded with determined desperation. Then she clothed the baby, eying her handiwork ruefully. But if not artistic, at least it was an improvement.

During all this time, none of them had spoken. Myra had watched, bright-eyed, obediently swallowing the soup, choking once or twice, as though eating were a habit to which she was no longer accustomed.

"There, at least she's clean and fresh," Vivian observed. Carrying the baby, she crossed to look down at Myra. "You poor kid!" she added. "You've had it rough, haven't you? But it's going to be better."

Myra smiled, but her concern was for her baby. "Is she all right?" she asked.

"Couldn't be better, considering, though I suspect she's hungry again," Vivian said. "But we can do something about that."

She poured out more of the can of milk and started to warm it. Johnny turned to the door.

"I'll go out," he said. "You can tend to things here for a while."

Vivian nodded understandingly. After some searching, Johnny found what he sought. Even the discovery was a minor shock.

The shovel was a hundred feet from the cabin, behind the clump of screening chokecherry brush. It had been used, not many days before, to dig a grave—the grave which he had expected to toil over. Clearly, on one of his last visits there, Leavitt Vascom had been certain that Myra could not last much longer. So he had made grim preparations.

Burial in the hole which he himself had dug was poetic justice, and Johnny wasted no time in ceremony or in consulting the others. Myra was in no condition to take any part, and he was sure that Vivian would not want to. He filled in the hole, then, feeling a strange compunction, picked a handful of wild flowers and placed them on the fresh ground. Strange are the ways of the heart, and whatever Leavitt had been, Myra had loved him. The bouquet was for her.

He found Vivian's horse and brought it up, along with his own. With the thoroughbred, that made three. He was pondering the next problem when Vivian came outside.

"They're both sleeping," she reported. "What shall we do next? Myra is dreadfully thin and weak. She should have several days of rest and care before she is moved. And the baby will be hungry—often. I think you fed her just in time to save her. Do you have any more canned milk?"

Johnny shook his head. "I just brought the one can," he admitted. "I didn't count on finding anyone—or anything like this."

Vivian nodded. "Neither did I. My horse nickered—and that warned me as well as him," she added grimly. "So I didn't ride blindly into sight, for which I'm thankful. You've taken care of him?"

"Yes. He had a grave already dug."

Understanding for whom it had been intended, Vivian's eyes sparkled.

"Give him one good deed, for which he gets no credit!" she snapped. "But Myra and the baby must be gotten out from here as soon as possible. That will be the baby's only chance."

"I'll fix up a team," Johnny agreed, "if you think Myra can stand riding in the wagon."

"She's endured so much already, I'm sure she can." Vivian nodded. "It has to be done."

The team was the real problem. Johnny had been unable to find any harness, but he could contrive a passable set, using lariat ropes. The difficulty would lie in persuading riding ponies to pull a wagon, working as a team. He couldn't afford to have them kick or run away, not with a sick woman and a baby as passengers.

By riding his own horse, as a part of the team, he figured to control them. He made a harness, then set about gathering grass and sagebrush as padding for the wagon bed. Meanwhile, Vivian prepared a meal. It seemed a long while since he'd helped himself to the bowl of stew and listened to Howard Denning explain his plan to bring sheep onto the range. His brow wrinkled anew as he remembered Leavitt's slurring reference to sheep.

When other things were ready, he hitched the team, not without difficulty, choosing his own and Vivian's ponies in preference to the thoroughbred. As he swung to his saddle, they took off at a wild run. The wagon wheels creaked dismally, but no grease was available. The spokes, dry and unused while the wagon had sat out in storm and sun, rattled loosely. Still, it would probably hold together as far as Wagon Wheel. It had to serve.

The ponies were skittish and uncertain, but after a circle of a mile, they lost much of their fright at the squealing vehicle at their heels.

Vivian had ransacked Leavitt's pack and, coupling the contents with supplies from Johnny's, had contrived a good meal. Myra had been completely out of food, even of bare necessities. Ill, in no condition to set out on foot across endless miles, she had been effectively trapped.

They ate; then Johnny carried Myra to the wagon.

She was amazingly light, but hope was replacing the despair in her eyes. Vivian carried the baby.

"Where are we heading for?" she asked.

"I think Wagon Wheel's best," Johnny said. "It's closest. What do you think?"

"I'm sure of it. Do you have a housekeeper?"

Johnny grinned. "Not now. Howard hired Lavinia Taylor, after Ma left, and put up with her for a week. Lavinia has a heart of gold—"

"And a tongue that's hung in the middle and works both ways," Vivian agreed. "I know. Her talk would drive most people crazy. But there will have to be a woman to look after Myra until she's stronger. She's endured a fearful ordeal, and it will take quite a while."

"Howard won't object to Lavinia, as long as she has something to do besides talk to him," Johnny promised. He understood what Vivian meant. In one way, Myra belonged to Axe, but in others she was alien there. For a while, at least, she would be better at Wagon Wheel. Seeing that she was asleep, he spoke.

"You heard what Leavitt said. Myra told me that he came back here and informed her that the marriage ceremony had been a mockery. But she went through it in good faith."

Vivian's lips thinned, gazing down at the now contented child in her arms.

"Then why should we tell it any other way now?" she asked. "Let it stand that she is his widow, this baby a Vascom—not that it's much of a heritage! But it's all she has." She went on thoughtfully:

"Myra won't be able to look after this little tyke for quite a while. So I think I'd better take her until she can."

"Would you?" He admired her spirit. "What will your father say?"

"He'll end up by inviting Myra to come to Axe when she is able. He's fair, as he sees things."

That was probably a correct assessment of Barney, though Johnny could not say as much for Leavitt, or for Slade Vascom, Vivian's brother. Slade and Leavitt, double cousins, made a pair. They had been dubbed the Twins, both because of their physical likeness and their manner of action. The wildness and arrogance of the Vascoms was in both, exaggerated by the lawlessness of the Slade side of the family.

...

There were no springs in a lumber wagon, and the mattress of grass would not absorb nearly all of the joltings, but that could not be helped. Johnny tied the one horse behind, then swung to the saddle and set out.

The team had run off their skittishness and soon settled to moving ahead in matter-of-fact fashion. It was necessary to hold them to a walk except for occasional good stretches; otherwise the going would be unbearable. But at that pace, it would mean camping that night and traveling on for a while the next day.

In mid-afternoon he knocked over a prairie chicken with a quick shot from his revolver. It would provide a passable supper for Vivian and himself, and the bones, boiled, would make a broth for Myra. The sun shone warmly, and but for the grim background, the trip would have been pleasant. Myra was uncomplaining. Vivian, sitting beside her, holding the baby, would be scarcely more comfortable.

They camped, and he surprised a strange look in Vivian's eyes as she cooked supper.

"So Denning is going into the sheep business?" she

asked.

Leavitt's initial greeting had been to call him a sheepherder, and she had mentioned overhearing all that had been said between them. Johnny nodded.

"Howard has decided that this never was cattle country, but should make good range for sheep. He doesn't like the notion, but he's doing it on account of Ma."

Somewhat to his surprise, Vivian accepted this without comment or further question, with none of the animosity which was ordinarily to be expected, especially from a Vascom.

"How is Ma?" she asked. "I heard about her accident. I always admired her spirit."

"Ma has to have another operation," he explained. "If it works—she may walk again, may even come back home. If it doesn't—" He let it go at that.

"Then let's hope and pray that it works," Vivian said. She raised her head, and then he too heard a sound. "Someone's coming." After a moment her voice took on an anxious note. "I think it's Slade," she added. "Don't be tricked again!"

6.

On the Western Wyoming range they had long been called the Vascom Twins, though less complimentary terms were often applied. Leavitt was Old Barney's nephew, Slade his son.

In appearance as in nature, they had been so alike that it had been difficult for strangers to tell them apart. A knife fight had changed that, about a year before. Slade's left cheek had been sliced like steak in a saloon brawl. On healing, the white rim of the scar looked surprisingly like the head of the Axe. It was a mark of which Slade professed to be proud, perhaps to hide his secret distress.

The scar was livid as Slade pulled his horse to a stop and looked about at the preparations for a night camp. Vivian was bent over the cook fire, while

Johnny was putting the finishing touches to a make-shift shelter above the wagon box, using a couple of the blankets. Slade Vascom leaned forward, and his breathing matched his horse's. The cayuse showed dark streaks of sweat, and its lungs heaved from running.

"What's this?" Slade rasped. "What are you doing here, Vivian? We've been wondering why you didn't show up at home—"

He broke off as the baby wailed, as though in protest against the demanding voice. For a moment his face was a picture of astonishment.

"I'm trying as best I can to make amends for Vascom brutality," Vivian answered. There was no word of greeting, though Slade's eyes followed her jealously. "Leavitt deserted Myra when she was sick. She was almost dying when Johnny Malcolm and I found her, to say nothing of the baby."

Slade swallowed. Clearly this was news to him, and it rocked him. The effect, however, was brief. He fixed quickly on another thing she had said.

"You and Malcolm found her! What are the two of you doing, off here together?"

"I don't know that it's any of your business," she

informed him disdainfully. "Only we weren't together. We met by chance at the cabin where Myra had been left by Leavitt. Johnny was about his own business. I'd had a letter from Leavitt, asking me to meet him at Lampases Spring. He said it was important."

The axe-head scar seemed to jerk, almost in a chopping motion. Slade remained in the saddle, his big hands clenched about the horn.

"Blast him!" he breathed. "And you fell for that?"

"I should have remembered that the Vascom Twins were liars," Vivian returned bitingly. "He made it sound important. I rather supposed that you'd been up to more of your usual tricks."

Slade let that pass, intent on what to him was clearly the main issue.

"And what happened? What did he say?"

"Nothing. I haven't spoken to him for a year. I'm sure he didn't intend for me—or anyone—to find the cabin and Myra. Apparently he had been staying away from it on purpose. Myra was starving, along with all the rest."

"Starving?" Slade repeated, and for the first time these references seemed to get home to him. He dropped the reins and swung to the ground, crossing to the wagon to look at Myra, still ignoring Johnny. "I didn't know what the devil Leavitt was up to," he confessed, "though he's been acting like a coyote with a hidden den for a long while, and away for weeks at a time. But that was nothing new."

He stared at the baby, looked more sharply at Myra, and became momentarily agreeable.

"This is bad business," he admitted. "He'll have to make amends, or Dad will kill him. And if he doesn't, I'll have a try at it!" he added with a click of teeth, as if the prospect afforded him real pleasure. "Where is he?"

Myra's voice was tired. "I don't know. I haven't seen him for weeks."

"He'd better stay out of sight," Slade growled, then seemed to lose interest in the subject. "You're camping here for the night?"

"What else is there to do?" Vivian countered. "We have to get Myra and the baby where they can be taken care of, but Myra is too weak to go any further today."

Slade asked more questions, ascertaining that they planned to take Myra to Wagon Wheel, at least temporarily, while Vivian would care for the baby. His face darkened.

"Dad won't like that, and I don't," he said shortly. "A sheep outfit is no place for a Vascom!"

Here it was again, the taunt and evidence that the news had spread. Johnny had held silent, keeping a tight rein on his temper, but he could not refrain from an answer.

"Your cousin brought her onto Wagon Wheel range without permission," he pointed out. "I'm accepting your word that you didn't know where he was or what he was up to. But there are points where Wagon Wheel draws the line!"

"There's no line so low as that of a sheepman!" Slade retorted instantly. Vivian flushed angrily.

"Slade, you're insufferable!" she protested, and his temper blazed.

"Are you taking his part against me?" he demanded. "Are you forgetting that you're a Vascom?"

"I'd like to," she admitted bitterly. "After all that's happened, I'm ashamed of the family."

The tension was eased slightly as another rider came galloping up. It was Cy Robbins, who had been an old hand on Wagon Wheel when Johnny had first gone to work for Denning. He looked about in some bewilderment at sight of the wagon and the Vascoms.

"So here you are, Johnny," he said. "Howard was beginnin' to get a mite worried when you didn't show up, so I set out to see what might be keepin' you."

It was decided that Robbins would remain with them until morning, then would ride ahead with word of their coming. Slade was obviously intent on staying also, not at all worried by lack of an invitation. He was barely civil, though he did help gather wood for the fire, and contributed to the supper from his own supplies.

By mutual if unspoken consent, nothing had been said by either Vivian or Johnny concerning what had happened to Leavitt. Myra had been too sick to realize that he had returned. Sooner or later, questions concerning his whereabouts were certain to come up, but it seemed better to add no more fuel to the fires of animosity at this time.

Slade had already saddled when Johnny threw off his blanket the next morning. He rode closer.

"I'm heading back for Axe," Slade announced. "One

word of advice, Malcolm. You can ride out of this country if you like. I'd suggest you do. That'll keep your nose clean. Wagon Wheel ain't going to be popular in these parts from here on out!"

He put his horse to a fast gallop and was gone. Johnny rubbed at his stubbled chin, watching him disappear. Coming from such a source, the word might be intended as friendly counsel. Only somehow he couldn't feel it to be so. It was more in the nature of a threat, a warning to get out. Johnny turned to gather wood for a fresh fire.

He left Robbins to drive and rode ahead himself, taking the word to Denning, who listened in understandable amazement.

"I've heard a lot of wild tales about those boys," Howard confessed. "And I've seen plenty with my own eyes, but nothing to match this." He gave Johnny a searching glance. "I figured there'd be trouble when I decided to run sheep. Now it's a sure thing."

Johnny answered his unspoken question. "I'm staying," he said.

"I knew I could count on you," Denning commended him. "You never run away from trouble. I don't need to tell you that I'm glad. But I figure we'll have our hands full."

Johnny despatched a messenger to bring back Lavinia Taylor. A widow, Lavinia lived with her married sister, and was always available for a job of nursing or whenever a competent woman was required. With her to look after Myra, the business of driving the cattle to the railroad could continue.

"I guess I can duck out enough to keep from bein' jawed to death," Denning said resignedly. "One thing about Lavinia, she can be depended on to help where she's needed, even if we're already being called a sheep outfit. And it takes character to do that."

The wagon made it in about noon, and Lavinia arrived at the same time and took efficient charge. Myra had stood the journey better than Johnny had thought possible, buoyed now by hope.

The baby was again complaining hungrily, and the three women put their heads together over it, assembling an outfit before Vivian went on to her own home, taking the baby. Slade had prepared the way, but it was a strange homecoming when she finally rode up, to be greeted by Barney, his face set and still.

"I'm glad to see you back," he observed, which was all the welcome she had expected. "But what's this that I'm told about Leavitt, and him having a wife, and writing to you. Give me the straight of it."

She responded with an unvarnished account, omitting only the part that Leavitt had been there when she arrived, and what had happened between him, Johnny and herself. Barney listened to her account, looked silently at the baby, then asked a single further question. "How long before Myra can be brought here?"

"She'll need to rest and get her strength back. Several weeks, I should think, at the least."

Barney nodded. "We'll try and have her clear of the Wagon Wheel ahead of the sheep." His face twisted. "I never figured to be beholden to that outfit. But life plays some queer tricks."

He said no more, but one question was answered, and Vivian was relieved. For all her outward air of assurance, she had been far from certain as to how Barney might react to her bringing the baby with her. She sensed that he was not merely accepting what she had done. In his own way, he was proud of her.

7.

The scar on Slade Vascom's face twisted as he rode. It appeared more a grimace than a smile, but to those who knew him it would have passed for a satisfied grin. He'd been jolted by the revelations the evening before, but his suspicions and fears had turned out to be groundless. Some of the developments were even pleasing.

"This time, Leavitt, you really put your foot in it!" He chuckled. "Which is what comes of grabbing, when you've got both hands full already! Now you've hog-tied yourself, and I won't have to worry any more about you. I was beginning to think I'd have to kill you, but it's a safe bet that someone else will take that chore off my hands."

For a long while, there had been increasing jealousy between them; each had the same prize in mind. Both played a dangerous game for high stakes. Until now, Leavitt had possessed two advantages. One was his unmarred face. Making a virtue of necessity, Slade could boast that as a scion of Broken Axe he wore the brand of Axe, but he was keenly sensitive on the point of his good looks. For appearance, he was convinced, counted heavily in such a game. Women, like men, were often fickle.

The second reason he kept carefully to himself.

He'd been suspicious, frustrated and furious, when Vivian had failed to return home as expected. Though she was far from realizing it, almost everything depended on her. Putting together vague whisperings and rumors, he'd followed a hunch and headed toward Lampases Spring. But he had not been prepared for what he had found.

Since Leavitt had so obligingly eliminated himself from the contest, he could take advantage of the breaks. During the night, lying sleepless, he had evolved a plan. Now he was losing no time putting it into operation.

A small, barren butte thrust ambitiously above the surrounding landscape, three miles north of the buildings on Wagon Wheel. It was still early when a thin wisp of smoke, as from a campfire, rose lazily above the hill.

The smoke hung, drifted, and faded in the brightening glare of the sun. After what seemed a long while, a horseman appeared, riding up a draw, coming without being easily visible to possible watchers. Actually, as Dinty Toole pointed out, he had made good time after discovering the signal.

"I had to get away without anybody noticin'," he pointed out. "And that takes a bit of doing."

"No matter," Slade shrugged, "now that you're here. I want answers to a few questions. It's sure, then, that Denning is buying sheep?"

"Reckon so. Howard says he's made up his mind. We're to start drivin' the cattle to the railroad any day now. Once they're sold, he'll use the money to buy sheep, and ship them back."

Slade grew tense.

"Do you know what arrangements he's made to get sheep?"

Dinty gave him a snaggle-toothed grin.

"Happens I do," he admitted. "After I got word to you of what he was up to, and you asked me to do some snoopin'—I snooped. Not much trouble about that, with Johnny gone, and the Old Man out ridin'— which he don't often do these days. I pried around in Denning's desk and found a letter. Sev'ral letters, in fact, but only one that was worth lookin' at."

"Get on with it," Vascom said impatiently.

"I'm comin' to it. It was from somebody back in Iowa—I got it all wrote down here, a copy of what I figured you'd want to know. This feller has a lot of sheep for sale. He quoted prices and everything on nine thousan' head. What he was doing was confirming Denning's agreement to buy that many from him, after the cattle are sold. Forty thousand dollars for the sheep, loaded on the cars, ready to ship west. That includes ten experienced herders, who'll go along to look after the sheep."

"Nine thousand head at forty thousand dollars," Slade repeated. "It sounds to me as though he's getting a good buy. Let me see what you wrote down."

He studied the copy of the letter, frowning, then

74

tucked it in a pocket.

"You've done a good job," he said and, with unexpected generosity, thrust half a dozen bills into Toole's eager hand. "This is a bonus, in addition to your regular wage," he added. "You say the drive starts in a day or so?"

"That's what the word is. We're just waitin' for Johnny. He rode off on some business and ain't got back."

"Fine. Be on the watch for another signal. Maybe you can earn another bonus."

"I can use it," Toole admitted. "One of these days, at this rate, I'll have money enough to buy me a business and settle down. Got my eye on a saloon at Lampases."

"The Silver Dollar," Slade guessed. "The gambling games there pay more than the liquor the way they're operated."

"Nothin' wrong with that, is there—so long as a man owns 'em?" Toole grinned. "I take it that I'm to stay on, workin' for Denning for a spell longer, even as a sheepman?"

"You'd be of no use to me if you left him," Slade

retorted. While Toole returned to his own work, he rode on, keeping out of sight of the buildings of Wagon Wheel, or any rider who might chance along. He paused briefly at Axe to inform his father what had happened, or as much as seemed expedient; then he went on, following a straight line toward the town of Lampases. That the town was roughly half a hundred miles from the spring of the same name seemed to hold no significance or to strike anyone as odd.

There was a bank at Lampases, and Barney Vascom transacted his business through it. Even more vital to Slade's plan was the knowledge that his father had an account of slightly more than forty thousand dollars to his credit.

That discovery, made largely by chance a few weeks before, had intrigued Slade. He had considered a score of plans for getting hold of part or all of the money for his own use, as he had done with lesser sums many times in the past. Certain of those schemes he had worked alone, others in conjunction with Leavitt, who was clever when it came to any planning of doubtful legality. Their success along those lines had led to a memorable blow-up on the part of Barney something more than half a year before. His anger could be terrible, and even the hot-headed Twins had been awed and cowed.

But not for long. There were two imperative reasons, the money in the bank and Broken Axe itself, for further conspiring. Now opportunity was at the door.

It was evening when he reached the town. Slade stabled his horse, found a restaurant and ate, then, under the cloak of settling night, walked to the banker's home.

Slim Bestwick had been a cowboy in his younger days. A riding injury had made it necessary to turn to other less arduous pursuits, and for a score of years, while he lost his nickname and erstwhile learnness, Bestwick had congratulated himself on his mishap. He had discovered an unsuspected talent for business, and for the past dozen years had been president of the bank, as well as its chief owner. He looked up in surprise and with a certain wariness at sight of his caller. But because Slade was a Vascom, he courteously asked him in.

Slade wasted no time.

"I doubt if you'll have heard the news yet," he said. "But sheep are due to put in an appearance on our range—at least on Wagon Wheel," he amended.

Bestwick listened with interest. Though once a cowboy, his years as a banker had conditioned him to think impartially. Once he understood the situation, he nodded.

"I would say that Denning is showing good judgment," he observed. "Your range is better suited to sheep than cattle. He'll encounter opposition, no doubt, but in the long run, it should prove an excellent investment."

"We on Axe think the same," Slade surprised him by agreeing. "That's why I'm here. For I don't need to tell you that there's no love lost between Wagon Wheel and Axe."

Bestwick smiled dryly. "No," he agreed. "You don't need to."

Since Axe was his client, rather than Wagon Wheel, he could be depended on to respect such confidences.

"Denning has made arrangements to buy forty thousand dollars worth of sheep back in Iowa—nine thousand head. Here is Dad's order on the bank for forty thousand dollars. He wants you, acting as his agent, to send a draft to the owner of the sheep. Denning can buy without knowing the difference. We'll even give him a good break—a quarter of the amount down, the balance in up to ninety days."

Bestwick considered the implications of the deal for a while, and smiled a slow smile of approval. There were those who in recent years had dubbed him Slick Bestwick, in lieu of the former Slim. He did nothing dishonest, but he approved of cleverness, and this deal had all the earmarks of a profitable transaction.

"I understand, and you may tell your father that I'll handle the matter with discretion," he responded. "You may even tell him that I think this is an excellent idea."

"I think so, too," Slade agreed, and modestly refrained from explaining just how clever it was, or his own part in it.

8.

The drive got under way at dawn. Having been penned for days in the corrals, the cattle were torn between impulses, anger both to run and to graze the new grass. The cowboys were kept busy controlling them, keeping the herd on the move. It would take ten days for the slow-moving dogies to reach the railroad, where Denning had the promise of cattle cars.

There were good points and bad to such a transaction as he had in mind. Receipts at the Chicago market were usually scanty at that season of the year, which tended to improve the prices. On the other hand, the herd had come through a long winter, and the leanness of the cold months was still upon them. They would not shrink much on the drive, but neither would there be any reserve of fat to render them attractive to buyers.

Denning was not unduly worried. Chicago was becoming the prime livestock marketing center, and a new practice was springing up in the mid-west, something until recently unheard of. Farmers who had a surplus of corn were discovering that they could buy western cattle, hold them a few weeks or months, feed them bountifully, and round them into fatter, more tender beef than the average customer had ever known. Corn sold in such fashion paid a premium price.

Most of the Wagon Wheel herd would go that way —the calves, cows, yearlings, even some of the older steers. As feeders, they should bring a fair price. Whatever the sacrifice, Denning was hopeful of getting enough to pay needed bills and finance his venture into sheep. Thereafter it would be a greater gamble. If it worked, the big spread which was Wagon Wheel might finally pay off.

Denning had hoped to make the trip back with the cattle, complete his business and visit Ma again. But traveling of any sort was becoming increasingly hard for him, and he had regretfully decided to stay behind, to supervise the work which had to be done in preparation for the sheep, including the building of the corrals and cutting wild hay.

"I'm leaving it all up to you, Johnny," Denning informed him. "You'll make the decisions—including what is best for Ma. The doctors have written me, and so has she, but they don't like to say for sure whether or not to risk another operation, and neither does she. I gather it's considerable of a gamble. Well—next to me there's nobody she thinks more of on this green earth than you, and I know you feel the same about her. So I'm shoulderin' that onto you, too. I know you'll do the best you can."

With a couple of exceptions, all of the crew had agreed to stay on, after Johnny had made known his intention to do so.

Johnny took time to look in on Myra. She was white and thin, but the sickness had run its course. Now, having the hope of life after she had resigned herself to dying, she managed a smile.

"I'm fine, Johnny," she assured him. "And I'll never forget what you've done for me." Her face held a dreaming look. "I don't know where Leavitt is, but he'll probably try to make trouble. So—take care of yourself, Johnny."

"I'll do that," he promised, and said nothing concerning Leavitt. If he was past causing trouble, Slade and others were not. "I want to see you up and around when I get back," he added.

"Of course," she agreed. "I may be at Axe by then—but if I am, I'll still want to see you, Johnny, whenever you get a chance to say hello."

"I'll sure keep that in mind," he agreed, and went out and gave the order to open the gates.

He made lazy progress for a few days, until trouble came from an unexpected source. The trail had grown routine. On this day, following several spurts of sunshine, the sky was obscured, a smell of rain drifting above the dust. The cattle stepped out at a livelier pace, as though suddenly eager to reach whatever destination might be in store for them. They seemed to scent adventure along with the rain, and found both equally welcome.

Watchful riders held them until, at mid-afternoon, there was the sudden belch of a revolver. The blast jarred on the heavy air, and the next instant, bawling, the whole herd surged into motion. It was a stampede, and stampede could be another word for disaster.

Johnny jerked his hat low and settled himself as his cayuse broke into a fast run, understanding this job as well as he. Then he noted incredulously that it was one of his own men who had triggered the catastrophe. Dinty Toole was blowing smoke from his revolver, staring from it to a flopping gopher, then on to the running cattle, which were swiftly leaving him behind.

Returning the gun to his holster, Dinty gazed expansively at the running herd. The clap of sound had worked as well as he'd hoped, producing the same sort of consternation as the rattle of a sidewinder coming from beside a man's foot.

It would be impossible to head the herd or stop them. None of the other drovers were in position to move fast enough. By the time the cattle had run themselves out, they would be widely scattered, and a couple of days lost. These were the sort of aggravations which the Twins paid him to engineer. With luck, he might receive a bonus of up to a hundred dollars for this one, and never would money have been more easily earned.

Strictly speaking, he was not in the employ of Broken Axe; Barney Vascom knew nothing of the deal whereby Leavitt had contracted with him to spy and report anything which might be of interest or possible use against his nominal employer. The idea had been all Leavitt's to begin with.

His own bungling had somewhat altered the situation. Dinty had encountered the other Twin prior to the accident which had resulted in Slade's distinguishing scar; assuming that he was talking to Leavitt, he had given a report, only to discover that it was Slade. But the error had worked out nicely. For a while, at Slade's suggestion, he had reported to both of them, not telling Leavitt of the new arrangement. Later, they had become joint employers.

He turned in time to catch Johnny's stare on him, and some of the pleasure of the moment drifted away like dust before the wind. He'd get told off properly for such apparent carelessness. But the bonus would make it worth a tongue-lashing.

A new note, in the rising thunder of hoofs and excited bawling of the herd, jerked his head around.

Working among cattle as long as he had, Dinty had come to know them well, to recognize the nuances of sound both of individuals and of massed animals. In certain respects they were like people, angry or contented, nervous or placid, and they expressed their moods. Sometimes it was by silence, again by soft lowing, or, as now, by maddened bellowing. Even the tempo of hoof-beats and the clash of horns were full of meaning.

Despite the length of their horns, those did not often clash. A big steer, with a wide sweep of horn, could thread his way at surprising speed through a tangle of trees or brush, scarcely disturbing a branch. Massed, a herd could travel without interfering with one another, save when they chose deliberately to hook or gouge.

Now there was a clash, the shock of bodies. Dinty stared with sagging jaw, bewildered. Here was another change, as swift and unlooked for as the situation his shot had produced.

From where he rode he could not see the cause, but it was clear that the wildly running vanguard of the herd had tried to stop, to turn back upon those who followed, to surge in almost the opposite direction. The gunshot had not really panicked them; it had been more like a signal for a wild dash.

Now their panic was real. Horns rattled as the mass tangled; bawling rose to a thundering crescendo. Then, driven by the sheer weight of fear, they made the swing and came surging back, straight toward Dinty, spreading as they ran, an enveloping, maddened wave of tons of flesh and driving hoofs.

From his own position, Johnny had a better view. The sudden thunder of stampede had surprised a big grizzly placidly going about his own business, with no thought of trouble on so pleasant a spring day. It had been only a few weeks since he had ended his winter hibernation and looked upon the world with a somewhat jaundiced eye. Age carried with it the realization that awakening to new life brought fresh responsibilities, not the least of which was the finding of sufficient food to replenish shrunken flesh and placate gnawing hunger.

Intent on the latter, he had been after a mouse, turning over a rock under which it had sought refuge, capturing it in mid-flight with a darting reach of his paw. The mouse made a tasty but discouragingly tiny morsel.

The grizzly was distracted by the sudden noise of stampede. Rearing high for a better look from nearsighted eyes, he loomed massively in the path of the oncoming herd.

At the same moment, the freakish wind veered. Until then it had carried the grizzly's scent away from the cattle. Now, even as he reared fearsomely, the rankness of bear odor flooded their nostrils.

Sight and smell combined were too much for the cattle. They stampeded back upon themselves; a few of the calves and even a yearling were overwhelmed and trampled in the rush. Then, spurred by terror, not knowing that the equally startled grizzly was hastily scrambling in the opposite direction, they roared toward the petrified Dinty.

His cayuse seemed equally astonished, frozen like its rider by indecision. When the two of them decided that they should be elsewhere in a hurry, the horse started to turn, to swing to the right. Dinty gave a wild jerk on the reins, trying to pull it around to the left.

Jerked savagely in mid-stride, the cayuse swerved, staggered and fell. Dinty went down heavily.

The horse regained its feet in a plunging scramble. Its training had taught it to stop and stand when the reins dropped, but terror of the oncoming herd was greater than discipline. The horse hurtled ahead and was gone.

It had happened in a space of heartbeats. Dinty came scrambling to his feet, tried to run, stumbled and rolled.

Johnny was the only one close enough to see or to do anything. There was a strong suspicion in his mind that the cause of the trouble had not been bungling or thoughtlessness, but treachery. Regardless of that, death was on the move, and such a fate would be a high price, even for a traitor.

He sent his own horse toward the fallen man, forcing it into the path of the herd. The horse new nothing of statistics, of the countless men and animals who had perished under pounding hoofs in similar circumstances, but its instinct was sure. However, so was its rider, and it obeyed, though unwillingly.

Dinty came a second time to his feet, dazed, his

mind numbed by panic. The onrush of the herd was like a high tide sweeping from the sea, threatening to overtop all previous boundaries. He tried to run, but his ankle had twisted in the second fall.

He saw Johnny heading for him, and his guilt was compounded by fear. The foreman had seen and understood his treachery, which had triggered the stampede. An when aroused, the wrath of John Malcolm could be a terrible lash.

Fear supplanted reason. Frantically, Dinty jerked his own gun again, firing at point-blank range.

In that stretch of country there had been no rain for days. The grass was a sparse fringe of green, and dust churned through and around it, stirred by thousands of hoofs. The choking cloud was shoved by the wind, carried ahead of the onrushing herd. In such fog, it was difficult to see.

Johnny watched the raised gun in disbelief; its strike was as swift as a rattler's. Haste caused a partial miss. Johnny had been the intended target, but the bullet buried itself instead in the cayuse. The horse faltered in its stride, staggered and went down, its body a flimsy barrier in the path of the onrushing herd.

Dinty did not shoot a second time. He stared, still with an expression of bewilderment. The barrier erected by his shot might have been imaginary, for the rolling tide did not even falter as it was reached. The cattle were too closely paced, too hard-pressed by their own mates, even to swerve.

Dinty went down a third time, and he did not get up again.

9

Instinctively Johnny kicked free of the stirrups, half-jumping, half-rolling clear as his horse went down.

Rolling, he hit the ground, and that part was not too bad, except that the herd was up with him before he could come erect. As though sensing that this might be their last opportunity to run free, they were making the most of it.

A hoof drove like a pile driver beside his face, flicking dirt into his eyes. Johnny grabbed blindly, clutching at a long horn on his other side. His fingers closed near the tip, and the steer reacted violently. A jerk of the head helped Johnny to gain his feet, but also sent him staggering to the side as his hold was lost.

He was bumped from behind and jostled forward, and bumped again, this time from the side. The double motion kept him on his feet, and he grabbed again. This time his fingers found a tail.

For a dozen lurching steps he was jerked along, barely able to hold fast. The press of bodies was steadily thickening, and he could not endure long in so exposed a position.

A fear-frenzied steer ran with half-closed eyes and half-opened mouth. From its throat dribbled a continuous bawling, the sound compounded of anger and terror, along with a sort of resigned acceptance.

Alien scent sucked into the steer's nostrils, only partly smothered by the dust. Reddened eyes made out something alien and therefore to be feared and hated; its head lowered still further, rapier-pointed horns set for a vicious sweep.

The press on either side thwarted its intent. All that the steer could manage was to jerk head and horns upward in violent thrust, not quite where they had been intended. That was a bit of luck. Johnny was caught on nose and bullet-like head between the points, lifted and boosted through the air.

He fell sprawling on the back of the animal whose tail he had been clutching, and again he instinctively wrapped his arms around its neck and clung. Once more the tight press of bodies favored him. His steed bucked as wildly as circumstances allowed, but there was no real chance to show what it could do.

How long or far he could keep riding would be a matter of luck. Skill on a sunfishing bronc was no more than a mild asset here. Even if his mount grew resigned, and he stayed with it, his weight would burden it severely in the long run. Stampeding as these were doing, cattle ran until stopped by exhaustion.

The steer would tire soon. Then it would stumble and go down. If that happened while the press remained heavy on every side, his chances of escaping would be slender. It would be crowding luck past the ragged edge.

His ears caught a mutation in the sweep of sound, a slight ebb at his right hand. Dust was like fog, but the wind sucked some of it away and he could see where the press had thinned and why. Almost beside him was a gulch, its steep side dropping away, the bottom concealed as by fog. The running herd had split almost by instinct, veering to each side to avoid being crowded over the brink.

At least most of them were managing to turn. A scrambling sound, punctuated by a despairing bellow, indicated that at least one had been shoved over the edge. Others might be entering at its mouth and filling the bottom of the draw past the safety point. That was a risk he'd have to take, and Johnny made his choice. He jumped, bunching again to roll, giving himself to the not always tender embrace of lady luck.

His heels struck first, digging into a steep, grassless slope part way down. Branches slapped him, where a bush clung to the slope. A root resisted his plowing spur, holding it an instant before breaking and upending him. He hit the bottom of the gulch on back and shoulders and lay an instant, the breath shocked out of him.

A ghostly cow plunged past, barely missing him, and he clawed and scrambled upright. Farther along the gulch, a scrambling, coupled with the sliding of dirt and small stones, indicated that such animals as had fallen into or entered the gulch were trying to get out.

He put his back to the wall of dirt behind him, able

to breathe again, taking up as little space as possible. The dust obscured his sight, even as the thunder rolling overhead and on both sides smothered lesser sounds.

Dirt rattled from above, a small cascade pouring over him. There was a possibility of the hoofs which had loosened it coming along, but there was no shelter, nowhere else to go.

The steer came down, sliding, fighting for footing, barely past where he stood. The animal lay a moment, dazed, the whites of its eyes rolling. A horn had caught somewhere, twisted and broken in the descent. Blood poured from the wound, while agony glazed its eyes. Then it got up and went on, weaving drunkenly.

Gradually the thunder gave way to separate, distinct sounds, and the these began to subside. Feeling as shaky as the steer, Johnny followed the draw. He found a calf with a broken neck, then a cow with two broken legs. Surprisingly, he had not lost his gun in all those wild gyrations. He despatched the cow, and ahead was a steep slope, torn ragged by scrambling hoofs.

As he climbed out from the gulch, Cy Robbins rode up. Dust coated him like a blanket, his eyes and mounth making uneasy slits in the mask. He pulled to a stop and stared thoughtfully, fumbling in a pocket for a remnant of tobacco plug, worrying off a corner between teeth which no longer quite matched.

"Thought I heard a shot. Are you real, Johnny, or am I mebby beholdin' the remnant o' your ghost?"

"Now that's a good question," Johnny conceded soberly. He had no heart for smiling. His near-brush with death and the memory of Dinty Toole were too fresh. The man had been a fool or a traitor, perhaps both. But across the years, Johnny had counted him, if not as a friend, at least as a member of Wagon Wheel and more or less his responsibility. He wouldn't have wished such an end, even for his worst enemy.

"Better climb up behind me," Robbins suggested. "Folks 'll think I'm bringin' in a scarecrow."

The rest of the crew had escaped unharmed. They buried Dinty. Only his gun, which had fallen under him, had escaped unscarred, a crowning irony. As foreman, Johnny spoke a few words above the grave, doing the best he could from memory.

He made no mention, one way or another, of the shots which Dinty had fired. The others, examining the gun, noted the empty shells. They had all heard the first and observed the result, but they, too, kept their thoughts to themselves.

With a fresh horse, Johnny joined the others in the gather. It took a lot of riding, through the remainder of that day and most of the next, to round up the scattered herd. Half a hundred head had died or were so badly injured that they had to be despatched. The stampede had carried them back almost to Termagent Creek, and that meant two days' extra loss.

Those were some of the hazards of the cattle business. A man accepted drought, blizzards, wolves, rustlers and all the rest. Johnny wondered if sheep raising could be any worse.

There was not much doubt but that this was a gesture of warning from some of their neighbors, men who not only resented sheep, but also hated sheepmen. Dinty's final acts had confirmed his suspicion there was a traitor among their own crew. Well, Dinty had collected his reward.

So, too, had Leavitt Vascom, who had been the first to taunt him with the epithet of sheepherder, who had been a prime mover in the hatred of Axe for Wheel. But such deaths would only spur others to even greater animosity.

Chastened by their tantrum, the cattle behaved circumspectly for the rest of the drive. They even grazed back the pounds lost in running, and appeared in reasonably good condition for the ordeal of the long train ride. There was even a dividend: the cattle cars awaiting them when they arrived. These had pulled in only an hour ahead of the herd; thus the delay due to stampede was no real loss.

Not that time much mattered. A man grew old at a riding job, but so did he if hammering nails or digging ditches, and days and years had a way of blending into the whole, losing significance. There was still plenty of time to sell the cattle, then return with sheep, so that they would be established ahead of the snows of winter.

It was a long chore to load the cattle onto the cars. Again, as during the peak of roundup, the branding and excitement, there was much bawling and concern. Once more the cattle were in a mood to break and run, but now the chance was past. They could fight and resist, and they did. It took nearly two days, and dusk was closing by the time the last car door was slammed in place.

There were two trains. The first one, loaded, had moved out ahead. Another locomotive, which had shunted a few cars at a time to the proper loading pens, now nudged the cars into a single string and moved to the head. A caboose was at the opposite end.

Four of the ranch crew had gone with the first section. Kid Coffee, Jim Heath and Cy Robbins, along with himself, would go on this one. Johnny did not look forward to the ride with pleasure. Their task was to watch alongside the cars whenever the train stopped, running to cover the length of the train, prodding with poles to force upright any animals which might be down and in danger of being trampled, feeding and watering when they unloaded.

Sometimes a train would start up when a man was halfway along its length. That meant grabbing, climbing to the top and making a precarious way back to the caboose, while the train swayed and jolted.

The remainder of the crew mounted their horses and were lost in the gathering night. In another couple of days they'd be back on the ranch. Far up ahead, the engine hooted.

The train started to move, and Johnny grabbed for

the handrail of the caboose. The others, including the
trainmen, had already gone inside. There was no one to
see him trip on the small wire, invisible in the gloom,
which had been stretched taut across the lower edge of
the steps. It had not been there a minute before, but it
threw him sprawling, writhing, half under the suddenly
turning wheels.

10

Surprise, coupled with the sudden jerk of the train, almost proved his undoing. As Johnny tripped and rolled, the hand rail at the front of the caboose caught his shoulder and knocked him partly forward, also under. Only his own reaction, twisting desperately, shoving back with both hands, saved him. A wheel crunched alongside the high heel of his right boot; then he rolled and was back from under. He came upright in time to snatch the last rail of the caboose, and this time he swung aboard.

For a minute he stood, not opening the door, listening, waiting. But no one came to see, or exhibited any curiosity.

Inside the caboose, the others looked up without

surprise, and a comment made it clear that they'd known that he was loitering on the back platform, that he had not missed the train. Kid Coffee was washing his face and hands, making a prodigious splash in a small basin. Cy Robbins was stacking his luggage, and Jim Heath, always a trencherman, had opened a package of lunch and was eating voraciously. None of them noticed his boot heel was scraped.

Checking the next morning, Johnny found the ends of the broken wire still in place. But that again proved nothing. It might be that the man who had affixed the wire was on the train, but too crafty to risk betraying himself by removing it.

The run to Chicago was as tiring as he'd expected, and uneventful. They made a couple of stops to unload, rest and feed the cattle. Even with extra trainmen assising, it was a long, slow chore each time. They were all dead beat when finally they pulled into Chicago.

There, the news was discouraging. Drought was beginning to lay a heavy hand on some sections of the range, and a lot of ranchers were unloading stock which normally would have been held at least until fall. The market was glutted; it had been having a bad week, and the coming one threatened to be worse. It was a buyer's market, not a seller's.

Like nearly all the other shippers, they had no choice. They had to sell for what they could get.

The decision was up to him. There was no way to reach Howard, and he already had troubles enough. Only a handful of buyers were interested. One, after looking over the bunch, made an offer of forty thousand dollars, which was the minimum that Denning had hoped for. Even then there was a condition. The man would pay ten thousand dollars down, the remainder in thirty days.

The proviso was not hard to understand, conditions being as they were. Time was needed to break up the herd into divisions—beef animals, cows, calves, feeders, and culls—and to find separate purchasers for each bunch.

If he wanted cash, he'd have to take a ten percent discount. They couldn't afford that, so Johnny took the first offer, hoping he could persuade the owner of the sheep to grant them time. He didn't expect much trouble, for ten thousand in cash could be a powerful persuader.

Returning to Iowa, he had a look at the sheep. Even to his inexperienced eyes, they seemed to be in good condition, though he had a moment of doubt as he moved among them. There was a difference, almost as wide as the miles between, between the sparse grass of Wagon Wheel range and the lush meadows where the sheep were now running. Texas-bred cattle didn't always adjust to the rigors of a northern range. The sheep had an innocent, helpless look. Would they be able to make such a transition and thrive?

He was surprised at the readiness with which his terms were accepted. Before the cars were ready, he'd go up to St. Paul, where Ma had spent so many weary months, and see her. Howard had been back twice, but the intervals between were long.

The antiseptic smell of the hospital, its hushed corridors, were disturbing. It was an alien world, and it must be an added ordeal for Ma. Then he tip-toed into the room, as a nurse cheerily announced, "Mrs. Denning, you have a visitor."

It was plain that Howard hadn't written that Johnny was coming, or if so, he'd beaten the letter. The surprise on her face testified to that. He'd remembered

Ma as a husky, hearty woman, a bundle of energy, always flouncing about, equally at home on the back of a horse or in her own kitchen, cheering everyone from Howard to the newest hand who might be nursing a touch of homesickness. The thin form under the sheet, with a touch of gray in her hair and her face to the wall, couldn't be Ma. Then she turned and looked, and as the amazement vanished her eyes lit up.

She didn't rise up, as she would once have done, nor did her voice boom in greeting as in the old days. But it was still hearty, though she choked in the middle of her greeting, and her hand, reaching for his, shook as though its thinness had left it unduly weak.

"Well, forever more, Johnny Malcolm You old horse thief, you're a sight for sore eyes—and I'll be blessed if mine don't feel like a salt lick!"

She'd toned down her vocabulary as well as her tone of voice to fit her surroundings, but she was the same old Ma, though he sensed how desperately lonely and homesick she was. They talked a streak for a while, interrupting each other. She asked a multitude of questions, which he answered as best he could, until she wanted to know what he was doing there and what was going on at Wagon Wheel.

"I know something *is*," she added. "I had a letter from Howard two or three days ago. What did I do with it? It was here somewhere—I've read it often enough. Trouble is, he didn't say anything. Just sort of hinted at changes, and got my curiosity all riled up. What *is* going on?"

Howard hadn't been able to find the words to tell of his decision, and the news would be a shock. But in the face of so direct a question, Johnny couldn't dodge.

"Brace yourself, Ma," he advised. "This has jarred us all—but I think it's the right decision. We've sold off the stock—every last steer, cow and calf. I'm taking back a couple of trainloads of sheep. Nine thousand head."

She took it better than he had expected. She had always been an understanding woman, and the reason was clear enough to her.

"You're doing all this for me." She sighed. "I know Howard. He'd have been willing to struggle along as well as he could, even if he never had a cent to spare. But he's right: it's not good cattle country. Whether sheep will do any better or not—I guess we can only make the try and find out, eh? If the neighbors will let us. Sheep *could* be a real money-maker."

"I feel that they will be."

"They'd better." Ma was herself again, keen-minded, competent. His visit was doing her good. "I'm that excited at seeing you, Johnny, I'm selfish and forgetful. I've a letter here about you—it came yesterday." She fumbled under her pillow and this time came up with what she wanted.

"It's from Myra," she explained. "Myra M'Ginnis— or Vascom, maybe. I used to mother her a bit, poor motherless lass, and I had a few letters from her, though they stopped a long while ago. Now I'm beginning to understand why. She writes of being stranded on a far corner of Wagon Wheel, of the worthless coot she took up with, and how you showed up in the nick of time to save her baby and herself. There's no word about sheep, or of you making a trip back here. But the things she says about you, Johnny—she makes me proud to know you!"

Johnny was surprised. It had never occurred to him that Myra would write to Ma, as almost her first act once she was strong enough to manage a pen. Apparently the letter had been written so soon after his own departure from Wagon Wheel that there was no fresh news.

"I never had a daughter," Ma added. "If I had, Myra would about have filled the bill. Of course she made a sad mistake, taking up with that Leavitt Vascom, but there's no denying that he's handsome as you'd expect a devil to be, and he could be nice enough. I remember the time he tried to butter me up, when first he was making eyes at Myra! But she's had her eyes opened to what a real man is, though it's late— poor lass!"

"She's lucky to be alive," Johnny said uncomfortably.

"And well she knows it, and gives full credit to you, Johnny, and remembers you each day in her prayers, which is right and proper. But the Vascoms don't stay squelched, which is what worries me. Old Barney never turned tail or ran for man or devil. Leavitt and Slade will duck for cover, but they always come back. That's what worries Myra—and me—especially with you taking back a band of sheep!"

"We'll deal with the Vascoms," Johnny promised. "You have that operation, then come along home and kick up your heels!"

"If you say it's the thing to do, I'll try it," Ma agreed. "Seeing you has perked me up so I can fight again. Bla—bless me, but I feel the same as Myra when she talks about Leavitt. She says she has about made up her mind to stay on at Wagon Wheel, preferring it to Axe. Leavitt hasn't turned up yet, and she hopes he never does!"

11

They were somewhere west of Laramie, and the train was climbing and twisting, crawling through the mountains in the uncertain gloom of midnight, when it happened. Malcolm had fallen asleep, stretched uncomfortably, half on a seat and half in the aisle, with only his boots removed. Even after many days and nights of such journeying, he had not grown accustomed to such quarters.

A jarring crash brought him awake, to find himself on his back in the aisle. The train had stopped with unpleasant abruptness, and loose objects were showering and rattling around and over him. From the outer night came a confused medley of distressing sounds—the terrified blatting·of the sheep, along with a grinding noise which gradually subsided. Lesser noises beat like a pulse.

Confused, Johnny fumbled for his boots, and found one of them. He tugged it on, pawing vainly for the other. Not taking time for a further search, he stumbled over obstructions. The interior of the caboose was as black as some of the tunnels through which they had passed. Wrestling open the door, he caught himself just in time, as he was about to jump out.

High white stars in a dark blue blanket of sky revealed the dim outlines of mountain country. They shed just enough light to show that if he got off here, it would be a long way down.

On that side of the track, the slope of the hill fell away, almost sheer. He could not see the bottom.

Other men were fumbling about, cursing at the gloom. A trainman approached, trying to find a lantern which was no longer in its accustomed place. Johnny struck a match, and the glimmer of light revealed not only the lantern but also his missing boot. While the brakie got the lantern lit, Johnny tugged on his boot. On the other side of the car, it was possible to descend to the ground.

Up ahead, confusion attested to the fact that part of the train was wrecked, though for as far as they could see, all the cars seemed still to be on the rails. The air was chill near the top of the divide.

The brakie turned back along the track, breaking into an urgent run as a mournful whistling echoed through the night. The second section of the train was not far behind. A curve shut off the view of their own stalled cars. Unless he could get around it and flag the engineer to a stop, they would come plowing into the rear of their own train.

Since he could do nothing about that, Johnny set off toward the front, picking his way cautiously in the gloom. A few cars were deep in a cut, but most of the train poised on a high grade, with none too much room even to walk at the side.

A whistle indicated that the swinging lantern had been seen; then the beam of a headlight flickered beside Johnny and became stationary. There would be help now from the crew of the second section. And from what he could see, there was need for it.

Sheep were packed in the cars, huddled in a dark mass, some murmuring plaintively. Most of them showed no sign of panic, but waited with a stoic patience.

The track curved again, beyond the radius of the headlight, but he could tell that the hill sloped sharply down at one side. The locomotive of their train, and an unknown number of cars, had been derailed. A dozen cars stood, like drunken derelicts, still upright but with wheels partly off the tracks. Beyond them, several more had plunged and rolled down the mountain. They were scattered in confusion, two or three hundred feet below, and sounds still emanated from them.

This wreck might be due only to a mischance, but there had been too many accidents since the news of Wagon Wheel's plan to change to sheep had become known. What had happened was bad, though it might have been worse. Only a little more would have sent most of the other cars off and toppling.

Had that happened, probably none of the sheep would ever have reached Wagon Wheel; that would have spelled ruin for Howard Denning. It might well be that it had happened already.

Down here, in the deeper gloom, sheep were blatting, some loose and running about in confusion. Several of the cars had broken open, allowing the occupants to escape. Others were still struggling to free themselves. Steam hissed and belched from the locomotive, which lay on its side like a wounded but still dangerous animal.

Johnny found the engineer hobbling about on a strained akle, nursing a bruised arm with his other hand, but otherwise not appearing to be seriously injured. The fireman had fared even better, which was surprising. They had ridden the engine in its plunge, and both seemed amazed to find themselves survivors.

"What happened?" Johnny asked.

The engineer shook his head.

"Sure and I'd like to know," he confessed. "We was rollin' along as sweet as a baby being rocked to sleep, just over the hump, see you, and I was reachin' to ease the throttle a mite as the pull leveled, congratulatin' myself that we'd made the top so easy-like with such a load. And the next thing I knew, we were rollin' and crashin' down the slope, and never a thing to see nor the least bit of warnin'. And Sam was watchin' from his side of the cab, and saw no more than I."

"Sure, and that's the gospel truth," Sam confirmed.

"There was a sort of jar, and the old rummy took off and tried to fly, as you might say, and all for no reason that we could tell."

"What's that?" The voice was sharp, querulous, but authoritative. Several other men had come up, hurrying from the second train. Listening, Johnny discovered that the man who was asking the questions was no less a personage than Van Sickle, the superintendent of the railroad. As chance would have it, he had boarded the second section of the train at its last stop, intending to ride with them as far as Green River.

Van Sickle was in an evil mood. The conductor, with whom Johnny had become friendly, whispered that the superintendent was new at his job; there had been an over-supply of trouble along the mountain division for more than a year, and he had been appointed to make sure that such things as had just happened should not take place. He seemed to regard the wreck as a personal affront.

The running, bleating sheep added to the confusion and his rage. If he was not a cattleman by training, apparently he was by instinct, and he made it clear that he hated sheep. Such business was not good for the country, the railroad, or anyone.

Apparently no one had been seriously hurt, which was something to be thankful for, but Van Sickle was in no mood to be thankful for small favors. They all climbed back, returning to the spot where the engine had jumped the track. It did not take long to find what had caused the disaster.

Upon leaving the rails, the locomotive and cars had torn things up as they went, but enough was left to tell the story. Van Sickle apparently knew his job.

"Somebody loosened a rail and shoved one end of it out of place," he pointed out, showing where the big spikes had been pried from many of the ties. The spikes had been tossed carelessly about. At night, there was not enough amiss so that a watcher could detect it; and even had the engineer spied the loose rail, there would have been no time, when swinging around a curve, to take action. One set of wheels had found no rail on which to run.

"This was a deliberate trick," Van Sickle growled. "They aimed to wreck this blasted sheep train, and they did. Somebody must have known what was coming, and they took this method of seeing that the sheep didn't reach their range."

Van Sickle issued rapid-fire orders. One man was instructed to climb a pole, tap the telegraph wire, and get a wrecking crew on the move east from Green River.

"We'll clear the track as fast as possible, make repairs, hook on to what cars are still standing, and move them ahead," Van Sickle explained. "It's the best we can do for the present."

"What about the others—and the sheep in 'm?" one man asked.

"Open the doors and let them run," Van Sickle exploded. "The sooner we're rid of them, the better."

Johnny had listened in silence. Now he intervened.

"You can't do that," he protested. "That would lose up to a couple of thousand head of sheep, here in these mountains. If they strayed, they could never be recovered."

Van Sickle swung on him. "Do you think that would worry me?" he asked sarcastically.

"It should," Johnny returned. "The railroad is responsible for delivering the sheep, in good condition, to their destination."

"Not in the event of wreck, fire or other disaster

beyond our cause or control, we're not."

"Probably you're right about that, though it might take some arguing in a court of law," Johnny conceded. "But if you aggravate the disaster and compound the loss by such methods as you've suggested, the railroad will be responsible, and you'll have to pay."

Van Sickle turned and thrust closer, to peer at him in the uncertain light.

"What business is this of yours?" he demanded. "Who the devil are you?"

"I'm Malcolm, foreman for Wagon Wheel, and we own these sheep. I don't object to your releasing the rest of those which are trapped in the cars down below. That will be necessary, of course. But I do want them watched and kept from straying, and our herders will help with that. We'll also have to have help rounding up those which have already strayed. Then they have to be reloaded and sent on, as soon as the track is fixed and the train can run."

Van Sickle regarded him with bitter animosity.

"You want this and you want that," he growled. "You want a wet nurse, don't you? You blasted sheepmen are all alike. No wonder everybody hates you. But if you think that we've nothing better to do than to help chase strays, you can think again." He stalked away, but Johnny noted that he did not implement the order to allow the sheep to run at will.

From their standpoint, it might have been worse. This way, they might lose up to a thousand head of sheep, and whether they would be recompensed for them or not was a doubtful question. Such a loss, on top of other expenses, could be a crippling blow. He was sure that it had been planned that none of the sheep should get beyond that point.

Howard Denning had been right when he'd predicted that there would be trouble. But they had expected it to be open, not underhanded.

Van Sickle was coming back, vaguely recognizable in the gloom. He was alone. A shadowy figure suddenly materialized from the darkness between two cars, a club raised to strike. There was not time to make a warning count, though Johnny found himself yelling as he jumped.

12

The older hands on Broken Axe shook their heads
and wondered. For almost the first time in their memory, Slade Vascom was cheerful, even smiling. Still
more unusual, he was hard-working, attending strictly
to whatever needed to be done. Knowing him, they
deduced that something was in the wind.

Knowing himself to be an object of speculation,
Slade grinned and was not at all bothered. So far as he
was concerned, everything was going well. He had
taken a series of steps to insure that it should continue
that way. True, John Malcolm had evaded or survived
several traps set for him, but luck was bound to turn.

The sheep train would be wrecked in the mountains,
and that ought to finish Malcolm and Wagon Wheel

121

at one and the same time. Out of the confusion, arrangements were already made to take over the sheep and dispose of them at a nice profit. It was a change from his original plan, but this was better. There would be a faster return, all going to him.

He knew that his father regarded this change with suspicion, but that was all right, too. It didn't matter overly much how it was managed, just so that he occupied the limelight. The Twins had always been inordinately vain, leading to an increasing rivalry, even for notoriety. Slade took secret pride in a collection of "Wanted" posters, in which, under various aliases, he was the central figure. He doubted if his cousin could match them.

One of these days, everyone on Axe, even Barney—particularly Barney—would find who was really in control.

As he rode by himself, it came as a double shock to encounter a stranger who edged his pony out from the shelter of a clump of brush, a gun held carelessly. Its muzzle, centered on Slade's chest, looked no colder than the eyes behind it. They held the same impartial animosity as a rattler's.

"Suit yourself," the stranger observed laconically, seeing the temptation in Slade's face, the hesitation as to whether or not he should make a desperation try for his own gun. "The dodgers read, 'Dead or Alive.' It's a sight easier to pack in a dead man than a live prisoner. So make your grab—if you feel lucky."

It had been too good to last, such a streak of luck as he'd been enjoying. Slade decided against sudden suicide.

"If you collect any money on me, you'll do it the hard way," he promised grimly.

The stranger nodded calmly, kneeing his horse closer. He reached and helped himself to Slade's holstered gun, then frisked him expertly for a hide-out weapon, either blade or shell. Satisfied, he leaned closer a second time, and before Slade could jerk back, handcuffs clicked coldly into place.

" A bold, bad man!" the newcomer jeered. "*And* a desperado, who rambled through the West like a big tornado! That's what they said about you. Why, this will be the easiest thousand dollars I ever collected."

"I suppose you've a warrant?" Slade asked, controlling his apprehension behind a show of indifference.

After all, they were in the middle of Axe range, and there were more ways than one of handling a situation.

"Right here." The lawman shook his gun before returning it to holster. "It works."

"I know you know," Slade agreed. "You're Simmons, the bounty hunter."

"You've got me wrong. I'm Wardlaw." It was an even more chilling name; it meant that this man had come all the way from California. He had a bulldog reputation.

Wardlaw fished a folded paper from a pocket, flipping it open with a jerk. It was the mate of one of those in Slade's collection.

Wanted—among other things—for highway robbery, with murder. You figured you'd be safe here on your home range, didn't you? But when I go after a man, Vascom, I don't stop until I get him."

"I've heard of you," Slade acknowledged, and tried a distraction. "Only this time you've got the wrong man. You really want my cousin, Leavitt Vascom."

"I'll take your cousin if I can get him," Wardlaw conceded. "He's worth just as much. But it was you I came after, and you I've got. That scar isn't to be mistaken. And now we'll turn and head out, avoiding anyone who might be so ill-advised as to try and interfere. Especially ill-advised for you," he amplified, "since you're worth as much dead."

Slade gulped. He'd heard about Wardlaw many times, never suspecting that the bounty hunter would stray so far or dare to invade Slade's home range. The man was as relentless as a weasel, as dangerous as a wolverine. Panic almost mastered him.

"Wait a minute," Slade pleaded. "Maybe we can talk this over. I'm worth a thousand dollars if you take me in—but I could be worth more if you don't."

Wardlaw regarded him inscrutably, and Slade knew that he hadn't been mistaken.

"You figure I can be bought?" Wardlaw asked.

"Any man can, if the price is right," Slade flung back. "You've a reputation as a bounty hunter, not as a lawman."

"Well?"

"So it doesn't make any difference to you, as long as you get your cut. I haven't got the money now, but I will have in a few weeks. Leave me alone, and a little later you can collect two thousand, instead of one—and no trouble about it."

Wardlow shook his head.

"Hh-uh. I'm not that cheap. Besides, I've come a long way."

"Three thousand, then," Slade said desperately. "You can stick around and take a little vacation. You can't make money any faster."

The bounty hunter fumbled in a pocket, then twiddled the key to the handcuffs.

"Five thousand, cash, in a month," he offered. "I don't haggle."

Slade gulped, then nodded.

"Five thousand it is," he agreed.

Wardlaw edged closer, gun at the ready. He unlocked the handcuffs, returning them to his pocket.

"A month," he warned. "And keep in mind that I don't take excuses; only cash. If I don't find the money waiting, I'll take you in—and there are ways of getting the difference out of your hide. Of course, I'm hoping that won't be necessary."

Nodding, he rode away, forgetting to return Slade's gun to him. Or perhaps it was not an oversight.

Slade was surprised to find himself shaking as he

rode home. That had been close—far too near for comfort. That particular murder poster had been plastered all up and down the coast. Because of it, he'd headed back to Axe months before, seeking sanctuary, confident of finding it, as on other occasions. Only things, meaning Barney, hadn't worked as in the past. And now this.

A month wasn't much time to gather such a sum of money, unless he chose highway robbery or a bank stick-up, and he hated to use such methods in his own territory. But thanks to the plan he had already set in motion, it should work out. Still, he had to move fast, instead of with caution, for the stakes were too high to hesitate. His neck was in the balance. The bounty hunter would be back, and it would be impossible to temporize or bargain a second time.

He might denounce the deputy, proclaiming that Wardlaw had agreed to take a bribe. The trouble with such a course was that it would be only his word against the bounty hunter's, and the knowledge of just how badly he was wanted by the law in several other places would come into the open.

A horseman was taking his leave as he approached

the buildings; a visitor who obviously had been palavering with Barney. Slade scowled. What the devil had caused Slim Bestwick to ride so far from town?

Drawing a deep breath, Slade entered the house. His hand was being forced, but the show-down might as well come now as later.

In his own room, he kept an extra gun. With his holster refilled, he was outwardly indifferent when Ching Lee, the cook, brought word that Barney wanted to see him.

His father wasted no words. His face was expressionless, but such inscrutability was more threatening than a scowl.

"What's this I hear about you buying sheep?" Barney demanded.

Slade shrugged.

"It seemed too good a chance to pass up," he explained. "There wasn't time to consult with you—so I went ahead in your name."

"So I've been informed. Go on."

"I got to thinking it over, and decided that maybe Denning was smart. This isn't good cattle country. It ought to be fine for sheep. This was a chance to get hold of the sheep that Denning was aiming to buy. We own them now, though he *thinks* he does. He'll bring them into the country—which others won't like. Wagon Wheel will get the blame. And in the process, it will go broke."

Barney waited. Slade swallowed and went on.

"We'll end up with the sheep, and they'll cost us next to nothing. By then people will be used to the idea. We can take over the whole range, with no particular opposition. We've fought the Wheel for a long while. This way we'll smash them."

"Maybe." Barney made a surprising admission. "I'm inclined to agree, too, that Denning's right about sheep. This certainly isn't good cattle country. So maybe you're right to that extent. But there's one big difference between you and me, mister."

Never before had he used the term with Slade. Anger glowed in his eyes.

"I've fought Howard Denning and Wagon Wheel ever since the two of us came to this country, just about together. I wanted the whole range, and so did he. And we always seemed to rub each other the wrong way. But there's one thing about our way—and we've had plenty, one time and another. Denning has always fought fair—and so have I—not in the sneaky, underhanded way that you're proposing!"

"If you're going to cut a man's throat, what's the difference if you do it with a knife or an axe?" Slade demanded. "Either way, he's just as dead."

"That I grant. And I don't suppose it makes too much difference to him in the long run. But it can make a lot of difference to the man who does it—whether he's fought fair or dirty. You and your Twin have always preferred to take the dirty way, to stab a man in the back or shoot him from ambush. Oh, don't fool yourself that I don't know what the pair of you have been up to. You've cheated and connived and stolen and even murdered. I suppose it't partly my fault, since I'm your father, and Leavitt has some of the same blood. I tried to bring the two of you up to fight, but to fight fair. I've failed, and I've tried to accept that responsibility, too. But this time you've gone too far—both of you!"

"Preaching comes rather strangely from you," Slade returned.

"Maybe it does. But I called the pair of you in here

nearly a year ago, and warned you that you had to mend your ways or I was through with you. You both promised. You've always been good at promising, but you never keep your word—which is another thing. Until the pair of you came along, a Vascom's word was good. There were no liars in the family. But I suppose that lying goes with all the rest."

Slade merely grinned. But the cold voice did not change it inflection.

"Months ago, the two of you came sneaking back, after things had gotten too hot for you wherever you had been. I told you then that you could still have a home here if you turned over a new leaf and behaved yourselves. I did it partly from pride of family, partly because I felt that I owed you that much. But I warned you then that as far as Axe was concerned, you were through; that I had cut you out of my will, and neither of you would ever have anything.

"I meant it. My mistake was in giving you another chance. You've both kept on as before, only worse. God help me, I'm ashamed of the name of Vascom, after what Leavitt has done! And now you commit my money, without permission, and plan to double—cross

Wagon Wheel as well. This time you've both gone too far. I'm giving you until tomorrow to get off Axe, off this range. And if you ever show yourselves around here again, either of you, I'll turn you over to the law myself."

Slade did not seem perturbed at the outburst. He was smiling, and suddenly his gun was in his hand.

"At last we understand each other," he murmured. "I don't know where Leavitt is, or care. But from now on I'm taking over here—and there doesn't to be room enough for the two of us."

Barney watched. The shocking thing to Slade was that there was not even surprise in his eyes.

"Put your hands up and turn around," Slade commanded. "You'll have to reside somewhere else temporarily. Afterward, we'll see whether you show sense or not."

He advanced, lashing out suddenly with the barrel of the gun. Barney tried to avoid the blow, but it was too swift. He went to his knees, then onto his face without a sound, while a trickle of blood showed amid the white of his hair.

13.

Either he had struck harder than he had intended, or else the old man wasn't as hard-headed as he had always supposed. Barney breathed jerkily, a rasping deep in his throat. Pallor covered his face like a shroud, and his pulse was a feeble flutter. Even when water was flung in his face, he showed no sings of reviving.

Slade worked over him for a few minutes, his uneasiness increasing. Then, when there was no change, he shrugged. Perhaps this was for the better. It could certainly make his plan easier, and it wouldn't be polite to spur a gift horse. A sardonic grin touched his mouth as he turned, making a quick tour of the house, then going around the buildings.

Except for Ching Lee, busy in his kitchen, no one else was around. The old Chinaman was too nearsighted to see beyond the windows of the cook house, too deaf to notice anything less than a gunshot. Vivian had gone for a ride, taking the baby.

Slade was thankful that she was not around. Being alone simplified what had to be done. He wrapped his father in a blanket, picked him up as though carrying out an old bundle of clothing, and walked to the barn. He deposited the unconscious man on some hay, deep among the shadows of a remote stall. Next he saddled Barney's favorite horse and concealed it among a clump of trees and brush behind the barn. When the crew rode in, they would notice that the horse was gone.

He had barely completed his preparations when Vivian returned, riding slowly. She looked surprised when Slade hurried to meet her, exclaiming as though she had been a stranger.

"I've been wondering where you'd gone to, Vivian. That ride certainly put color in your cheeks—not that they needed it! Did I ever tell you that you're getting to be a remarkably handsome woman?"

Vivian looked at him, startled. This was so unlike his usual attitude that she wondered if he had been drinking.

"Why no, I don't remember that you ever did," she admitted.

"I shouldn't be that blind—and I'm not," Slade protested. "Here, let me help you. I'll take care of your horse. I'll help you down."

"My, you *are* polite," she remarked, and handed him the baby, then jumped quickly down. That was not what he'd intended, and Slade scowled, but changed to a twisted grin as she met his look. He even essayed a smile for the baby, who was regarding him with wide-open eyes. The baby promptly gave a wail of displeasure.

"Now what's the trouble?" Slade demanded. "Most young ladies like me." Somewhat hastily he handed her back, then protested as Vivian promptly turned toward the house. "Hey, don't be in such a hurry. I want to talk to you."

"She's hungry and needs changing," Vivian returned. "I'll be in the house."

Shrugging, Slade cared for her horse, then followed her inside. The baby was occupied with a bottle. Vivian shot a question at him.

"Where's Dad? Have you seen him?"

"Not lately," Slade said carelessly. "I believe he rode out somewhere a while ago. Why?"

"Nothing—except that he's been staying pretty close around the house lately. I don't think that he's very well."

"You must be imagining things," Slade protested. "I haven't noticed anything wrong about him. Anyhow, this gives us a chance to talk to each other. Don't you think it's about time that we did have a talk? You've been away for nearly a year, and I haven't heard anything of your experiences, or how you liked school, or anything else."

Vivian looked surprised. "There's nothing to tell," she said. "School was all right, I suppose, though I felt rather out of place back there. But I didn't suppose that you had the slightest interest in what I did."

Slade looked pained. "Whatever gave you that idea?" he asked. "Of course I'm interested in what you do, or have been doing. I care more about you, and what happens to you, Vivian, than anyone else. I always have."

That was news to her, and again she wondered if he had been drinking. Slade went on eagerly.

"I guess I understand, and I suppose you got the notion that I didn't care too much about what went on around here, because I didn't take much part in helping with the ranch. But that's not because I didn't want to. You know how Dad is—he always likes to run everything to suit himself. At least that's the way it was. I think things are changing some now. We've had some talks, and I'm to do more from now on, take a bigger part in running things."

Vivian regarded him uneasily. He sounded nervous and disconnected, but he had been unpredictable most of his years.

"Dad can use more help, I'm sure," she murmured. "Axe is a big place."

"There's no question about him needing help. From now on, I'm going really to take an interest—and that includes you, of course. For this affects both of us, Viv."

She could smell no liquor on his breath, but he was increasingly strange. Vivian moved to put a table between them.

"Does it? Well, of course we're both interested in things, I suppose—"

"Of course we are, but it's a lot more than that."

He moved quickly to one side, and as she countered by turning the other way, darted back and was beside her. "Don't you understand? I'm interested in *you!*"

She was suddenly frightened, but strove not to show it. She managed to laugh.

"That's certainly a change, that you should know I'm alive, Slade. But I don't understand—"-

"You might as well then, and now is as good a time as any. For I can't go on the way I've been doing any longer. You mean too much to me. You're not really my sister, you know."

This time she was really surprised.

"You're my half-brother, if that's what you mean," she returned. "I've always known that, of course—"

"But that's just it. We're not," he said triumphantly. "I mean, I'm not your half-brother. Actually, we're no relation at all. I suppose that technically we'd count as step-brother and sister, since Dad married your mother. But you're really no relation at all. You were a baby at the time. I remember you—and how you wanted your own way even then!"

She stared at him, beginning to comprehend, and all at once a number of matters which had puzzled her became understandable.

"I didn't know that," she admitted. "I didn't realize. I just took it for granted—"

"Sure you did, as was natural," Slade agreed, and grinned at her triumphantly. "But that's the way it is. Now do you see what a difference it makes?"

She understood clearly enough, and her dismay increased. But it wouldn't do to let him see that she was afraid. She shook her head.

"I can't see that it makes much—after all this time." She was careful to hide the sudden feeling of elation which countered other emotions. It made no particular difference that Barney was not her father. She had always respected him, but had sometimes felt guilty that she could feel no real affection for any of her relatives. That was more understandable now.

As to Slade and Leavitt, her feeling for them had been one of active dislike, increasing rather than diminishing as time went on. Leavitt now lay in a nameless grave, and indirectly it was because of her. But she could feel no sympathy or contrition, when she remembered how he had held a knife at Johnny Malcolm's throat, the way in which he had treated

Myra, and the rest.

"It makes a lot of difference." Slade broke in on her thoughts. "I never said anything about how I felt before you went away—I guess I was too scared of the Old Man to dare speak up. And since you've come home, I haven't had a chance. But now you understand how things are, and I can admit that I've always loved you, Viv—and not as a brother! Now we can get married, for there's nothing to prevent it."

He grabbed for her, and she dodged behind the clothes basket in which the baby lay. She could not hide the horror and revulsion in her face.

Slade tried to dodge again in the opposite direction to intercept her, but this time the baby set up a wail. Frustrated, he stopped and she bent to soothe the baby.

"Now see what you've done!" she protested, and managed to keep her voice even, almost light. "You'll have to give me time to think about this, to get used to the notion. It's all so new! We're still brother and sister—at least—"

Slade scowled at the baby. "We're not," he growled. "We never have been and never will be. I thought you could tell how I felt about you, even if I didn't come right out and say so. Why, Viv, I've been crazy about you for almost as long as I can remember—"

"You're talking crazy now," she protested. "I couldn't even think of such a thing—"

"Why couldn't you?" Slade's voice was thick with sudden jealousy. "What was there between you and Malcolm, when I found you together off there? Don't tell me you've fallen for a dirty sheepherder like him—"

"That will be enough, Slade!" She had been raised as the daughter of Barney, and no one had ever suggested that she lacked the Vascom pride. On occasions, as now, her anger could match theirs, too. She blazed at him, and Slade retreated, discomfited. But his suspicion was fanned to a virtual certainty.

He retreated to another part of the house, then went on to meet some of the returning crew members. Some of them were loyal to Barney, and would react suspiciously to anything which he might suggest. But there were others, in addition to certain employees at Wagon Wheel, who had taken his pay for a long while. The time was at hand for such men to earn that money.

14.

Johnny's yell mingled with a triumphant exclamation from the club wielder as he jumped and swung at virtually the same moment. He could not forbear to vent his spleen in words as well as action.

"So far, Malcolm, you've had the devil's luck, but try and get out of—"

There was no path, there at the rim of the railroad grade where Van Sickle walked. Below that, the hill fell away steeply. A likely spot for murder.

Johnny's shout warned the killer that he'd misjudged his man in the dark, but frustration only spurred him on. Malcolm's shoulder hit the railroader, twisting him partly about and shoving him back, but there was no time to avoid the blow originally intended for himself.

Johnny took it on his upflung arm, grabbing.

His fingers met the club, and it came free in his grasp, while he reeled at its shock along his shoulder. He staggered; his legs twisted and his feet fumbled. Then a hand caught him and pulled him back as he reeled, and he realized that it was Van Sickle, aiding him.

Their antagonist was gone, ducking between two of the cattle cars and through to the far side of the track, immediately lost to sight. Van Sickle pursued, but presently came back. By then, the numbness in his arm was receding, and with only a torn shirt and swelling bruise, Johnny decided that it could have been worse.

"You all right?" Van Sickle asked gruffly. "He got away," he added.

"I could be worse off," Johnny returned. "That was what he aimed at."

"He mistook me for you, and would have smashed me off there if you hadn't jumped in," the superintendent fumed. "What the devil's going on, anyhow? First this wreck—then this. They must have a connection."

"Seems likely," Johnny conceded dryly.

"I lost my temper and made some uncalled-for remarks," Van Sickle confessed ruefully. "But it strikes me that this is going pretty far, even for a row between rival outfits."

"I'll go along with you on that," Johnny agreed. "A lot of it seems pretty personal, which has got me to wondering. I'm only foreman for Wagon Wheel, but it seems almost as if the sheep were only being used as an excuse."

"That's an interesting notion. You have some special enemies, or something?"

"I didn't know of any. That's what keeps me guessing." He was searching his memory, trying to place the voice, but without success. It has sounded familiar, but the impression was as elusive as it was hazy.

"My guess would be that whoever tampered with the rail was still hanging about, and when that failed to get you, he saw this chance and took it," Van Sickle observed. "At it is, I owe you an apology, as well as a solid skull. Maybe it's too thick to have been damaged," he added with a grin. "But I'm partial to keeping it that way. We'll look after the sheep as well as we can.

You give the orders where they are concerned."

The herders were arriving by then, and by morning, under Van Sickle's steady drive, most of the strays had been rounded up and the track cleared. By mid-morning they were ready to roll again.

He was somewhat surprised to find neither Howard or any others of the crew awaiting them when they unloaded the sheep for the drive to the ranch. There would be a lot of work on Wagon Wheel, building corrals, putting up hay for winter, doing a score of unaccustomed chores in anticipation of the new role for the ranch. Still, he'd expected some word.

The sheep, divided into two big bands, moving a day apart, were not so hard to handle as he'd feared. The herders and their dogs were skilled.

They had covered half the distance to Wagon Wheel before real trouble loomed on the horizon. A dozen mounted men rode into sight, well armed. An eager look dashed Johnny's hope that some might be from Wagon Wheel. And while none beyonged to Axe, it required no imagination to guess that Axe would have influenced the men to undertake the mission. Some of them had been friends, but that, he suspected, was definitely in the past.

Johnny rode to meet them, Cy Robbins beside him. Big Bill Leseur led the deputation. He held up a hand in a flat gesture as Johnny approached, the signal as negative as his voice.

"You've come far enough with those sheep, Malcolm," Leseur warned. "You ought to know that we won't allow anything of the sort in this country."

"I've been expectin' some such word," Johnny returned with equal frankness. "But aren't you overlookin' a couple of factors, Bill? All the land hereabouts is open range—and we have as good a right here as you or anyone else. And I mind me of an old saying in this country: that it's a free country for everybody."

Leseur shook his head.

"That don't apply to sheep or sheepmen."

Johnny looked surprised. "You mean you're settin' yourselves up as judge, jury and law—above the government?"

"I mean we ain't going to allow sheep to reach our range."

"They won't be on your range any of the time. I'll

promise you that. Once on Wagon Wheel, we'll make sure they don't trespass or bother anyone else."

Big Bill's headshake was uncompromising.

"No!"

"I could suggest, Bill, that you might be first cousin to a Missouri mule—but one or the other of you might take that as being uncomplimentary, so I won't." Johnny grinned and looked around.

The herders had left the sheep to be held by the dogs, and were coming up. Johnny had said nothing to them, but they had a good idea of the situation. For the first time, he noticed, they had buckled on guns. With them, the two forces were approximately equal. And it didn't really make any particular difference whether you thought of things as a cattleman or from the point of view of a sheepman. Your reactions were the same.

"I don't intend to start trouble, Bill," Johnny went on, and was conscious of a surprising feeling of kinship with herders. "But you know that Wagon Wheel has never been pushed around."

The others hesitated. As he expected, this show was by way of warning. It seemed to come home to them that they were being used as cat's-paws, and they had no relish for what might prove a bloody clash.

"Our job was to warn you that you've come far enough," Leseur said. "We've done that. You keep on at your own risk." He led his men away, retreating with reasonably good grace.

As evening came on, there was still no sign of Denning or any of the main crew. But other men came out of the night in force, shadowy figures on horseback materializing suddenly, outnumbering them three to one. Most of them Johnny recognized, and knew that the preliminaries were over. These were riders of Axe.

The first intimation of their presence was a voice, calling warningly from the gloom.

"Don't make any wrong moves and nobody will be hurt—aside from your boss. Every man of you there is covered by a gun. Start trouble, and you and your sheep are finished. This is by way of warning, since you wouldn't heed a friendly word. We don't want bloodshed."

A hush followed. In it, everyone could hear the clicks as hammers were thumbed back on six-guns or from rifles. The sounds echoed from every side. The voice spoke again.

"A couple of your men can walk around and check, if you like, just to see that we ain't bluffing."

Johnny knew that it was no bluff. Broken Axe, like Wagon Wheel, never bluffed.

"You see how it is," the speaker added. "Start anything, and you haven't a chance. But we aren't hurting anyone—not even the sheep—right now. Nobody but you, Malcolm. You're boss here—as well as being a traitor and a dirty turncoat. So we'll make clear what we mean."

A quartette of shadowy figures advanced out of the gloom, each with a leveled gun. It would have been suicidal to resist. As one man helped himself to his gun, Johnny's nostrils caught a new odor—sticky and almost pleasant, save for its connotations. It was the smell of hot tar.

15.

The ranch house on Wagon Wheel was a sprawling but comfortable two-story affair. The weather had turned hot and dry, and Myra's room, on the second floor, was breathless. Through the open screened window, a cool night breeze tempered the room's atmosphere. Lying wakeful, Myra thought of many things.

There was her baby. Vivian had sent word that the child was doing well, and she would bring it back some day very soon. Myra's strength would permit her to care for it again. She was able to be up for several hours each day, even to take walks out of doors. It was almost like a miracle to be alive.

Slade Vascom had come to Wagon Wheel and

asserted that he was taking Vivian home with him, to Axe; he'd demanded to talk to her. Myra had overheard the altercation, the raised voices as Howard Denning refused and warned him to get off Wagon Wheel and stay off. Slade had sounded so much like Leavitt that she had shivered in fear. But he'd gone away again.

She had come to like Howard even to respect him. Now she admired him, for he had stood up to Slade, although he was a sick man, scarcely able to stir from the house. He was waiting for Johnny Malcolm to return, to look after affairs. She hoped Johnny would not be long in coming.

Myra started, hearing his name, Johnny Malcolm. Someone had spoken it in the darkness outside the house. Two men were talking, speaking in hushed voices, but sound carried in the silence of the night. Since her window was up under the eaves, they could not see it, or suspect that it was open, that anyone might be able to overhear.

"Yeah, he's on the way with the sheep. But they've come about as far as they'll get. Axe is set to see to that. They're going really to take care of the sheep—

and Johnny—tomorrow night."

The voices drifted into silence, but terror was in the dark room now. Axe wanted to get Johnny. Axe had become a symbol of fear, something beyond scruple. They would kill him.

She must do something, but what? Those men had belonged to the crew of Wagon Wheel, but their words had made it plain that they were in the pay of Axe, turncoats, traitors. Who could be trusted? She dared not tell Howard, for he'd try to ride himself, even if it killed him.

She was up, fumbling for her clothes, dressing hastily in the darkness, not daring to strike a light. There might still be time to ride, to reach Johnny, to warn him, to help. She was not too strong, but well enough, and this was a task which had to be done. Silently she let herself out into the night.

Night had fallen when Slade Vascom rode out from Axe, leading a second horse on which Barney slumped like a half-emptied sack of grain. He had not regained consciousness, which under the circumstances was convenient. Though he had struck harder than he intended, Slade had no compunctions. Not only did this make the present operation easier, but this was a long overdue payment for wrongs, real and fancied.

His hatred for his father, coupled with sometimes passive, often open rebellion, dated back to a spring blizzard when he had been eight years old. He remembered vividly, partly because it had been his birthday. His mother had baked a cake. For a present, and because she had been raised a Slade, she had given him a six-shooter—a woman's model, small and dainty, but deadly. It was the first gun he'd ever had. Slade remembered his wildly exultant thrill when he had held it in his hands.

For his Twin, Leavitt, who thought his cousin was so like him, there had been a gift also, by way of compensation. Leavitt's mother and his own had been twin sisters, Slades. In their eyes, that was like a badge—not a blue ribbon, but a red.

Leavitt's gift had been a small, perfectly honed model of a standard bowie knife. Already, Leavitt had shown his fondness for such a weapon, practicing endlessly with an old jackknife, literally chopping a board to splinters. That same evening, in the gathering dusk, he had transfixed a rabbit with his new blade, blooding it properly.

Along with the cake and the gifts, Slade's mother had told them the story of her father—their grandfather Slade and his exploits, as a young man. Like most of the Slades, he had died young, at the end of a rope. But she had made him appear a heroic figure, one to be emulated. Both boys had listened, enthralled.

Barney, who had been young then, had been out on the range all day. He had returned, soaked and chilled and in a bad mood, in time to hear Leavitt's squeal of glee as his knife transfixed the rabbit, to find the boys dancing about the victim, shaking knife and gun in a sort of ritual. The sight of the weapons in their hands had enraged him.

He'd stormed into the house, accusing his wife of wanting her children to follow in the steps of their grandfather. His tone of voice, more than the *word*s, had conveyed his contempt and disapprobation for the man the Vigilantes had hanged.

Slade's mother had screamed back at him. Then, while he went to change to dry clothes, she had moved swiftly, slipping out of the house with both children, fumbling in the gloom of the barn, saddling two horses, one for them, one for herself. Slade still remembered the creaking and groaning of the boards in the wind, the thickening storm. He had been frightened, but like Leavitt, he had obeyed without protest when she loaded them onto one horse and mounted the other herself, heading out into the darkness.

It had been raining as they set out, but soon the rain had changed to sleet, then to driving snow. A late spring storm could sometimes be worse than midwinter blizzards, and this was such a storm. Before an hour had passed, all three had been shivering, chilled to the bone and lost. He suspected that they would have turned back, had any of them been sure which way to go or what to do.

It had been past midnight before his father had found them. By then, one horse was down with a broken leg, the other shaking with exhaustion. The injured horse had caught its rider when falling. It had come to both boys, shockingly, and only minutes earlier, that she was dead.

From that day, they had hated Barney with a bitterness which never wavered, holding him responsible, clinging to the teachings of Slade's mother as the only true faith. Their goal had been the emulation of their grandfather, and whatever Barney Vascom had done, all that he had tried to teach them, had been scorned.

Had his second wife lived longer, she might have made a difference, even in them. She had been a proud woman, fitting well into the tradition of the Vascoms, but gentle, with a sweetness which, against their will, had won the boys. But that was two years later. Her small daughter, who had become Slade's stepsister, had been a toddler, just learning to walk.

Their stepmother had been with them only a couple of years, not long enough to overcome former memories or deep-hidden resolutions. Pneumonia was as swift a killer as it was deadly.

Slade found himself remembering as he rode, and feeling an odd sort of regret. Like an imperfect kitten, it had taken him a long time to get his eyes open. By then it had been too late.

He no longer thought of his grandfather as a heroic figure, or one to be emulated. Plenty of men remembered and still spoke of him and his exploits, seldom realizing that he had been any kin of the Vascoms.

Drew Slade had been a gunman and killer, too cowardly to give opponents an even break. Slade recognized his own heritage, the taint in his and Leavitt's blood.

As for his mother—well, the less said of her the better. She had been beautiful, wild and tempestuous, and such qualities had appealed to the hot-headed Vascom boys, Barney and Phil. Phil's wife had left him and her son, to run off with a wagon train boss headed for California. Phil had caught up, only to find that he was up against a faster gun than his own.

Barney had wanted them to amount to something, which had probably been his reason for risking marriage a second time, to give them the influence of a good woman. During most of the time she had been with them, they had resented their stepmother, remembering a stark figure in a driving blizzard.

Slade shrugged, glancing toward the slumped figure in the saddle. It was too late for such thoughts, much too late, with the bounty hunter set to return. He could see now the rightness in Barney's philosophy, how much better it was to be the honest, respected owner of a spread than to be a man on the run, always looking over your shoulder. There was no glamour in such an existence; only misery.

But he, like Leavitt, had journeyed past the point of no return. Barney had finally drawn a line, after repeated warnings, and they had overstepped it with cool deliberation. Regrets were as useless as tumbleweeds. He was his mother's son, his grandfather's scion, not Barney's, and it was his neck, like his grandfather's, that was in danger.

The simple way, and perhaps the best, would be to strike again, then dump the body into some draw where only the wolves would ever find it, and be done. Two things stayed his hand. He had already set plans in motion, and Axe's crew was riding. Life was unpredictable, and events. Barney might possibly prove useful.

The other, less tangible, was the memory of how Barney had taken off his own heavy coat and wrapped him in it on that long-ago night of blizzard, after wrapping Leavitt in his aunt's coat. Somehow he had contrived to carry both of them in his arms, on the horse, back to shelter in the grayness of dawn.

I might even give him a chance, if he comes around

and agrees to be reasonable, Slade reflected. Just so I control Axe and Wheel.

Twice chilled to the bone in a matter of hours, staggering with exhaustion, his father had been unable to ride back to where the dead horse and woman lay in the blizzard's path; or even to give coherent orders to his crew to go after his wife. He had come down with pneumonia, and lived. But by the time he had become rational again, the weather had turned warm, the snow had gone, and the wolves had ranged widely. That too, the boys had held against him. Yet now, for the first time, Slade grudgingly admitted that he had done all that was possible.

It was past midnight when they reached the cabin beyond Lampases Spring. Slade had never visited the place, but he knew about where to look. Leavitt had taken Myra there, had held her hidden and a virtual prisoner for half a year, and no one had been the wiser. It would be ideally suited to his own purpose.

He untied the still unconscious man and half-carried, half-dragged him inside the cabin. With the door open, a thin glimmer of moonlight came through, enough to reveal the bunks along one wall. He got his father into the lower one, and his thoughts turned sardonic. This was where Myra had preceded them.

The sun had taken the place of the moon when he awoke, at a sound from the lower bunk. Barney was not only conscious but awake, which attested to the hardness of his head and the toughness of his constitution. He'd come through a lot which would have killed lesser men; under the circumstances perhaps that was a pity.

Reaction had left him weak and a little dazed. He looked about uncertainly as Slade swung down from the upper bunk. His glance ranged the cabin, and understanding came into his eyes.

"So this is where you've brought me."

Slade nodded, and erased all weakness or sentiment from his tone.

"I'm giving you one more chance. If you give *me* another, you can go on living. It's as simple as that."

Barney contrived to shrug. The gesture brought a grimace as pain raced through his skull, and he sank back. But his whisper was defiant.

"There's an end to the longest rope."

"Think it over," Slade advised. "I can get along

without you—but you can't without me. Not this time."
He took a considering look around the cabin, making
sure that it was as barren as the others had reported.

Outside, he studied the door, walked around the
cabin, and was satisfied. It was old and ramshackle,
but still sufficiently sound for his plan. There was no
window. Once the door was barred on the outside, it
would be an effective prison. Lacking any tools with
which to dig, cut or batter, even Barney, tough as
he'd proved himself, could not escape.

Slade barred the door, then looked for the spring.
It was not difficult to locate, but what he saw not far
beyond startled him. He needed only a glance to be
sure that it was a new-made grave.

Its significance was clear. There was even a dried
bunch of flowers on the dirt, had additional proof been
needed. Here, almost certainly, was the answer to the
continued absence of Leavitt.

And it makes sense, Slade reflected. Malcolm found
him here—or the other way around. In either case,
Malcolm killed him, which is surprising, considering
Leavitt's way of fighting. But I guess I owe you a
vote of thanks, Malcolm—not that I'm going to give

it. This simplifies matters in more ways than one, and I certainly won't shed any tears.

He returned to the cabin and cooked breakfast from his supplies, giving some to his father. Barney had no appetite. Recovery would be slow, even under good conditions.

There was an old shovel in the brush, which had already been used to move the dirt. Disliking his task, but knowing that it might be useful, Slade set to work. At least it was easy digging, and once he had come upon the body, the wound was clear enough so he was certain of the cause of death.

It would be convenient to have witnesses, but that was out of the question on several counts. He filled the grave in again, then returned to the cabin. Barney had apparently been asleep. He looked wan and feverish. Slade sat on a stool and reported.

"I found Leavitt," he explained. "Buried, off up the gulch. He must have tangled with Malcolm, and his luck ran out."

"Good for Malcolm," Barney observed. "It saves the hangman a chore."

Slade did not contest the sentiment. After what

162

Leavitt had done, he was inclined to agree.

"That solves part of my problem. I'll have to be getting back to Axe, taking charge. You know, I've been thinking. I guess I've been mistaken about you in some ways. That's neither here nor there, except that you can still have a place there if you want. Only I have to run things."

"The answer is still no."

"Suit yourself." Slade stood up. "Maybe you'll change your mind, after thinking it over a few days. There's water in the bucket, some grub in that sack."

He bolted the door again, and squinted at the sun. In another few minutes that side of the cabin would be in the shade, remaining so for the rest of that day. But on the morrow, the sun would shine hotly again.

From a pocket he took a small magnifying glass with which he and Leavitt had played as boys, starting more than one fire over which to roast game or fish, feeling like pioneers because they had no need for matches. He cut a crotched stick and thrust it into the ground, then fastened the glass in the crotch. It was a simple matter to focus the beam of the sun onto one of the tinder-dry logs near the corner of the cabin.

After a minute, a thin streamer of smoke started to curl, then died as the shadow shut away the sun until another day.

He gathered an armful of dry wood from among the brush of the gulch, piling it in place, and several handfuls of cured grass from the previous summer. These were about the stick, stacked against the logs. There would be no stick left as evidence after the sun focused again, and if the magnifying glass should ever be found amid the ashes, it would be so twisted and melted as to be unrecognizable.

It was unlikely that anyone would see flame or smoke on that remote corner of Wagon Wheel range and investigate. Should anyone do so, he would be back on Axe, busy about other matters, when the fire was discovered.

16.

Johnny stood rigid. The quartette from Axe had guns on him, and there were others all about, keeping a sharp watch on his own men to stop them from interfering. It came again, more forcefully now, that there was an element of the personal in this, directed against himself; something more than dislike for sheep or for the foreman of Wagon Wheel.

Now it was driving toward culmination. One of the four men carried a bucket, and it was from this that the sweetish smell of warm tar emanated. A second man had a bulky sack slung over his shoulder, and Johnny could guess its contents.

It was folly to fight back when the other fellow had the drop, when you knew that he had no scruples, and would welcome an excuse for pulling the trigger. To submit was common sense. But there was a point where good sense left off, and this was that point.

He went into action, jumping straight-armed, the drive of anger behind the blow. It caught one of the men and sent him sprawling, his nose gushing blood, his gun lost in the gloom.

Johnny spun, using a trick which had been tried against him and which was deadly if properly worked —kicking and twisting, raking with the spur. It could be as vicious as a bowie.

He aimed for the man with the tar, but another came out of the gloom and got in his way, then cried out sharply as the spur slashed with a ripping of cloth. He grabbed frantically at the tormenting leg, caught Johnny's foot and held, twisting. Johnny sprawled, and others piled on him like ants swarming over a bug.

Johnny outdid the insect struggling. Twice he almost broke away, and once he closed his fingers on a holstered gun and got it loose, but before he could bring it into action another gun barrel slashed alongside his skull. He fell back, his head feeling as if it had just been cleaved, pain bursting through the top of his skull.

As from a long way off, Johnny heard the voice of Cy Robbins, methodically cursing his captors. No one paid much attention. Wagon Wheel, the sheep and the herders were incidental. It was Johnny they were after, and they had him.

They ascertained that he was not too badly hurt, and that pleased them; they wanted him to feel, to suffer his degradation to the utmost. They dumped the bucket of tar over him, turning him so that he would be more completely covered. One man took hold of his boots, another caught his arm, and they lifted, twisting, turning, sloshing him in what had spilled.

It soaked into his clothing, clung and held. The sack was upended, spilled in a fluttering cloud. A torrent of feathers stuck and clung until he was like some grotesque fowl.

His head cleared slowly. Blood trickled from a cut in his scalp down the side of his cheek, along his chin. Some reached his mouth, rank and salty, flavored by tar.

The sheep stood uncertainly, an endless cacophony

of sound drifting like a wail from thousands of throats. The bleating held apprehension and fear of the unknown.

Someone got hold of and lifted Johnny, growling at the tar, and let him drop back. That gave them an idea, and they discussed it with the hunger of dogs for a fresh bone. He would not be subjected to the final indignity of being ridden on a rail. For one thing, there was no rail handy. And there was something better, or worse, according to the point of view.

A couple of men picked him up, trying to hold where there was not too much tar. They partly dragged and partly carried him, and again he heard the voice of Robbins, cursing, protesting, until it was suddenly cut off.

The sheep shied, but stupidly, not far. They were pressed too closely to move much. There were nearly five thousand head in the band, and the men were dragging him to the center of the mass. There they dropped him, then made their way back out. Wild yelling signaled the final act, to scare the sheep. They were to be stampeded into frenzied movement, with him helpless in their midst.

It seemed to Myra that she had been endlessly on the trail, finding no one, getting nowhere. Time had lost its meaning. Weakness ached in her bones and made her flesh flabby as a caught fish turns soft in the air. But she had endured worse before, and she kept going. They would be somewhere on ahead, down the trail: Johnny, the sheep and the riders from Axe. They could be nowhere else.

She was confusedly aware that the heat of the sun had given way to coolness, the glare of light to thickening dusk. She would have to stop soon, would have to rest. Flesh could take only so much, either her own or that of her horse. It stumbled now and again as it moved.

She blinked and looked again, and it was no mirage. That was not a low-hung star, but a fire—perhaps a cook fire on which fresh wood had been thrown. The red eye shone a long way in the night. As she glimpsed the beacon, she heard another sound, one strange and alien, but not to be mistaken—the steady, disturbed bleating of sheep.

Men were near the fire as she rode up, standing about in strained, unnatural attitudes. She had known that it would be this way; that was why she had come. She caught the glint of light on gun barrels, where some men watched others and held them like hounds on a leash.

A couple of men were dragging or carrying something, forcing their way among the sheep. She could make out the sheep, a vast gray mass in the uncertain gloom; the stars seemed more remote and aloof than she ever remembered seeing them.

The men had dropped whatever they were carrying and were pushing hastily back from among the sheep. Another was cursing, his voice shrill with anger and helpless rage. She caught enough of what he was mouthing to understand, and the night wind blew cold. Then a fist smashed against the speaker's mouth and silenced him.

It was Johnny they had lugged out there, Johnny, probably tied, certainly helpless. Now they were starting to yell, trying to run the sheep over him!

That much of their purpose was clear. Johnny Malcolm was to die beneath the hoofs of the sheep he'd brought to that land.

Myra cried wildly and drove her horse forward,

and no one tried to stop her. The sheep were hesitant
and uncertain, not quite ready to run. The shouting men
fell silent as some of them recognized her. It was
Myra M'Ginnis, or Vascom—and they were at a loss.

She reached Johnny and was off her horse and kneel-
ing beside him, crying out, cradling his head in her
arms, careless of the tar, shocked and enraged at sight
of the feathers, as understanding came. She turned
with a burst of anger which would have done credit
to any of the Vascoms, as some of the men pressed
closer.

Clayburn had been in charge of the night's work,
doing Slade's bidding efficiently. He'd gotten a job on
Axe a couple of years before, returning with Slade
from one of the latter's periodical forays on a distant
range. Discreetly, he had arrived alone, saying nothing
about any acquaintance with the younger Vascom
and, once hired, had demonstrated that he could do
the work required.

Since that day he'd served Slade rather than Barney,
having reason above and beyond the job for gratitude.
But for Slade, he'd have lain forgotten in his grave
for those two years. Slade had saved him from a

hangrope which had already been adjusted about his neck. It had been a risk, even though Slade had had the drop, to free him. Thereafter they had ridden hard to evade a vengeful posse.

He scowled at Myra, his voice a harsh boom from deep in his throat.

"Sure we've tarred an' feathered him, ma'am. What should he expect, bringin' sheep to this range?"

"Sheep?" Myra cried. "You're only using them as an excuse to mistreat a man you hate—a man who saved my life. And you're a cowardly bunch, so many of you jumping one man—"

"He had his own crew," Clayburn reminded her uncomfortably. "Only they was asleep on the job!"

"It amounted to the same thing, after you sneaked up on them! You must be proud of yourselves!"

Clayburn winced at the charge, as did some of the others. Coming from the lips of a beautiful woman, the indictment stung. Clayburn realized resentfully that Slade had left them to do the job and to take the full onus.

"Axe has had its way of doing for a long while, and I reckon it will keep right on," Clayburn returned doggedly. "And leavin' out the sheep, he's only getting what's coming to him. We've found out something that'll maybe interest you, Ma'am. He murdered your husband, Leavitt Vascom—stuck a knife in him, then buried him, out by Lampases Spring!"

17

Clayburn flung the accusation with calculated brutality. Report had it that this girl had been badly treated by Leavitt, coming very close to death. But Clayburn had seen how much she liked the fellow, and she had married him. Such news should overwhelm her, shut her up.

Myra heard the report without surprise. It came to her that she had expected something of the sort, really. Such an end for such a man was almost inevitable. It explained why nothing more had been heard of Leavitt recently, though he might have fled to another part of the country.

Far from being shocked, she was conscious of an overwhelming sense of relief, a lifting of the fear which had been with her against the time when he might return. As for what Johnny was being charged with— her breath caught as she saw how he had been mistreated.

She came defensively to her feet, facing them with head upflung. If this last year had been an ordeal by fire, she had come through it tempered and seasoned, with a beauty which until then had only been suggested.

"You're saying that Leavitt's dead," she returned, "even that he was killed. But all that you're doing is guessing, making wild charges to try and excuse yourself for something worse. If it's so, then he only got what was coming to him! He left me alone, to die, telling me to hurry up about it, because I was in his way! As for John Malcolm, I know this. He saved my life, and I'll stand by him. If you're going to murder him, you'll have to kill me first!"

Clayburn chewed his lip uneasily. His appeal to sympathy had backfired, even among his own men. Most of them knew Leavitt Vascom as well as he did, and they accepted her account, wasting no pity on him.

"You've done enough here," Myra pressed her advantage. "And what are you doing here in the first place? I don't believe Barney sent you on such a job.

He never resorts to such sneaky methods of fighting. So you'd better go."

Clayburn shrugged, eying his own crew, observing the building anger in the others. None of the riders of Axe were in a mood to continue the sport, and he knew uneasily that Myra was right, that the anger of old Barney could be terrible. He turned and swung onto his horse, then rode away without a backward look.

The others let them go. Myra dropped on her knees beside Johnny, her eyes wide with pity.

"Build up the fire again and heat water," she commanded. "Hurry. Oh, Johnny, Johnny, what have they done to you?"

Following her clash with Slade, Vivian moved restlessly, feeling increasingly trapped. Slade had overplayed his hand, lacking the patience which a true gambler should exercise, but he had made plain what he was after, and that she was the key by which he intended to obtain the big ranch. The thought was like a nightmare.

Even with him gone, the atmosphere of the house

seemed heavy, oppressively surcharged. For he would be back. Worse, Barney was not returning.

The knowledge that Barney was not her father somehow did not surprise her. It left her with a feeling both of relief and pity for him, a greater understanding and sympathy than she had possessed before. The knowledge that he planned to pass over his own son and make her his heir was both surprising and frightening. For that intent had placed them both in jeopardy.

There could be a dozen explanations for Barney's continued absence, but she had a feeling that more were valid in this situation. Slade had made clear that he played a game for high stakes, in which both she and her father were mere pawns.

Whether or not she was Barney's child, she possessed his ability to reason coldly and logically. There was danger here. She would do better to get away while she could. And it would be well to ride armed.

There were always extra guns in Barney's room. She went to it, noting that the bed had been smoothed neatly, then left undisturbed. In a drawer of the desk she found a small but deadly derringer and slipped it into her dress.

Slade had said that Barney had ridden away. Apparently he had told the truth, since the house was empty. She was about to turn away when her eyes caught an alien speck near the middle of the floor.

There was no particular reason her pulse should falter, until a closer look confirmed her suspicion. The speck was a spot of dry blood, and there were other spots scattered across the room. Even in the fading light, she knew that she was not mistaken.

It was starting to grow dark outside, but the night seemed suddenly more friendly than the huge, silent house. Something had happened to Barney, and her imagination was far too lively in speculating on what it was.

The crew had returned, or at least many of them were coming in following the day's work. Light showed in cook house and bunk house alike. She considered questioning them, even asking for help, instituting a search for their employer. But she as quickly rejected the notion. Many, if not most of the men, were Slade's friends. Someone would be apt to carry tales to him. She must not spoil what chance there was.

She made her preparations calmly, working swiftly.

She had to get to Wagon Wheel, and she prepared the baby for the ride, feeling a sharp twinge of regret. Its mother would be happy to have it again, but she would miss the baby. Still, she was its aunt, and this would not be a final parting.

That the outfit with which Axe had so long been feuding should offer sanctuary was not even ironical. One fact was clear. They were all in this together.

As she went out, she was surprised to see that the other buildings had gone dark. That was odd, since it was much too early for the men to go to bed. Usually they played cards and occupied themselves with small tasks for another hour or more.

The emptiness of barn and corrals confirmed a rising apprehension. The crew had gone off again, taking most of the riding animals. She found her own horse and saddled it. The night made a welcome shelter as she headed for Wagon Wheel.

It had been her plan to place the baby in Myra's arms, then to pour out her story to Howard Denning and ask his advice. But Lavinia Taylor gave her the disturbing news that Myra was gone. No one had any notion where.

As for Howard, he was asleep, worn out by worry and apprehension and the growing trouble of his own old injury.

"It'll be a mercy when John Malcolm gets back," Lavinia declared. "Howard's lost without him. And unless Ma gets better and comes back to look after Howard—my land, I don't know. The poor man is sick, and he needs better medicine than a doctor can give him!"

Under the circumstances, it would be cruel to disturb him, perhaps useless. Vivian thought regretfully of the bed she had counted on, then dismissed the temptation.

"There's something going on on this range," she said. "I don't now just what it is, but it means trouble. Can you look after the baby until Myra returns?"

"If I can't, I'm slipping," Lavinia asserted. "I've looked after more people, of just about any age or size you might mention, than I can count the years I've been around this country. And the one is all that makes the other worth thinking about."

"I'm sure of that," Vivian agreed. "I'll have to be getting right back, but I know that you'll look after her." In response to Lavinia's protest that she should not be riding at such an hour, her answer was simple. "I must."

Had Lavinia guessed that she was not returning to Axe and dared not, she would have been insistent. Swallowed again by the night, Vivian hesitated. Nagging fears were bad enough, but the worst part was that now she had to ride blindly, with only her instinct for guidance. Something was going on, but where or what she could only guess. Where would Slade have taken his father?

She swung north, with the stars for guidance, though she knew the country well enough to ride it blindfolded if need be. Her decision was based on what the men would call a hunch. Having chosen a course, she could only keep going, hoping and praying that she was right, and that she might not be too late.

The night wore itself away. Daylight was at once better and worse. The sun was friendly, but it could be pitilessly revealing, should enemies prowl these same wastes—and enemies might be riders from either outfit. She had brought no food, not having anticipated this additional journey. Hunger gnawed, and never had she felt so alone or friendless. The land lay wide and empty, beginning to burn under the sun of late June. Nowhere was there a cow or single stray, since the range had been swept clean.

The last time she had journeyed there had been with Johnny Malcolm. Remembering, her cheeks turned pink at the truancy of her thoughts. But there was no one to see or guess, and it was pleasant to lose herself in dreams.

She drank at the springs, and water was a big help. Having been raised in a saddle, she was making her way as straight as though guided by a compass. It was nearing mid-day when she glimpsed the cabin, and her breath quickened, half-fearfully, half-hopefully, at a sign of life: a thin trickle of smoke rising.

Since it was impossible to hide her approach, she put the horse to a run, and all it once it seemed that this must be an illusion; not the smoke, which was real and increasing, but the likelihood that it came from the chimney. The rusty snout of the stovepipe thrust above the roof exactly as it had done weeks before, but the smoke was coming from the opposite end of the cabin.

Apprehension gripped her, and she urged her tired horse to a still greater effort. Now it was clear enough, and she flung herself from the saddle, snatching at a larger stick which lay nearby, tearing at the piled wood against the side of the shack. After smoking in uncertain fashion, it was just beginning to blaze vigorously. A moment more and the flames would have been beyond control. Tinder-dry as the old logs were, the cabin would have gone fast.

She saw something else as she tore at the piled wood, not only how carefully it had been arranged, with small sticks near the bottom and larger ones above; but also how dry grass had helped ignite the fire, a small fringe of partly burned grasses having dropped away. Still more revealing was the crotched stick and what it held, just ready to topple into the fire—the magnifying glass, its thick lens focusing the sun into a tiny red spot.

She had seen that glass many times in past years, and she recognized it with a mingled feeling of dismay and shame. Leavitt and Slade had treasured their fire maker. Once they had almost set the barn on fire in similar fashion.

There was a sound from inside the cabin. She hurried around to the door, finding it barred with a log brace on the outside. It was no surprise, once she had the door open, to see Barney seated uncertainly on the edge of the lower bunk.

18.

The column of smoke lifted and hung in the still air like a funeral pyre. Slade, viewing the beacon from a distance, smiled at the thought. That was what it was, and now it was too late to turn back. He had burned, if not his bridges, then his cabin, which in this case was more final.

It was too late even for regret, and he sought impatiently to banish such shadows from his mind. After his discovery in the gulch above the cabin, he'd ridden hard, giving orders to Clayburn, despatching him with several of the crew. By this time those orders should have been executed, or be well on the way toward finality. They should, in fact, soon be returning, to report a mission accomplished.

So it was long past time for softness. If some parts of his program were tough, then it was because he'd been given no choice. When Barney had cut Leavitt and himself out of his will, he had in effect cut his own throat. He should have known that it was asking for trouble to leave Axe to Vivian.

The news had shocked Leavitt, too. Slade knew now that he'd had the same reaction, the same ambition: to marry Vivian, and thus possess the ranch. In Leavitt's case, the news had come at a most inopportune time, after he'd involved himself with Myra M'Ginnis.

Typically, Leavitt had set out to free himself of the incumberance. That he had eliminated himself in the process was a stroke of luck.

What remained was to turn his back on that slowly fading column of smoke, and go ahead with other plans. He was Axe now, as the smoke testified, with no one strong enough to challenge what he did. Vivian could be handled, one way or another. All that remained was to gather up the loose threads, then weave them into one strand, under his control—

Slade scowled, disliking the simile; in his mind it

suggested a rope, and a rope suggested a noose. Say rather, he'd pick up the pieces—

There was wind in the distance, wind which stirred small dust devils. But there was more than dust, gone into limbo. Something moved, momentarily glimpsed, lost again on the rim of the horizon. Unconsciously, Slade moved his tongue across lips gone suddenly dry and swung his horse, putting it to a run, heading in the opposite direction. Perhaps his imagination was playing tricks, and it was only dust; he hadn't been able to see too clearly. But no one should be riding off there, and he had to know.

After a mile, he slowed, going more carefully, like a man afraid—or a hunter stalking game. Brush and a few trees gave a clothed appearance to a gulch, and he followed along its bottom, almost to the crest of the slope where it began. Dismounting, he moved like an Indian.

From there he could see without being seen, and his breath caught in his throat. There was one horse, nearly a mile away, a single horse with two riders. Doubly burdened, it moved slowly, but as it approached he could see it clearly.

Barney Vascom was in the saddle, Vivian mounted behind him, her arms reaching forward on either side, steadying him as he rode. Far off to the north, the last smoke from the burning cabin was vanishing in the haze of summer.

Barney was far sicker than she'd counted on; by the time she had made sure of that, a tiny smoldering remnant of flame had taken fresh hold, and the old cabin had been too far gone to save.

Slade stared, his tongue nervously weaving patterns. Here was disaster. By some mischance, Vivian had gone to the cabin, reaching it in time to save Barney; but the evidence, even without what Barney could tell, was plain. The fire must have been burning when she arrived, already eating its way into the cabin.

How he had really burned his bridges.

Before, he had had a hard choice to make, but it was as nothing compared to what confronted him now. Slade returned to his horse and reached for the rifle in the saddle sheath, fingering it reluctantly. Two quick, well-aimed bullets would be enough. After that, Axe would be his. For a will, even if it turned up, wouldn't matter, with Vivian and Leavitt both gone, and himself the sole remaining heir.

It had to be that way, for more than the ranch was at stake. His own neck was endangered, and the strands were making a noose in more ways than one.

The horse and its riders were closer as he returned to the crest, coming withing range, yet far enough away so that they would not be able to sense anything wrong before he started shooting. Slade lifted the rifle, thrusting the butt of the stock hard against his shoulder, sighting along the barrel. His hands were clammy, and the front sight seemed to waver and blur.

He threw himself flat on the ground, resting the end of the barrel over a small stone. That was better. Both shots would have to be quick, before the horse could bolt, or any counter-action be taken. But to a man as skilled in marksmanship as he, there should be no problem. Slade closed one eye and curled a finger around the trigger.

Then he started and drew back, a curse rasping in his throat. Suddenly he was anxious to do the job, and now it was too late—though luck of a sort was with him, in that he hadn't pulled the trigger. Had he done so, the shots would have been widely heard, traced swiftly to him.

Off to the southeast, riders were coming into sight, men whose attitude indicated weariness. They had seen the single horse with its double burden and were heading to join Barney and Vivian. These were the men he'd despatched on a mission south, led by Clayburn.

They should still have been many hours and hours away, but something had sent them hastening back far sooner than he'd expected. Whether the news they bore was good or bad no longer mattered. It was too late even for bullets, too late for everything.

No, perhaps not too late for one final act on his part. Seeing the others and the way they rode, Slade had a feeling that John Malcolm must still be alive, still moving the sheep toward Wagon Wheel. One thing remained: to settle with Johnny.

19.

Blood dripped from the spear-tipped points of Slade's spurs and stained his horse's sides in ragged streaks. It was an outward indication of the raging frustration which he could no longer keep bottled. He pulled up in the shelter of a draw which was close enough so that, with luck, he might be able to hear what was said as the crew joined Vivian and Barney. Amazement and concern were in their voices as they greeted Barney, asking what had happened.

Barney grunted, not choosing to enlighten them. He was in a dour mood, still far from shaking off the effects of the blow which had come close to cracking his skull. His speech was thick and uncertain, but Vivian knew better than to try to take charge at such a moment.

"Never mind me," he growled. "The question is, where have you fellows been—and what've you been doing? And who gave you leave?"

Clayburn reluctantly undertook to answer.

"We rode a day's journey south," he explained. "Slade told us what to do, said he was relayin' your orders, so of course we followed them."

That wasn't quite true. Slade had made it clear that the others of the crew should assume that the orders came from Barney, but Clayburn had known better.

It sounded plausible enough, under the circumstances. Barney's tongue thickened.

"What did he tell you to do?"

"He said you wanted the sheep met—and stopped."

Barney was conscious of the sudden tightening embrace of Vivian's arms. He was equally aware of the increasing pain in his skull, as though the broken blade of the Axe had crashed there. Stubbornly, he gave no sign.

"And what did you do? You got a tongue to talk with?"

"We sent word ahead by Leseur that they'd come far

enough. When they didn't pay attention, we stopped them. Got the jump on them."

"Mister—" the use of such a title, even without the brittleness of the tone, was warning to any who knew Barney—" my patience is frayin' like a worn-out lasso. *What'd you do?*"

Clayburn shrugged. If the old man wanted it, he could have it.

"We gave Malcolm the tar and feather treatment." Again, Barney felt the convulsive clasp of the arms about his waist. "If he's fool enough still to try and keep coming after that—"

"Tar and feathers, eh?" Barney's tone lost its rasp, became almost conversational. "And I suppose he let you?"

"It took some doing," Clayburn conceded, "but we had the men."

"And the jump, like you said," Barney supplied dryly. "You make me proud to be the boss of Axe—of such a stinkin', cowardly bunch, that a coyote would turn up his nose at! You're fired, Clayburn. You've worked to double-cross me ever since I took you on, at Slade's recommendation. So from now on you can draw your pay from him—a pair of rattlesnakes! I—"

His voice rasped again, broke, and Barney slumped forward in the saddle. But for Vivian's clasp he would have fallen. Saliva drooled from the corner of his mouth, suddenly slack.

By the time the confusion ended and the silent, chastened group were on their way to the buildings, one thing was clear. Barney, if not already dead, was dying. Slade watched impersonally. He might still be able to take control.

Clayburn was prudently withdrawing, following Barney's final ultimatum. As soon as he could manage it without being seen, Slade took out after him. Clayburn was riding fast.

Slade was impatient for the rest of the story concerning Malcolm, the details of which had not been supplied. Tar and feathers alone could be a light punishment. But if the victim resisted and was severely manhandled, a man might not survive.

One or twice Slade shouted, but the distance was too great. Clayburn rode without looking back. Press his horse as he would, Slade was slow in narrowing the gap.

He was heading into rough, broken country. Slade

took a short cut, and Clayburn was lost to sight. Then the sound of voices, from close at hand, brought him up short. The one belonged to Clayburn. The other belonged to the bounty hunter, and it came as chill as December wind.

"Take it easy, mister." Wardlaw's voice was a drawl, but its authority suggested that he might be looking at the other man along the barrel of a gun. "I'd like a word with you—maybe two or three."

"Sure, as many as you like." Clayburn was cool in a pinch. "But you don't need that gun."

"We'll keep it, just the same. You see, I'm trainin' this Colt to be a wild horse. And it runs in my mind that I ought to know you, as though I'd seen you before. Or could it be that I've studied your likeness on a dodger?"

"Not likely. I'm Clayburn, foreman for Axe. This is Axe range you're on."

"Now I know you're a liar," the bounty hunter returned pleasantly. "Barney Vascom rods his own spread. And Clayburn ain't the moniker I've seen along with your likeness. But right now I'm not interested in you—all I want is some information."

"Fair enough. Only you've confused me with somebody else."

"I don't make mistakes. Can't afford to in my business. But you're small potatoes," Wardlaw added contemptuously. "There's only a hundred measly bucks reward for you, and I don't fish for minnows. You just had a meeting with your boss; then the rest of them went one way and you another. Why?"

"Barney seemed to have some sort of a stroke. He'd worked himself all up—firin'me. I figure he was really mad at his son Slade, who'd given me my orders. He claimed that they hadn't come from him."

"A stroke? You figure Barney's about to cash in?"

"Not likely." Clayburn was contemptuous. "He's tough."

Slade understood Wardlaw's interest. His own ability to pay the promised bribe might hinge on that point.

"You say he was peevish at Slade. Just what did he say?"

"Plenty. Sounded like he was just getting warmed up when that fit took him. As it was, he called Slade a rattlesnake. Reckon he'll be just about that popular around this range from now on."

Slade cursed under his breath at the man's volubility.

That word was damning, and no one knew it better than the bounty hunter. For a wild moment, Slade thought of shooting Wardlaw in the back before he suspected danger. But the crew might still be within sound of gunfire; it could be too risky.

Wardlaw had lost interest. "Better keep riding, like Barney told you," he instructed. "Just one thing. Don't try to find Slade, or side him. If you did that, I might find you worth enough—dead—to take you in, along with him."

"Don't worry." Clayburn shrugged. "I ain't so big a fool as to risk my neck for such as him."

Clayburn's estimate of Barney's toughness had been in error. The boss of Broken Axe was dead, and the world, none too cheerful at any time, seemed doubly desolate. Rain, coming when no one had expected it, added to the appearance of gloom. It was as though nature wept for the man who had inspired few tears while living.

Vivian was genuinely sorry. If anything, she was more grief-stricken than could have been the case if she had still believed him her father. Somehow the recent revelations made everything both better and worse, showing him to be the lonely man he had been. Of her own changed status because of these developments, she had no time to think.

Myra arrived in the midst of the confusion, bringing sympathy and news at once disturbing and startling. She was able to add details to what Clayburn had said about Johnny Malcolm and the sheep and the manner in which he had been treated. Vivian's eagerness for news was unmistakable, and Myra smiled at her through a mist of tears.

"That's the main reason why I hurried back and came to see you first thing," she explained. "Johnny's all right. But for a while he was so done in that he was delirious. While he was that way, he kept saying your name, Vivian—calling for you. I thought you'd want to know."

"Oh, I do," Vivian breathed. "It's wonderful of you to tell me."

Myra was understanding and sympathetic, gravely honest.

"He saved my life, and I think perhaps I may have saved his," she said. "That makes me feel better. I'll admit that since I've had my eyes opened—well, I've come to appreciate Johnny more than I did a year ago. And if things had been different—but at least I've some memories, and the baby, thanks to both of you for taking care of her. And it's you he loves, Vivian. I'm not going to give any advice, but I wouldn't let a man like that go—or find out that I owned a big ranch before he'd had time to tell me other things. For he's proud. And another reason why I wouldn't waste any time—I'd want to make sure that he got this far alive!"

Action had always been a characteristic of Barney Vascom. In that moment Vivian was definitely a Vascom.

"Thank you for everything, Myra," she agreed. "I've had my eyes opened, too, lately. I won't waste any time."

The unexpected storm caught Slade by surprise, drenching him, adding to the savagery of his mood. He found temporary shelter, then, as the rain settled to a lasting downpour, realized that he could not wait it out. It had become vital that he finish his own chores; he had to succeed where others had failed. If he could settle with Malcolm, there would be no one to stand long in the way of his control of this range. Under those circumstances, the bounty hunter could be dealt with—one way or another.

There was one good thing about the storm. He'd be less visible or open to discovery by Wardlaw as he rode. His horse had been grazing, finding the wet grass to its taste. He tightened the cinch, then, swinging to the saddle, glimpsed another rider, briefly revealed, then shrouded again by the storm.

Quivering, the cayuse poised an instant, then jumped to the rake of the spurs. Slade's mind, spurred by jealousy, fitted the pieces together. Either Barney was already dead, or desperately sick. Why else would Vivian set out at such a time, heading south—where Johnny was? It was only too plain to his inflamed mind.

The storm seemed to thicken, the rain continuing hour after hour. A couple of times, when the downpour slackened, he caught sight of Vivian well ahead. Try as he might, he could not narrow the gap.

Early darkness crept across the land as he neared the Termagent, running high and muddy. The sheep should be just about that far along, but at least they were still on the far side. This might be a good place to wait. Slade sought shelter, heading for the abandoned cabin of the former ferryman, a shack set somewhat back from the river, hidden among a clump of trees.

It had a musty smell, having been unused for more than a year. Rats and mice had made themselves at home, but at least the place was dry. Slade looked about hopefully for food, on the chance that some tinned goods might have been left behind. A loose plank in the floor responded to his efforts, and momentarily he believed that he had found such a cache.

There was a can, stowed where dirt had been excavated to make room. Then he saw that the can was too big for fruit or vegetables, and he scowled in disgust as he made out what it was—a sealed keg of black blasting powder. The ferryman had probably kept it on hand to knock loose drifting trees or logs, when they lodged at dangerous spots in the ferryboat's channel.

Apparently the keg had been left behind when the bridge was built. Since it was sealed, the powder should be as good as ever. A gleam came to Slade's eyes.

Near the can was a length of fuse. There was still perhaps half an hour of daylight, enough for his purpose. And the sheep were still somewhere on the far side of the river.

Carrying the keg, Slade walked to the bridge, then ducked beneath it. The Termagent was running high, showing the effects of the steady downpour, which was probably worse farther upstream. It had risen nearly a foot, creeping under the bridge so that there was barely room to place the keg and its fuse.

Lighting it, Slade followed the sheltering fringe of brush back to the cabin. There he waited.

The blast should come at any instant. He found a better vantage point and gasped, then broke into a run, shouting hoarsely. But even as desperation assailed him, he knew that he'd be to late.

While he'd moved back out of sight, a horseman had come along the road and was now near the middle of the bridge. Vivian. He'd suppose that she was well ahead, long past that point. Even as he yelled, the rending boom of the giant powder smothered the sound.

20.

Myra had not overstated the situation. John Malcolm had been badly spent after the tar and feathers and the beating. But Myra had come, like an angel of mercy, taking charge, soothing and restoring him in more ways than with food and warmth. Looking back the next morning, after his friends had cleaned him up and he'd fallen asleep, he had some uneasy moments. He'd been delirious, and he wasn't at all sure that he'd not mistaken Myra for Vivian, or what tricks his tongue might have played under those conditions.

But if so, Myra had been understanding and cheerfully friendly when she had set out on her return journey. She had parried his appreciation with a smile and a slightly shaky laugh.

"You saved *my* life, Johnny," she reminded him. "So now we're fairly even. Better late than never, they say." Not explaining that, she ended with a rush, "Being able to do something makes me feel as though I have some reason for being alive."

As he went on with the sheep, it was apparent that she had encountered others and spread a new gospel among them. Everywhere was a new and friendlier atmosphere.

After she had gone, Johnny remembered that first moment, when Clayburn had made his charges concerning Leavitt. She had asked no questions. Clearly she had disdained to. It was reassuring to know that such friends remained.

The unseasonable storm surprised them as much as anyone. The sheep did not seem to mind, but the men, riding soaked, were less appreciative.

"Sure the rain 'll do the range a lot of good," Cy Robbins conceded. "Couldn't be better for the country. But me, I ain't a duck, and I can't help but ponder some questions. One is, is any of this rain fallin' up on Wagon Wheel, where we really need it? And why should *I* get so much? I don't rightly figure to require so much bathin'."

"Maybe nature knows best. Or maybe it's just confused your smell with the sheep, not findin' no diff'rence," a companion suggested.

So prolonged a storm was unusual for so late in the season. The ground become almost a morass. They ate cold meals and slept in damp blankets. Even the sheep looked sodden.

It was late when they sighted the river. Even from a distance, it appeared high and muddy, boiling along as though angry at itself and eager to reach a milder land.

"She's a shrew for sure," Robbins observed. "Lucky we ain't got to face her raw, the way they used to before the bridge was built."

"Or back before the ferry," an old-timer put it. "She used to separate the men from the boys in those days. The good died young—and sudden."

Fresh thunder jarred the closing dusk. The bridge, just coming into sight, reared like a bucking horse. A giant cotton boll seemed to burst open at its far end. Then the bridge settled back, churning the river to a wilder frenzy.

The current slashed at the sudden barricade, wrenching in a frenzy. What was left of the far side of the bridge swung majestically. The nearer end, still anchored to the shore, yielded to the strain. There was a crack of timbers as it tore; then the bridge was gone, a plaything of the river.

That part Johnny observed without conscious effort. His attention was focused on the horse and rider who had been in the middle of the bridge when it went into convulsions. The horse raced desperately and was almost at the shore when its footing gave way, spilling cayuse and rider like straws.

At that point the road twisted downstream, so that the action was above him. And on that southern bank, the land stretched wide and easy, by contrast with the formidably rearing cliffs which circumscribed it on the north shore.

Johnny pushed his horse into the current, scanning it hopefully. Darkness was pushing a blanket over land and water, and the tangled mass of debris which had been the bridge made it worse. Then he made out something which no longer struggled, swept along by the current. The horse had been fatally hurt as it hit the water.

He had his lariat loose and ready, though no longer even daring to hope. Then he glimpsed the whiteness of an arm, as if in a beckoning gesture. He shouted and flung the loop, and drew it back as the hungry current fought against giving up its prey. Only as she was drawn alongside did he know surely that it was Vivian.

He pulled her up onto his horse, and her arms crept about his neck and clung.

"Johnny!" she sobbed. "Hold me close! Don't ever let me go!"

Slade made out the scene, dim in the distance, the rain and dusk. He lifted his rifle, his face twisting, but lowered it again. His hands were shaking too much for a shot, and this had to be sure.

Beyond a few bruises, Vivian had not been hurt. Her horse had acted as a buffer when they struck the water, flinging her clear. After making sure of that, Johnny headed toward the camp, which was already being set up.

The news she brought was both good and bad. Barney Vascom was dead, and the personal significance of that did not occur to Johnny for some time. He had made clear to Vivian, on the journey from the burning cabin, that his rage was not against the sheep or even Wagon Wheel. Now a reaction was setting in across the range. While the sheep would not be welcomed, they would be accepted.

If they could be gotten that far. That was the next question, with the bridge out. Even cattle, in the old days, had been forced into a week-long detour around that portion of the Termagent. Establishment of the ferry had saved many days, though crossing on it was a slow and sometimes hazardous job. The bridge had made a big difference.

Vivian had another piece of news. Ma Denning had sent word that the latest operation had been a success. It wouldn't be too long before she'd be coming home, to look after Howard and the rest of her boys.

The news about Barney decided Johnny. A week would be too long to go around by the ford, for then they'd miss Barney's funeral. And a man should have at least one of his kin and some of his friends to mourn him.

"Maybe we can use the ferry," Johnny said. "We'll

have a try. If it works, they can shuttle the sheep across as well. It ought to work."

Morning brought an end to the rain, though the clouds still clustered as though reluctant to desert the river. Johnny examined the ferryboat, still tied in a sheltered cove on their shore, the long, heavy rope running from it up to the steel cable which spanned the stream. On the far side, where the cliffs rose inhospitably, a sort of dock had been built, part way up the portal, with a road leading back. The ferry was sometimes even with the dock, sometimes a foot or so above or below, depending on the height of the river. But it had been a big improvement, prior to the bridge.

The ferryman, who had operated the big raft for more than a score of years, had left the country when the bridge had been opened. Oley had opined that his job was done, and decided to warm his old bones in the Arizona sun.

Without his skill, it wouldn't be simple to operate the ferry, but it should be possible. The process was relatively simple. Loaded and eased from its harbor into the current, the raft bobbed cork-like at the end of its pulley and heavy rope, while the cable stretched.

Those on board pulled it along, hand over hand, by another double rope, stretched from shore to shore, and still in place. The method was primitive, but it worked. Johnny had crossed there more than once.

Normally, it was a ten-minute passage either way. One man, with the strength possessed by Oley, could manage the empty ferry. Two or three could tug it along with a load. By some trick of the river, the current helped more than it hindered.

Johnny was for making the first crossing with a couple of the men, to make sure that it could be done. Vivian vetoed that.

"I'm going with you. If anything happens, I want to be with you. I think I've earned that right, Johnny."

There could be no question of that. And whether the hazard would be greater or less, there was no sure way of telling. Unless Slade had become a madman ——

They tied two horses on board, to ride on toward Wheel and Axe. The raft could be pulled back, with him at the rope on the far side, if they made it all right. They cast off, and the raft wobbled and weaved crazily as the current caught it and the cable stretched. The first part was easy, the river aiding, others pulling at the rope on the south bank.

Then, past the middle, it became grueling work, with the crosscable stretched taut like an inverted V, the river angry about them. Now it was hand over hand to win their way forward, a painful inching along. Vivian was helping, smiling as she pulled.

They were almost to the dock when a shot sounded, and the rope went slack in their grasp. The ferry jerked wildly, bobbing loosely.

The pull rope had been cut by a bullet. It was Slade's answer. Not daring to come down to the dock and cut it with a knife, where he would be in sight and easily targeted, he had kept out of sight on the cliffs above, timing his shot as he chose.

He had not put his bullet into Johnny, but what might yet happen was not pleasant to think about. It had suddenly become a cat and mouse game. The raft was already partly crippled, and Slade could stalk them from the shelter of the high cliff, keeping out of sight, venting his vengeance in whatever way appealed to him.

A second, more violent jerk showed that he intended to go all the way, though by indirect methods. The steel cable, holding the heavy rope which anchored the ferry, snapped loose and writhed wildly above the river.

Unlike the pull rope, the cable was anchored higher up and farther back, out of sight. It had been twisted twice around a tree and tied. There, unhindered, Slade had worked to loosen it, releasing it at a picked instant. Now there was nothing to hold them.

The pulley screamed along the steel strand and tore loose, and the raft plunged, rudderless in the grip of the current, heading straight into white water. Not far below, the stream narrowed, thundering through a gorge between high walls. Then, a mile farther downstream, it plunged in wild abandon over a deep waterfall.

21.

The raft lurched, twisting, then straightened and surged ahead. The horses were mad with terror. One of them leaped over the rail, then was brought up, threshing wildly, by its halter rope. It was on the lower side of the craft, and the current sucked it under and held it. The impediment seemed to make little difference in the force which the river exerted.

Free from the anchoring cable, there was no power which could stop or even slow the raft, short of the plunge which would splinter it into wreckage. There was no pole or sweep to steer with, and even had there been, there was no beach, as had been the case a short time before, no place to land. Now the gorge enclosed them, walls of rock rearing on either side. The hemmed

213

waters slashed back in fury at such confinement.

Vivian's face had gone white, more from watching the horse than from their own peril. Slade's action was clear enough to both. Once they were gone, there would be no one between him and control of Broken Axe. An extra killing or so made no particular difference to a man already in the shadow of the noose.

Vivian looked at Johnny, and there was sweetness in the set of her lips, the willingness to face even this along with him. His throat felt tight. But he was not ready to accept defeat. There was a chance, however slim. He snatched at the rope at which they had been pulling only moments before. He'd prided himself on his handiness with a rope; now was the time to put it to use.

Only partly understanding, Vivian watched as he built a loop in the end of the rope—an end showing ragged and torn. At least the rope was stout, barely rotted by the year of inactivity since the bridge had replaced the ferry. It should be good for any test to which it was subjected, and there was plenty of rope. After breaking, the loose part had whipped loose from the tree and pulley on the south bank, and part still trailed in the water.

"Be ready to take a snub around the post," he instructed, "if I make a catch." The post was a stout section of log, solidly anchored at one end of the raft. It had served to fasten the ferry when not in use.

Vivian nodded understandingly, pulling in some of the rope and coiling it, holding it so as to afford him such slack as might be needed. Johnny poised, looking up at the high cliff above. They were close to the northern rim, swept over by the current. The top of the cliff was a score of feet overhead.

This would require luck to begin with, as well as skill. The unhampered ferryboat was moving fast, but that was not too great a cause for worry. He'd roped moving targets many times from the back of a running horse, and this was roughly comparable. The rub now was that he'd never traveled through this canyon—nor had any other man made the journey and lived to report.

So he didn't know on what to depend. But if there should be some outjuting of rock near the top of the cliff, or a possible tree branch, anything which would serve as a target and might give reasonably solid

215

anchorage, there would be a chance. He saw what he'd hoped for even as he finished making a noose, and loosed the loop in a swift upward fling.

It was tricky roping, in that, while the target was standing still, it was overhead instead of on the level; and he'd have only one try. Tension was in him, and he seemed to jerk in sympathy as he felt the noose catch. "Now!" he yelled, and Vivian responded with the skilled speed of a trained roper. She whipped a double loop of the rope around the post, snubbing it, and braced desperately.

The jerk on the rope from above almost lifted Johnny from his feet, but almost instantly the strain was transferred to the rope and post as the line went taut. The raft spun in a wild gyration, and the remaining horse was flung over the side and under. Vivian was on her knees, still holding grimly. Johnny jumped to aid her, pulling in more of the slack, tying it fast.

The prisoned raft was in a bad spot, spray washing over it, drenching them with each raging sweep of the current. But at least the headlong race toward disaster had been checked. There was still a nagging worry that this might be temporary, however. Should the jutting thumb of rock crack, or prove less solid than it looked, they'd be on their way again; the rope might break in the savage tug of war with the current, or the old post rip loose.

The rope was stretched at a long taut angle, the raft making it twirl and dance. He guessed that they had come half the distance toward the waterfall. To swim was out of the question.

The loop had caught the outcrop about a yard below the top of the ledge. High enough, with luck. He fumbled for his pocket knife and cut off the extra rope, handing it to Vivian.

"Tie one end about your waist," he instructed, and fastened the other around his own. "I'll climb to the top. When I'm up, then you come."

She nodded comprehendingly, but her eyes closed tightly at the hazard of the web-thin, nervously twitching rope. Blindly she was in his arms, her hands eager, her lips salty. After a moment she pushed him back, managing a smile.

"You'll make it, Johnny," she said, and the declaration was like a promise.

The rope was like a wildly plucked fiddle string,

swinging and jerking to the bobbing of the raft. To climb straight up would have been easier, but he had to make his way along it at an angle.

The soaked strands were harsh, but he inched along; then the outcrop was ahead, above. He got a grip on an upper edge and lifted himself, preparatory to the final effort of pulling himself onto solid ground—and looked into the mocking face of Slade Vascom.

The shock was unnerving. It hadn't occurred to him that Slade would ride along the rim, to follow the progress of the cast-off raft and check so carefully on his vengeance. Save for the knife scar, like a red dimple, on Slade's cheek, it was as though he again stared into the face of Leavitt, knife in hand.

There were no fingers on his throat, and there was water below, instead of rock grinding into his back, but in such a current he would be like driftwood. And there was a knife in Slade's hand as he reached to slash the rope.

It was a tortured face, but Slade had gone too far to draw back. He swept downward with the knife, leaning, and Johnny risked his precarious grip and grabbed, closing his fingers on the knife wrist. The blade twisted, scarring his own wrist, a sharp prick which had a good effect. It enraged Johnny, lending him strength. He twisted and dragged downward, and the scar stood out more vividly against a paling cheek. The knife slipped and was gone.

Johnny still held his grip, and terror outran the pain in the eyes of the trapped man. He tried to pull back, and slipped.

A greater weight jerked at Johnny's arms, almost more than he could bear. Slade had gone over in a sudden tumbling scramble. One of Johnny's hands clasped the rope, close to the rock anchor, a far from sure grip, but one into which he put all his might. He was leaning crazily, his other hand still holding Slade's wrist, keeping him from making the plunge.

He wrenched air back into straining lungs, wondering if he could manage. Neither of his hands could hold out very long. But if they forgot their differences long enough to work together, they might get out of this alive. And Slade possessed the same ambition, the same hate and terror and wish to live.

He was about to suggest the idea to Slade, to explain what he would need to do. But Slade writhed upward with a frantic twist, and his teeth tore at Johnny's clasping fingers. It was too much.

The relief from strain as he lost his hold was enough to enable him to reach and get a fresh grip on the outcrop of stone. He clung for a minute, resting, then pulled himself up and flopped on the ground. Again he lay a while, then turned, reassured by the tautness of the rope about his waist. Vivian's face seemed small and white amid the spray on the still tossing raft. He waved, and she climbed to him, with his help.

The sun broke through the clouds as she stood beside him. Slade's horse cropped the grass not far away.

From the landing, they waved in signal to the crew on the other shore. They would have to take the long drive around, but that no longer made much difference. It wouldn't be too far to a place where they could find another horse. Not that Johnny minded riding double, with Vivian in front in his arms. Even the horse seemed to find it a good arrangement.

On their ride north, Vivian confided one fact which was a fitting epitaph for Barney.

"He thought that sheep might be a good idea for this range," she explained. "He said that if they were run right, with plenty of pasture, so that the grass wasn't eaten too short—it should be the answer to a lot of problems. And he pointed out that Axe and Wheel together would make just such a spread. He wanted peace and prosperity; not trouble."

"We'll work it out," Johnny promised. "And I like that word: together."

THUNDER TO THE WEST

TROUBLE ON THE WIND

1.

Brick Gordon's mood was evil, his temper short, and he was well aware of it. He glanced toward O'Rourke's Saloon, seeing it as a symbol of the change which was sweeping the country, finding in it an added cause for irritation. It was about time for a man like himself to be moving on to a new range.

The transformation of O'Rourke's Saloon was just about complete. Inside, carpenters were still sawing and hammering, but on the outside it was newly painted, the color a garish pink which was an affront to the eyes as well as to the sensibilities. A sign, bearing the name "Grand Theatre," had just been erected, replacing the name of O'Rourke. Culture was coming to Long Rain, bestowed upon it by the largesse of Curt O'Dion; a sort of forced feeding, as was true of everything done by the boss of Quirt.

Gordon shrugged, wavering between amusement and disgust. He'd been with O'Dion a couple of months before, riding into town along with Felix Yankus and Monte Yuma. It was not by chance, as they and everyone recognized, that O'Dion chose the three best gunslingers when he took his rides. It had been that day, he guessed, that the idea for the theatre had come to O'Dion.

At the time, there had been two saloons in town: The Silver Dollar, patronized by Quirt, and O'Rourke's, favored by the riders from Slash Y. Only the week before, by some deal undisclosed to the general public, O'Dion had acquired control of The Silver Dollar.

Then, instead of entering his own saloon, he'd headed for the rival establishment, with the trio at his heels, startling O'Rourke by their appearance. That had been nothing compared to what followed. O'Dion had ordered a drink and downed it; then he'd coolly informed O'Rourke that he was buying him out.

The declaration had been as much of a surprise to Gordon as to O'Rourke; it still left a bad taste in his mouth, as he thought back and remembered the dismayed helplessness of the paunchy big man, forced to sell at a ruinous price. There had been no overt show of force; the guns of Quirt were persuasion enough, even when they remained holstered. O'Rourke had indulged in one bleat of complaint.

"But what do you want with another saloon, O'Dion?" What about the place you already have?

And where will Slash Y go for its drinks?"

"Now that is a good question." Curt O'Dion had stroked his silky mustache and smiled. "As to what I want with it—" He'd made up a high-sounding answer on the spur of the moment, since his pride would not admit to the bald truth: that he wanted to force all competition out of business.

"It's not as a liquor dispensary that I'm interested in the building, O'Rourke. Not that at all. What runs in my mind is that Long Rain should have an opera house of its own, a classy place for entertainment." Liking the notion, he had pursued it enthusiastically.

"Why should we, here at the county seat, take a back seat to such an upstart town as New Cheyenne, which boasts such entertainment and makes slighting remarks about us? You, my friend, will be hailed as a public-spirited benefactor for having donated this building for such a purpose!"

Bitter but helpless, O'Rourke had not remained to watch the transformation of the saloon into a theatre. He was gone, like the many others who had crossed O'Dion's path or simply happened to be in his way.

A large hand-bill, printed on pink paper, had been tacked to the board fence adjacent to the former saloon. Faro, the town drunkard, was studying it with the impersonal gravity of a somnolent owl. He glanced up at the man from Quirt, his eyes raking him slyly, the hostility carefully veiled. O'Rourke, out of the goodness of his heart and the softness of his head, had usually been good for at least one free drink a day. Now there were no free drinks to be had.

"So Long Rain is to acquire culture," Faro murmured. "The Great Lakes and Seaboard Players are to come among us—*after* showing their wares at New Cheyenne! Now that is something, that these old eyes should live to see the day or to behold when Selway's is crowded with a thirsty crew from Slash Y—denied their whiskey at O'Rourke's and refusing to patronize O'Dion's—but hungry, and on a Thursday!"

Having planted the barb, he shuffled away. Startled, Gordon glanced farther along the street, his eyes narrowing. It might be true, for this was a Thursday, and the hitch-rails on both sides of the street were lined with horses bearing the brand of Slash Y. The only horse with a Quirt brand was his own.

Quirt and Slash Y had been the big outfits in the valley of the Bitter Sage for almost as long as anyone could remember. Old Abe McKay had chosen the eastern section, then had built Slash Y to formidable proportions—a man who minded his own business and made certain that others did the same. Tom Landis had preempted the western half of the valley for his own at about the same time, making Quirt an equal power.

As long as Landis had run the Quirt, there had been no trouble. The rumblings of unrest had come when Curt O'Dion had arrived in the country, claiming Quirt as his own, explaining that he had bought it from Landis when the latter had been on a trip to Chicago with a shipment of cattle. Landis had never returned to contradict him, and only one man had had the temerity to question O'Dion's account or claim to ownership. Boot Hill had acquired another tenant.

From that day, two years before, hostility between the two big outfits had increased, despite O'Dion's bland insistence that he wanted only good relations with all men.

Like most of Landis' crew, Brick Gordon had stayed on at Quirt. The pay was good, and O'Dion had quickly demonstrated that he knew the cattle business.

When trouble had threatened to erupt, it had been averted by a truce. Long Rain was trading headquarters for both outfits. Slash Y went to O'Rourke's Saloon, Quirt to The Silver Dollar. But at The Mercantile or at Selway's, the one good restaurant, trouble might erupt if they came together. So it had been agreed that Tuesdays, Thursdays, Saturdays, and the first and third Sundays of any month should be Quirt days in the town; the others were reserved for Slash Y. For more than a year, the truce had been observed.

But this was a Thursday, and Slash Y seemed to be

in town in force. Which was hardly to be wondered at, with their saloon summarily closed and the rival liquor store owned by O'Dion. This show of resentment had probably been sparked by Driscoll McKay, the son of Abe, an ambitious man who was more and more taking over the running of the outfit.

From an impersonal point of view, Gordon could scarcely blame them; but he was a Quirt rider, and he felt a surge of annoyance, directed as much at his employer as at Slash Y. What the devil was O'Dion up to?

O'Dion knew that he'd been a good friend of the former owner; but they had gotten along well enough, at least until the last few weeks. Of late, there had been a subtle change in O'Dion's attitude toward him, shown in small but significant ways, such as sending him into town today, alone, on an errand which had turned out to be trivial. He was certain now that it had been merely an excuse.

Now he was in town, the sole representative of Quirt—and Quirt's crew were always expected to uphold the rather nebulous honor of Quirt.

O'Dion must have gotten wind of Slash Y's intention to show their contempt for the old agreement; but instead of meeting force with force, he'd sent Gordon in, alone. Why? He knew of Gordon's heady temper, and he knew what might happen to a man in such a situation. What was he up to?

Gordon pondered. He could ride out without his supper, but the word would run at his heels that a Quirt man had been bluffed away from Selway's on a Quirt day. After such a show, or lack of it, he wouldn't be able to stay on at Quirt.

As far as staying was concerned, he wasn't at all sure that he cared to, the way things were going. On the other hand, as a Quirt man, also with his personal pride, he couldn't turn his back on a bluff. Besides, if was time to eat.

Gordon pushed open the door of Selway's and his irritation mounted as a survey confirmed his suspicion. All but one small table were occupied, and most of the customers belonged to Slash Y.

Looking around, he was conscious of the sudden silence. He'd been seen, and even those who didn't know him recognized him instinctively as belonging to Quirt. There was the flaming red hair, the casual look of gray eyes which seemed always to hold a hint of challenge.

A glance encountered his and locked briefly; blue eyes against gray, faintly mocking. The blue eyes belonged to Driscoll McKay. Gordon knew him as an aspiring man, resenting the fairly loose rein with which Abe had tethered him, greedy now to boss an outfit which he already looked upon as his.

He can't wait, Gordon thought, and found in that

a clue to this invasion of the town on a Thursday. "Quirt's given him a good excuse—but he's looking for trouble and anxious to find it!"

He shrugged, feeling impatience and self-anger, then strode to the one table still unoccupied and drew out a chair. There would be no pleasure in eating there tonight, under the circumstances. There might well be trouble.

But he couldn't run, and in any case, he was hungry. And Selway's was the only restaurant worthy of the name.

A waiter came to take his order, eyes staring from a suddenly bloodless face. Disregarding his manifest nervousness, Gordon ordered.

"Steak and spuds, with tea."

He caught the titter of amusement at the final item. Almost everybody drank coffee. Few had the temerity to order tea, even if they preferred it, among such a gathering. But he didn't care for Arbuckles, and he'd been having tea too long to quit now.

"Shut up, you fool! That's Gordon!"

The warning was a whisper; a man at the next table lost color, and the ripple of laughter subsided. Most men knew better than to laugh at Brick Gordon. Tonight he chose to ignore it. He was attacking his steak when he became aware of a newcomer hesitating at his table, and glanced up. It took an effort of will to forestall a sharp intake of breath when he saw who stood there.

He'd seen Mary McKay two or three times since her return from the East, but always at a distance, never to speak to. On this or any other range, she was unforgettable. It was not that she was outstanding in figure or had any unusual combination of good looks. It was simply that she was Mary McKay, as he was Brick Gordon; and there was no one else quite like her.

Most women with yellow hair had hair merely yellow; Mary's was rich with the gold of autumn leaves, the richness extending to her cheeks. The effect was enhanced by the way her mouth turned up at the corners, the gleam in her eyes. The combination was arresting.

"Do you mind if I sit here?" She smiled, then took the other chair as he came to his feet.

"Happy to have you, ma'am."

"Thank you." She studied him carefully, clearly wondering who he was, noting the gesture, for not every man bothered to rise on such an occasion. "I think I'll have the same as you," she added. "It looks good, even to the tea. I grow tired of coffee."

"Coffee's fine in the morning," he observed. "Come evening, though, I like tea. Guess I must have some English in me somewhere."

"That wouldn't be so bad, would it?" she asked, and to his surprise, Gordon found the conversation flowing along as though they had been old friends. He was aware that the rest of the room had more or less paused, watching, considering, as she took a seat at the table alongside a man from Quirt. But since she was the daughter of their boss, no one intervened. Even her brother, across the room, contented himself with sharp watchfulness. Since her back was to him, Mary did not notice.

She was plainly unaware that she was eating and visiting with a Quirt rider, though Brick found himself wondering if she would care, even if she knew. From all reports, Mary McKay was an independent-minded young lady. She'd been away most of the three years that he'd worked for Quirt, attending an Eastern school. She had returned to Slash Y only a couple of months before.

Under the circumstances, he'd better ride a tight herd on himself and not allow himself any notions. Those would be easy, with so pretty a girl. But this was no time to be a fool.

Abruptly she leaned forward, smiling.

"We haven't even introduced ourselves," she said. "I'm Mary—Mary McKay."

"I know, ma'am. And I'm pleased to meet you."

A small frown appeared between her eyes.

"I said that I was 'Mary,' not 'ma'am,'" she reminded him. "And you haven't told me your name."

"I'm sorry, Mary. Folks call me Brick—Brick Gordon."

"On account of your hair, of course. Anyhow, Brick, it fits." Clearly she had not heard of him, or if so, did not recollect the name now. Again she leaned forward, a hint of mischief or challenge in her eyes.

"I'd like a glass of beer," she observed, "But they wouldn't bring it to me if I ordered it. Some folks are easily shocked. But you might do me a favor—by ordering it."

He studied her a moment, his face expressionless, not bothering to tell her that he too was shocked at the request. Then he too began to feel reckless. The others would see—and they might be spurred to action. But if that was what she wanted—

"Whatever you wish," he murmured, and signaled to the waiter, giving the order. A moment later, when a bottle and glass were brought, he filled the glass and shoved it across the table.

She smiled her thanks, then paused with the glass half to her lips. If she had done this to get action, she was not to be disappointed. At least a dozen chairs were scraping back, Slash Y men coming to their feet and converging on the small table like an avenging horde.

Driscoll McKay was not among them, but he was watching, plainly approving. Jim Lomax, Slash Y foreman, acted as spokesman. He ignored his employer's daughter, and his voice rang harshly.

"Do you think you can get away wtih that, Gordon? We've put up with you eatin' at the same table with Miss McKay—but when you offer her liquor you go too far. Not the whole crew of Quirt could make that stick!"

Brick crouched tensely on the edge of his chair. His impulse was to heave to his feet, to face the bunch and outface or outfight them, but this was a time to keep a tight rein on his temper. The fact that they were there, on a day when only Quirt was supposed to have eating rights in the restaurant, rang as warningly as the shake of a diamondback's tail.

Was the girl in on the plot also? She had precipitated the trouble by her request, but the look on her face left him in doubt. She seemed to be astonished as well as dismayed at the reaction, and he was ready to withhold judgment where she was concerned.

Which was more than the others were in a mood to do with him. A hand fell heavily on his shoulder, fingers closing like claws. He tried to shake it off, and felt a jerk as another hand grabbed at his revolver and twitched it from the holster. His clutch for it was a fraction too slow; then, furious, he heaved to his feet, sending his chair crashing back with the violence of the motion.

The man who had grabbed his gun was spoiling for trouble. As a part of the same motion, he brought it up and aimed a smash of the blued steel barrel at Gordon's head, a rap which, had it landed as intended, would have dropped him like the bludgeon of an axe. He dodged, coming up under the blow, lashing out with bared knuckles, and his swing connected with the rim of a craggy jaw.

Long pent violence exploded in that swing, and the man who had appropriated his gun landed on his back in the middle of the adjoining table, his hair momentarily pillowed in a plate of gravy, spilling a cup of coffee over one of the occupants. His clutch on the six-gun loosened as he struck, allowing it to drop. Brick pounced and came up with it before any of the others could prevent him.

They were all around him. There was no chance to get his back to a wall, and the moment held the threat of unpleasantness. But there was a way to counter-attack. If you couldn't control a roomful, someone close at hand would do as well. He jabbed the muzzle of the gun into the ribs of Lomax, countering the foreman's move for his own gun.

"If anybody gets roughed up, Lomax, you top the list!" he warned.

The other man was getting off the wrecked table, feeling gingerly of his chin, shifting exploring fingers to the spot where the back of his head had come in contact with the plate. Everyone in the room was now on his feet, half the men with hands on guns. Not until that moment had Gordon taken account of the fact all of them were armed. That was unusual, though not unknown, when Slash Y came to town.

"Make your choice," he warned Lomax, and shoved with the gun point. "Should I have to pull trigger, it would mean your death!"

It was the plight of Lomax that restrained the others. Apparently they had come to town on this particular day looking for trouble. But tempers had not yet outrun caution. Driscoll McKay shouldered forward.

"Easy, boys," he warned. "I'll handle this. Put up your guns, everybody."

They hesitated, then obeyed as Lomax nodded confirmation. Shrugging, Gordon returned his own gun to its holster.

"The men are touchy about what you just did, Gordon," Driscoll growled. "Though you should have known better, Mary," he added reprovingly. "You were asking for trouble—"

Mary McKay had come to her feet with the rest, then stood, her eyes bright and watchful. Her face was faintly puzzled; there was clearly something in this which she did not understand. Now she tossed her head defiantly.

"I was asking for something for myself—and there was one gentleman in the room—only one," she observed pointedly. "Does it require all the rest of you, jumping like a pack of wolves, to deal with one?"

Blood coursed darkly under the skin of most of their faces at her question. Lomax attempted to answer.

"What made us mad was havin' a Quirt rider cozyin' up to you, Miss Mary. And when he tried to get you drunk—"

"Are you from Quirt?" Her attention returned to Gordon, her interest quickening. "I didn't know that. As for the rest—" Her glance, blazing now like sun sweeping from behind a cloud, scorched Lomax, then came to rest on her brother. "Are you a McKay, or even a man, to permit such insinuations to be cast? I came to his table, not he to mine—"

Driscoll managed a shrug. His voice was heavy.

"Now, sis, let's not indulge in a public airing of differences," he suggested. "There's fault on both sides." His heavy-lidded stare fixed on Gordon. "Only get one thing straight, Gordon, for your own good. Just because my sister made a mistake—don't go getting any notions where she's concerned!"

2.

Riding home in the settling night, Gordon strove to sort out his emotions and impressions, and found both curiously tangled. Agreeing with Driscoll McKay on one point, he had clamped his jaw on the flood of words eager to spill off his tongue, turned in silence and walked out of the restaurant. Since a lady was involved, it was neither the time nor place for a public airing of differences.

And, in spite of her request for a drink, he was convinced that Mary McKay was a lady.

He was angry as well as confused, his anger directed chiefly at Slash Y for invading the town and restaurant on a day reserved for Quirt, at their arrogance and eagerness to stir up trouble. Still, Quirt had given plenty of provocation. In their place he would have done the same.

Apparently it had been partly chance, and partly the fact that there was no other place to sit, which had brought Mary McKay to his table. She had taken it for granted that he was one of the Slash crew.

Unwittingly, she had gotten him into trouble. But

by the same token, she had gotten him out again. Except for the restraint imposed by her presence, he'd certainly have been involved in trouble from the moment he entered the restaurant.

Actually, he knew little concerning Mary McKay, scarcely more than she seemed to know about him. Along with Driscoll, she was heir to Slash Y, and it might not be long before they would be coming into their inheritance. Thinking back, Brick realized it had been quite a while since he'd seen old Abe McKay, either in town or riding his range. Abe was getting old, and he kept increasingly close to his fireside. Between them, Driscoll and Lomax had been taking over the running of the ranch, deciding policy. Today's trip to town was almost certainly Driscoll's decision.

Mary was a relative newcomer in the situation, after being away for some years. Yet he couldn't understand how a girl raised on the range could lose touch with reality as completely as she seemed to have done. She had acted like a tenderfoot, to whom everything was strange.

His face burned as he recalled Driscoll's warning not to get any notions where she was concerned! The brass of the man! Did they think he was a fortune-hunter, or interested in anything connected with Slash Y, even its women?

Well, they could go to the devil, he told himself

violently, all of them—then found himself amending that in his mind. Actually, it appeared as though Mary had been challenging the rest of them, being deliberately provocative in asking him to order the drink for her.

He hadn't approved, any more than they had, for a man didn't like to see a woman indulge in liquor—not her kind of a woman, at least. Even so, there was something about her which he admired, the flash of spirit, as well as the way she had condemned the rest of them sweepingly and scathingly.

He had taken note that her cheeks had bloomed scarlet when Driscoll had made that last biting remark about him not getting any notions.

To the devil with them—also with Quirt. He wouldn't run from trouble, not if it was legitimate. But what was brewing in the valley of the Bitter Sage threatened to be bitter indeed, and not at all to his liking. He was fed up. In the morning, he'd ride out and leave them to stew in their own juice.

Even though his decision was made, he was still seething when he unsaddled. Mary he could pardon on various grounds—either of ignorance, or the age-old excuse that she was a beautiful woman. But the men—

The buildings of Quirt were set in a secluded meadow among the hills. O'Dion's big house stood dark, looming monstrous by comparison with the other buildings, even the barn. A crew had worked nearly two years to build the house, hauling stone, erecting a massive dwelling which looked almost like a medieval castle. It seemed incongruous for an unmarried man who had spent the first three decades of his life in soddies or long shacks, when not curled up in a blanket on the open range. But the house was O'Dion's, a symbol of the power for which he was hungrily on the reach.

The old bunk house, standing in the shadow of the bigger one, was alight and crowded. Gordon tried to slip in unobtrusively, but heads turned at his entrance, and even a poker face was not enough. They read something of his anger in the glint of his eyes, and clamored to know what had happened.

"A little trouble," he admitted. "When I went into Selway's for supper, it was crowded—with Slash Y riders."

That stirred them. The fact that Quirt had been increasingly provocative made no difference. Slash Y had taken up the challenge and flung it back in their faces.

"What happened?" Felix Yankus asked the question. He usually spoke for Quirt, unless O'Dion was present.

"We had a few words." Gordon shrugged. "Nothing serious."

"I'll bet!" One man laughed shortly.

Knowing Gordon's temper, the others too seemed

to accept his disclaimer with reservations. But he had no intention of giving a full account, which would involve dragging in the name of Mary McKay. They discussed this move on the part of the Slash, and its possible implications, then went to bed.

They were finishing breakfast the next morning before Curt O'Dion entered the room and slid into his accustomed place. He was slight of figure for the power which he represented on the range, so that the big gun at his hip had the aspect of a burden. There was a flaunting twist to his mustache, and his voice could boom like a bellows.

His eyes swept the table in a quick survey, pausing an instant on Gordon, turning speculative. Whatever his thoughts, he gave no inkling of them.

"Take your time and keep your seats, boys. I've a word for everyone before you go."

He helped himself characteristically to flapjacks, simply upending the platter which held a stack of a dozen onto his plate, sloshing syrup over the pile, and spearing a steak at the same time. He ate rapidly, with huge appetite, and it occurred to Gordon, remembering the darkened big house, that he looked like a man who might have spent the night riding rather than sleeping.

No one questioned him. On Quirt, men had long since learned not to show surprise when O'Dion gave an order.

He shoved his empty plate away, drained a third cup of coffee, and leaned back with a gusty sigh of satisfaction. For a second time his glance fixed speculatively on Gordon, and it was clear that he had been told what had taken place in town. But he made no direct reference to that when he spoke.

"There is in the Good Book a place where the Man of Wisdom speaks. He proclaims that there is a time for everything—a time to be sad, a time to be merry, a time to be born, a time to die. Everything in its proper time and place. No wonder he was called wise."

No one answered. To them, it did not appear incongruous that O'Dion should quote from the Good Book. They had heard him do it too often.

"So it is that I've been biding my time, waiting for the right time. And now it has arrived. The natives are restless." He smiled, a tight grin which held no humor. "As you know, Slash has been getting notions. Yesterday they chose to break the truce. That was their doing, not ours, and such vainglory on their part must be curbed. Also, it is time for Quirt to expand, and now they have given us the signal to move ahead. Therefore we shall gird up our loins and take possession of the land."

Expectancy showed on every face, but no one interrupted.

O'Dion's voice took on the purring quality of a puma. He leaned forward, arms on the table. With the sleeves rolled above his elbows, they were revealed to be as hairy as his upper lip.

"Your duties will include more riding, and there will be some branding to do—even the altering of brands, if those already on the hide show wrong. It is my intention that one brand shall become predominant on this range. And that brand is Quirt."

There were quick intakes of breath as his meaning became clear. This was a declaration of war, an assertion that the Slash must be driven from the range. To men who knew O'Dion, the pronouncement was not surprising. He had grown accustomed to having his own way, and those who got in it were apt to be stepped on.

"There may be some trouble," he added. "But I don't think that will worry any of us. The warrior sniffs the battle from afar and glories in it. I tell you, so that you will be ready. One other thing. The laborer is worthy of his hire. As Quirt profits, so will you who ride for Quirt."

Heads nodded with satisfaction. This was O'Dion's way of replying to the insult and challenge offered Quirt the evening before. Slash had asked for war, so war it would be, to the finish.

No one doubted O'Dion's assurance that they should

share in the rewards. He asked a lot of his men when occasion demanded, but he was never niggardly in paying them. The trouble was that the bonus always came from someone else's till, as when he'd gotten the idea of turning O'Rourke's Saloon into an opera house.

Moments before, he'd forced O'Rourke to accept a niggardly five hundred dollars in cash for his building and business. Then, smiling blandly, he'd emptied O'Rourke's till of more than a thousand dollars, announcing that the money would be O'Rourke's contribution to the new enterprise, to pay the costs of alteration.

Someone would be expected to pay for this now. Slash Y, perhaps. Certainly someone other than Curt O'Dion. His open-handedness never extended to his own pocketbook.

O'Dion paused, eying his crew, and seemed satisfied. This was a rough, tough crew; all others had been weeded out, and replacements were handier with guns than with the tools of a cowboy's trade. He'd been getting ready for this ever since he had acquired Quirt.

"Be ready for anything," O'Dion added, "starting today."

Some started to shove back from the table. Gordon's voice halted the exodus.

"In that case, O'Dion, I'll be taking my time now," he observed.

The others looked at him in surprise, almost with shock. For anyone to question the boss at such a moment was unusual, but that the rebel should be Brick Gordon was doubly so, particularly after what had happened the day before.

Curt O'Dion was a hard man, and proud of his reputation. He had long boasted that he kept a tough crew of fighting men, and it was universally accepted that Brick Gordon was the toughest of the hardcase crew. Not that he went about looking for trouble, as some of them did, or provoked it unduly. But when it came, no one had a better capacity for dealing with it.

O'Dion's gaze swiveled to him, and again there was a speculative expression in the back of his eyes. There was something here beyond his understanding, and that bothered Gordon.

"Your time, did you say, Brick?" O'Dion put the purr back in his voice, but the claws of the cat scratched through. "Was it that which you said, or were my ears playin' me tricks?"

Gordon shrugged.

"Your ears are good enough. I'll have my time."

"But I don't understand. You wouldn't want to quit when there's trouble on the wind, a bit of thunder to the west. Not when the war horse sniffs the battle from afar—"

"This horse doesn't like the smell," Gordon retorted

bluntly. "So I'm quitting."

"The devil you are! After what happened last night, I'd think you'd relish the chance to get back at the Slash."

"I might, at that. But when it comes to going outside the law, count me out."

O'Dion's color matched the hair on Gordon's head. Not even his foreman had ever had the temerity to talk to the boss of Quirt in such a fashion.

"You are saying that you do not approve of the methods which I have outlined?"

"Whether I approve or not is beside the point. I don't care to be a part of such a deal. That's all."

"Oh, and that is all, is it now? It appears that we have one righteous man in the congregation of the sinful—behold him! And should we crawl on our knees and change our ways on that account?"

There was something here which went far beyond the surface, an acrimony, almost a personal hatred which were new in Gordon's relations with his employer. What was happening now was being used by O'Dion as an excuse; it was not the cause. Well, whatever his reason or motive, to the devil with him.

"I'm not asking you to change your ways or telling you what to do. I'm merely taking my time."

"The man is taking his time, he says—and riding out, after what I have revealed of our plans—doing so frankly because I supposed myself surrounded by a loyal crew of trustworthy men. But of course it's not that easy nor simple."

"Do you think I'd run to Slash Y and tell them what you have in mind?" Gordon's temper was also rising.

"A man who would quit at such a time just might play the part of a Judas," O'Dion returned grimly. Triumph threaded his tone, as though in spite of his disclaimer, the turn of events was to his liking. "On that score we take no chances. No one quits at this juncture—least of all you."

Gordon felt a mild astonishment at himself. Certainly he had been seething at the treatment accorded him by Slash, and here was a perfect opportunity to get back at them. Only the evening before he had been one man against an entire crew, and had come dangerously close to being manhandled. Now he was taking a stand against a crew of equal size, and as lacking in squeamishness. And for what?

Certainly not from any love for Slash Y. He'd always given a grudging respect to old Abe McKay, who was a hard man but fair. He was also tough, as a man had to be to hold his own on such a range, particularly when confronted by an outfit such as Quirt had become under O'Dion.

As for the rest of Slash Y, they were competent men who did their job, and were ready to fight, if need be, at the drop of a hat.

At the top now was Driscoll McKay, backed by Jim Lomax, spoiling for trouble, apparently as eager as Quirt. Driscoll he considered more a fool than a leader, even though Driscoll had restrained his crew the evening before. Perhaps he'd done so out of consideration for his sister, though more likely it had been because he'd realized that Lomax would be the first to suffer.

Certainly Brick had no reason for gratitude, either to Driscoll McKay or his outfit. Nor was he doing it for Mary McKay—who, whatever her intention might have been, had gotten him into a bad fix and all but made a fool of him. He wasn't concerned with her one way or another—and never would be, he reminded himself angrily.

If he took his time and rode out now, he'd keep going on to some distant range. The plain truth was that he drew the line at rustling, at blotting of brands.

"I'll overlook what you're suggesting, O'Dion," he returned. "But I'm taking my time—now. This is a free country, and I'm a free man—and don't forget it!"

This time there could be no doubt. The flicker of triumph in O'Dion's eyes could not be hidden. Gambler though he might be, he was no poker player, and all disclaimers to the contrary, he was pleased at the turn events had taken.

3.

Only a double-barreled chump, Gordon reflected bitterly, would fail to learn a lesson the first time. In
town, the evening before, he had allowed them to get
the jump on him; in part, that had happened because
there was a lady present, and he, in a sense, had been
her host. In addition, he hadn't supposed that Slash Y
was so eager for trouble as to send their whole crew
against one man .

The fact remained that they'd sneaked his gun and
had had him at a disadvantage—and he should have
profited by that lesson.

Yet now, for a second time, he'd been caught off
guard, not supposing that the men who had been his
trail mates for years would turn so suddenly and savagely. Mitch Noland worked the trick, lunging in from
the side, slamming shoulder and arm into Gordon's
ribs, throwing him against the man on the other side.
While he was off balance, Yankus pinned his arms;

then it seemed that the whole crew were swarming over him like ants on a strayed beetle.

One took his gun. He fought back, but the odds were too great. They twisted his arms behind his back, and Yankus drove a jarring fist into the middle of his stomach. The blow was so savage that it left him gasping and breathless. While he was helpless, it seemed that every man sought to hit him at least once, as though by such a show to court the approval of O'Dion.

The boss watched with no change of expression, speaking no word of restraint. It was Mitch Noland, eying with sudden revulsion the blood on his fist, blood not his own, who cried out in protest and shoved his own considerable bulk as a shield, grabbing two men who still came on and holding them, struggling but helpless.

"That's enough," he said thickly. "What are we—wolves? After all, he's one of us."

Gordon was still on his feet, held by a man on either side. The red haze was not due to his own anger.

"You're right, Mitch," O'Dion murmured. "He's had a lesson—perhaps enough of one. Maybe our ears were deceivin' us, Brick. Could it be that we didn't hear quite right? Are you going along with the rest of us?"

It wasn't often that O'Dion gave any man a second

chance. For him, it was a big concession. Gordon's face was a bloody smear, the agony of the savage attack still rocking through him. He spat defiance.

"This is the sort of thing I expected from Slash," he returned: "a whole crew jumping one man! Now I'd sooner work with the devil!"

Yankus moved threateningly, but Noland raised a big paw, and O'Dion continued to regard Brick almost sorrowfully.

"Some are slow to learn," he observed. "Having eyes, they can't see the shape of things to come, and their ears are plugged." He tugged at an end of his mustache, his facial muscles twitching in sympathy with the jerk. "Perhaps he needs a bit of cooling off, a chance to think the matter over. Let it not be said of us at Quirt that we are lacking in patience."

An answering gleam flickered in the eyes of Yankus.

"Maybe the bear pit would be a good place for thinking," he suggested.

O'Dion regarded his foreman with approval.

"What could be better?" he agreed. "A quiet place —a secret place. When you are ready to come out, on our side again, you have but to say the word, Brick."

"And if I don't choose to come crawling?"

"There will be no crawling required." A second time the mustache jerked. "But it runs in my mind that perhaps we have been careless in leaving such an open pit

—that maybe it should be filled in again—like a grave."

With the threat ringing in his ears, they dragged Gordon away, and he knew O'Dion well enough to be sure that he had heard his doom pronounced, unless he changed his mind. The bear pit was a mile from the buildings, a yawning hole in the middle of a tiny meadow, among a scraggly growth of jack pine. The irony, which would not go unappreciated by O'Dion, was that Gordon had been the one to suggest the pit in the first place.

It had come about because Quirt had been suffering depredations over a long period at the paws of a renegade grizzly. The bear had been dubbed The Beef Eater, because of his fondness for cattle. His toll was an average of one cow or steer each week, and he had a disconcerting habit of striking at widely separated points, often miles apart. Efforts to shoot or trap the bear had failed.

Gordon had made the discovery that on several occasions the big grizzly had followed the same trail, venturing close to the buildings of Quirt, as though taking a close look at the situation. One bull had been killed in the corrals.

Other methods having failed, Gordon had pointed out that a pit, dug where the trail crossed the open meadow, then carefully covered over, might bring the cow killer to destruction. The pit had been dug, sheer-walled and deep, roofed and left in place.

On the very next morning, going for a look, they had approached with high hopes, noting that the roof had collapsed, that something was certainly trapped in the pit. Then elation had given way to disgust, as they found at the bottom a deer with a broken neck. The sign around the brink of the hole had offered mute testimony that now the grizzly would never be taken in it.

Claw marks were all around the rim, obviously from the twisted foot of the bear, injured in a trap years before. Apparently The Beef Eater had been approaching, exactly as hoped; a deer had fled before him, falling into the pit, and the grizzly had examined the trap in detail. Knowing of its existence, he would not be fooled by it.

In one sense the pit might be said to have worked, for oddly enough, the depredations had stopped. Whether the killer had taken the hint and left the country, or been overtaken by misfortune in the wilds, there had been no more sign of him. A wire fence had been built around the pit to keep cattle from falling in, and it had gone almost forgotten.

Dragged along by a man clutching either arm, Gordon was dumped unceremoniously into the hole. If he, like the deer, suffered a broken neck, they were in no mood to care. By the time he picked himself up, shaken but no worse than bruised, only the receding sounds of footsteps came to his ears.

A look around his prison was not reassuring. It was twenty feet deep and a dozen feet across. Weather and water had caused little erosion of the walls, and while some debris had fallen in, not enough had collected to afford any foundation from which to climb. A few attempts to escape convinced him of what he had known: that it was impossible. Once, working desperately, he made it to within half a dozen feet of the rim, only to have an outjut of soil and rock break loose and pitch him back. That time he landed hard and lay breathless.

The day dragged. Flies came to keep him company, attracted by the dry blood on his face, a constant irritation. There was plenty of time for reflection, to wonder if anger and pride were to be his undoing. He could still change his mind and work with the rest of Quirt's crew; he had no doubt that O'Dion would succeed. Old Abe McKay no longer bulked formidably in the way of his ambitions, and Gordon, like O'Dion, doubted that Driscoll McKay would prove much of an adversary.

They'd simply bleed the Slash, as a weasel sucks the blood of a victim, until it could struggle no more. Other small outfits could be counted on to stand aloof from such a struggle. Their own eventual salvation might lie in combining now to fight alongside the Slash, but for many reasons they would not. By the time they woke up to their danger, it would be too late.

The only other possible deterrent was the law, and O'Dion had made sure that he would have nothing to fear from that. The sheriff and the judge owed their election and their allegiance to O'Dion. Any gesture they made to stop him would be no more than a token one.

You have a chance to be in on the winning side—or to stay in this hole forever, Gordon reminded himself. And a sensible man would swallow his pride!

The trouble was that he was not sensible. He'd had his doubts about the deal by which O'Dion had acquired Quirt, and those had increased with O'Dion's subsequent activities. But he was a cowhand, and so long as he was called upon to do no more than a cowboy's proper work, he'd done so, though with increasing watchfulness.

Now O'Dion was demanding brand blotching and wholesale thievery, and that was something else. Also, there was O'Dion's inexplicable attitude toward himself, recent in origin but unmistakable. It was as though O'Dion were anxious to be rid of him, but not by allowing him to quit or go as a free agent.

That Mary McKay and her heritage were involved in this, he told himself angrily, made no difference.

It was evening before anyone came near. He heard the sound of footsteps, a single man, the creak of the barbed wire fence as the strands were parted to allow passage between. He was not surprised that it was Felix Yankus who gazed down at him, his heavy face gloating and resentful. In his foreman O'Dion had found a kindred spirit, though Yankus lacked the surface polish of his boss.

The foreman held a tray in both hands, and Gordon made out that it was laden with food and something to drink. Thirst had become a torture during the long afternoon.

"You have enough, Brick?" Yankus asked. "I've brought you some supper—if you're ready for it. And then you can come along back."

"Throw me a rope or something, then," Gordon replied.

Yankus set the tray down, then scowled suspiciously.

"You ready to go along and do as the boss says?" he demanded.

"Let's talk after I've eaten," Gordon suggested, but Yankus was not so easily fooled. He shook his head, grinning crookedly.

"No, sir. You give your word first, or you stay right there. And it can get to be uncomfortable, fillin' your belly on air. Make it quick, or I'm going to eat this grub. I just had a good feed, but I can enjoy another."

Deliberately, sitting down, he started to eat. He was obviously enjoying it, drinking noisily, and Gordon was forced to watch helplessly. They would take his word, because they knew that once he gave it, he'd stick to a promise. Short of that, O'Dion would abide by his threat, leaving him to die by slow degrees. O'Dion, of course, was sure that he wouldn't be so foolish as to hold out very long.

Yankus sighed gustily, wiping his mouth with the back of a hand, pushing the tray to one side. He got slowly to his feet.

"That was good grub," he observed, and proceeded to enumerate the bill of fare, from fried chicken to biscuits to apple pie, each item mouth-watering to his auditor. "Might be the cook could find some more for you back at the cook house. 'Course, if you ain't interested—"

"How does it feel to be a worm, Yankus?" Brick asked. "And so low that you could crawl under a rattlesnake without it knowing? Or are you so much a worm that you don't even know the difference?"

Night was beginning to settle, filling the little meadow among the trees with dusk, but enough light remained to reveal the dark flush on the foreman's face. His voice choked with rage.

"Who you callin' a worm?" he demanded. "Why, blast you, I'm just doing what I was told—"

"Sure you are," Gordon cut in. "That's all you know, to do as you're told. That's what slaves do. You couldn't think for yourself if you tried, or even act like a man. You're the sort who hits a man when he can't fight back, a gully-whuzzler that even a coyote would turn up his nose at!"

Yankus looked momentarily puzzled.

"I ain't nothin' of the sort," he protested. "What's a gully-whuzzler?"

"You are," Gordon retorted. "The lowest crawlin' form of gully-whuzzler."

He'd made up the term on the spur of the moment. As he'd expected, it enraged the slow-thinking Yankus simply because he didn't understand it. He glared wildly around, frustrated by the distance between them, then darted from sight for a moment, returning almost at once with a long, slender pole. Gordon had noticed it that morning, when his captors had dragged him to the prison.

Originally, many saplings had been cut and trimmed and used to bridge the pit, with grass and leaves fashioned above to conceal the trap. Most of those had disappeared in the year and more since the pit was built, but a few remained. He taunted Yankus in the hope of enraging him.

Now, torn between rage and wild glee, Yankus leaned forward, reaching down, thrusting with one end of the pole, trying to prod or hit him. A wild swing almost succeeded, but Gordon jumped aside.

"See what I mean?" he shouted. "A gully-whuzzler!"

Yankus raced halfway around the rim, surprisingly agile for so big a man, and took another swing. Deliberately, Gordon sprawled and lay as though he'd been hurt. Yankus chortled triumphantly and thrust viciously with the pole. Twisting, Gordon grabbed the end, and before Yankus could understand the trick, gave a savage jerk in return. If he could get possession of the pole, he'd have a tool to aid him in climbing from the pit. But what happened was even better.

Yankus was clutching his end of the pole doggedly and, taken off-guard, he came along with it, losing his balance and toppling. He landed heavily, then lay prone. A quick examination convinced Gordon that the wind was merely knocked out of him, but that was enough.

Setting the pole upright at the edge, using it both for balance and climbing, he was at the top by the time Yankus was able to sit up and take a renewed interest in affairs. Tossing the pole aside, Gordon looked down. By now it was virtually dark at the bottom of the hole.

"Somebody will probably help you out tomorrow," he said, then snapped his fingers in exasperation. He'd been in so big a hurry to get out before Yankus recovered that he'd forgotten to help himself to Yankus' gun. Now it was too late.

A bullet came so close that he heard it sing past his ear. He jumped back, then moved away. The shooting would be heard, and others would come on the run. Still worse, once the crew was alerted, he couldn't very well return to the buildings, either to get his horse or to help himself to some grub.

4.

Disgusted, Brick set off. At least he was free of the pit, and the settling night was in his favor. Curt O'Dion was a realist, so he probably wouldn't bother with much of a hunt, knowing how hopeless the effort would be.

On the other hand, if he remained in that country, O'Dion and the crew of Quirt would be relentless and unforgiving. Something had prompted O'Dion to send him into the town the day before, knowing that he'd probably run into trouble. Now, in the face of his defiance, O'Dion would be angry and apprehensive, because he'd expect him to go to the Slash, tell what he knew and offer his services.

It would be logical, according to O'Dion's way of thinking, first to get back at Quirt, secondly to be near Mary McKay. His meeting with her the evening before would loom in O'Dion's mind as the primary reason for Gordon's course of conduct. He'd probably assume that there was more to it than had actually been the case.

The thought brought Gordon up short. Certainly he didn't like the Slash or anything connected with the outfit—for even Mary, whether wittingly or not, had contrived to make a fool of him. Yet now Curt O'Dion's rage would be aimed at her as well as at himself, as he linked the two in his mind. That being so, did he have any right to pull out now and head for a new range, leaving Mary to face such a predicament?

It was easy to tell himself that none of this was his quarrel, that it would be the part of wisdom to go fast and far, leaving all of them to stew in the juice of their own brewing. The trouble was that Quirt had made it his fight, whether he liked it or not. And he'd never made a practice of running from a fight.

Nonetheless, a lot of pros were involved, as well as cons. The question was still unresolved in his mind when he heard the faint jingle of a bridle bit and saw the shadowy outline of a horse, cropping the grass. A faint hump above its back confirmed the rest; it was a saddle horse, with reins dragging, and certainly miles from where it should have been.

That might mean that its rider had been thrown and was somewhere nearby, perhaps injured and helpless. Or the horse could belong to a rider from Quirt, posted to watch for him. He hadn't expected O'Dion to go that far, but it was a possibility.

He was some five miles from the buildings on Quirt,

and by the same token about an equal distance from the headquarters of the Slash. This was Quirt range, but it wasn't far to the line between the two outfits.

The moon, nearly at the full tonight, would be up soon. Its glow was already spreading across the east. He could detect nothing suspicious, and a horse was what he stood most in need of. Not of a mind to blunder into another trap, he moved cautiously. He'd slaked his thirst at a small tributary of the Bitter Sage, but the memory of the long day remained vivid.

At his approach, the horse raised its head, but did not try to shy away. True to its training, it stood ground-hitched when the reins were dropped, though hunger had caused it to graze, moving about. That indicated that it had been there for some time. A look at its left flank confirmed his guess. The brand was the Slash Y.

Imprisoned as he had been through the day, he had no knowledge of what might have happened. There could have been a clash between the two outfits. He'd have a look before going on.

Moving in a widening circle, he soon found what he had feared. Half-hidden among grass and brush was the sprawled figure of a man. The sudden glow of the moon, rolling across the horizon, helped pick it out.

His first guess was that the man was dead, probably for some hours. Then, bending over and placing a hand on a shoulder, he decided that the fellow was still alive. At least he was warm, not rigid, though he lay face down in the grass. Turning him for a look, Gordon started back in shock.

It was Driscoll McKay.

The moonlight showed a face drained of blood, almost marble-white. But there was blood lower down, under an armpit—blood half-dry, yet still sticky. The wound did not look particularly ugly, being only a small hole which had not bled too much. That, he knew, was only the outward and superficial aspect.

It had been made by a bullet, which had gone in and was still embedded somewhere within his body. That in itself was apt to be bad. The lack of bleeding in this instance could not be considered reassuring. McKay was unconscious, and judging by the signs, he had been lying so for hours.

There was only one thing to do, and that was to get him on his horse and back to Slash Y, and then, if he was still alive, to send for a doctor. Moving him could be bad, but to leave him would mean certain death. One alternate was almost as grim as the other.

Driscoll's gun was not in his holster, and a brief search near the body failed to discover it. There was no time for a thorough hunt, even though a gun in his own pocket would have been comfortable insurance at this juncture. Gordon brought up the horse.

It was the manner in which the cayuse lifted its

head, ears cocked forward, which warned that others were approaching. By then, with the moonlight flooding the landscape, there was not time to slip away, no chance to hide. Half a dozen horsemen came suddenly into sight, cresting the slope above, then came on at a brisk trot. The glint of the moon shone on drawn guns.

They surrounded him, exclaiming, suddenly angry as they recognized him, then made out the recumbent form of Driscoll McKay. The six were from the Slash, Jim Lomax at their head.

Lomax bent above McKay, then straightened grimly.

"What you got to say for yourself, Gordon?" he demanded.

"I came upon him a little while ago," Gordon explained. "I was just getting ready to load him onto his horse, to take him to his home."

"That's a likely story," one of the others exclaimed hotly. "You shot him, and we caught you dead to rights. Why don't we string him up for the murderin' killer he is?"

Lomax lifted a restraining hand. His eyes remained fixed on Gordon's face.

"You and he didn't get on very well together the last time you met," he reminded Brick.

"True enough," Gordon conceded. "But use your head. He's been here for hours—his horse had done a lot of grazing. That wound is far from fresh. I've no horse—and no gun."

Lomax had reason to feel distrust and hostility, but he hadn't been made foreman at the Slash without possessing qualities of leadership. He nodded grudgingly.

"Go on."

"That's it. I found him, after sighting his horse. I figured the best thing was to get him to Slash Y. It would be risky, but to leave him would be worse."

There was another grudging nod. "If you didn't shoot him, then who did?"

"I could make a guess, but you can do that as well as I can. Quirt is on the war path against the Slash. That's not news to you. For the rest—" He shrugged.

Lomax made a decision. "Load him onto his horse," he instructed. "Gently, now. We've got to take him in. You'll come along, Gordon."

"Suits me," Gordon agreed. "When he's able to talk, he'll tell you what happened, which will clear me."

"It had better—and you'd better hope that he's able to talk again," Lomax grunted. "Otherwise I wouldn't want to be in your boots."

"You say you found him this way. But what the blazes are you doing here, that you found him?" another man burst out impatiently. "And on foot, without a gun?"

"Since you ask, I'm runnin' from Quirt," Gordon returned, "minus both those articles. All at once we didn't see eye to eye."

"You tryin' to tell us that you've quit and they're after you?" The other man snorted derisively. "You better make up a better story than that, or come daylight, we'll be decoratin' a tree."

Gordon did not bother to reply. A quick search seemed to confirm his claim that he was on foot, and, grudgingly, he was given a seat behind Sam Drake, a thoughtful man who had remained in the background at the restaurant the evening before.

They made their way back to the Slash, taking their time, since haste would be hard on the injured man. McKay remained unstirring, and Gordon's anxiety was reflected on the faces of the others. Lomax dispatched a couple of the crew, one to ride straight for a doctor, the other to get a wagon and return, meeting them along the way.

Most of the ride had been completed before the wagon met them, with blankets spread over straw in the box. The transfer was made, still with no visible change in the wounded man.

The ranch buildings came into sight, with lights everywhere, and there was a bustle of preparation. Mary McKay came hurrying to meet them, pale with dread. Looking up, her eyes widened as they met Gordon's, then mirrored both surprise and apprehension.

"You!" The word was so hushed that he could barely hear. "What are you doing here?"

Lomax answered for him.

"We found him 'side of your brother, Mary. Gordon claims he'd just found him—but we'd like some more explainin' about that."

"But I don't understand." Suddenly she did, and indignation replaced the perplexity on her face. "You don't mean that you think he might have done it?" she protested. "Oh, no! He's not that sort."

Gordon eased off the horse from behind Drake and managed a bow.

"I'm obliged for your good opinion, Miss McKay," he said. "As I pointed out to the others, your brother had been shot quite a while before I found him. Besides, I've no gun."

"He claims that he's quit Quirt—and that they're after him," Lomax added. "That's harder to swallow than the rest."

"You men!" Mary exclaimed impatiently. As though despairing of male stupidity, she climbed on to the brake hub of the wagon and peered down at her brother, studying him anxiously. "Get a door to move him on," she instructed, and watched while Driscoll was lifted from the wagon and carried into the house. Catching sight of a loitering figure in the shadows of the big porch, she hurried to him.

"It's Driscoll, Pa," she explained. "He's been shot—badly hurt. They've just brought him in."

Abe McKay asked no questions as to why he had not been informed sooner. Probably they had supposed him to be asleep. His voice seemed devoid of emotion.

"How bad?"

"We don't know," Mary confessed. "The wounds looks pretty mean. We've sent for the doctor."

"He's still alive, then?"

"Yes."

"Tell me about it."

Lomax had moved alongside Gordon. "Stick around," he said gruffly.

"I'm as interested in this as you are," Gordon reminded him.

Lomax supplied such details as he knew, including the account of how they had come upon Gordon. McKay stood, his back to the side of the house, his face hidden in the shadows. If any of the things he was told surprised him, he gave no sign.

"Better have a look at his wound," he observed, "see if there's anything you can do. Most likely be hours before the doc can get here. You have a look, Gordon," he added. "From what I hear, you've had experience with gunshot wounds."

It was true, and Gordon had taken charge on more

than one occasion when there were injuries at Quirt, before the doctor could come. What surprised him was that McKay should know about this.

He helped Mary wash and cleanse the wound as well as possible. Since the bleeding had stopped, there was not much else to do. Lomax suggested getting some whiskey between Driscoll's lips as a stimulant, but McKay, from the background, promptly vetoed that.

"No whiskey. Better to leave him as he is, if he's restin' easy. You agree, Gordon?"

Surprised at having his opinion sought, Gordon nodded. "Yes. To revive him now might kill him, once the effect of the stimulant wore off. Only a doctor can probe for that bullet, for it's uncomfortably close to his heart."

"My opinion, too." McKay nodded. "Keep a good watch on him, in case he shows signs of waking up. Better put on the coffeepot. Now what's this, Gordon, about O'Dion's plan concerning Quirt?"

"From what he told us yesterday, I gather that he is out to take over this whole range. He's been building toward that ever since he came, and now he thinks the time is ripe."

"Yeah, there's been plenty of sign along the way. Now he's coming into the open—and shooting from ambush?"

"This shooting has all the earmarks. He intends to

blot brands, whatever is necessary to smash the Slash."

"In other words, war?"

"He knows it'll come to that."

"And so you quit, rather than go along?"

"Yes."

Abe nodded, as though not surprised. Mary came with coffee, one of the crew following with tin cups. Gordon downed his with relish, accepting a couple of refills. In the yellow light of the kerosene lamps, Mary's face appeared drawn and pale, but she was steady and efficient. No one thought of sleeping. Abe questioned the others about Driscoll's movements during the day, but no one had seen him ride away. Only when night had closed down and he had failed to return had alarm been felt. Some of them had set out to search.

Ordinarily, no one would have been concerned, but the trouble at Selway's the night before had made them uneasy.

Abe had listened quietly, but now his face showed sharp attention. He rapped a question.

"What's this about you bustin' in on Selway's last night? That was Thursday—and a Quirt night."

Two or three of the crew exchanged startled, guilty glances. Clearly, they had betrayed something about which the boss had been in ignorance. Lomax sought to explain.

"Well, we were all in town yesterday, and it was

time to eat. There didn't seem to be anybody from Quirt around, so we went to Selway's. We're tired of being pushed around by Quirt," he added defensively.

"That was Driscoll's-notion, I take it—about being tired of being pushed around and eatin' at Selway's?"

"Well—yes, I guess it was."

"And somebody from Quirt *was* there?"

"Nobody to start with. Gordon came in while we were eating."

"Gordon, eh? And then what?"

"There was some trouble."

"I bet," Abe said dryly. "All of you against one. How much trouble?"

"Nothing to speak of. Not with Mary there—"

"Uh huh. And you and Driscoll didn't see fit to inform me of any of this. As foreman, you're workin' for Driscoll, eh, not me? I'm on the shelf, and what I say don't count any longer. That it, Mister?"

Lomax was sweating, acutely uncomfortable. He ran a finger around his shirt collar as though it choked him.

"That's not so, Abe. It was just—just—"

"Just that you and Driscoll figured to take over here on Slash, and you needed a diversion to make it look right—trouble with Quirt. So you asked for trouble, and now you've got it. Somebody coming?"

The others heard it then, though Abe had been the first to catch the sound. A surrey wheeled into sight, drawn by a team of high-stepping bays. Doctor Porter, pudgy and graying at the temples, tossed the reins to one of the crew, then moved briskly to the house. He paused for a word with the McKays, then followed Mary.

Silence settled, almost as heavy as the surrounding blackness. It was nearly an hour before the doctor emerged, followed by Mary. Her face was composed, but her eyes were red.

"We tried," Porter reported gruffly. "It was a chance— but a slim one. And it didn't work. He's dead."

5

Now that the verdict had been given, Gordon realized that he had expected nothing else. The thread of hope had been as slender as a spider's web; there had been little chance that Driscoll McKay might ever regain consciousness, to tell what he knew concerning who had struck him down—or who had not.

Angry mutterings arose from some of the men. Evidence or lack of it notwithstanding, it had been Brick Gordon whom they had caught at the scene of the murder.

"I say, let's string him up!" one rebel growled. "He's Quirt, ain't he—and they're all guilty!"

The even, quiet voice of Abe McKay cut across the rising clamor like a slosh of cold water. He had returned, unnoticed, to loiter in the shadows. His face was strained and drawn, but he was still the boss.

"Quit such talk! Now, Lomax, what you got to say?"

Put suddenly on the spot, Lomax was caught off

guard.

"Well, I don't quite know," he admitted. "But there's an old saying that seems to apply—an eye for an eye and a tooth for a tooth!"

Abe snorted derisively.

"Is that the best you can come up with? You're a fool," he added bluntly, "same as Driscoll was. I let him talk me into puttin' you in as foreman, though I knew it was a mistake. Not that it mattered too much, as long as I could look after things myself. Now it matters plenty. And there's no room for a fool to head up things on Slash."

Apparently the demotion was not unexpected, but Lomax listened incredulously as McKay continued.

"After what happened the night before in town, Driscoll should have known better than to ride alone, specially off on Quirt range. His trouble was that he never knew much—and he didn't live long enough to learn! So now we're in a mess."

"Quirt can't get away with this," Lomax protested thickly. "We'll hit back at them."

"They've gotten away with it," McKay reminded him. "Driscoll's dead. Nothing is going to change that. Sure we'll fight back—but doing it blind, striking senselessly, would finish us. That's what they're hoping we'll do; they're trying to goad us into riding into a trap. How do you figure it, Gordon?"

"I wouldn't be surprised if that was back of this shooting," Gordon conceded. "They aimed to be rid of the man they figured to be in charge, and driving Slash crazy mad at the same time."

"Sure, that's bound to be the reason. O'Dion figures he's got us on the run and half licked already. And he might have been right, with a little luck. Only he made a mistake by not knowin' a man when he saw one. I can't handle this fight myself, and he's countin' on that. With Driscoll out of the way, O'Dion thought we would be finished. We might have been if he'd used some sense at home. But now that you're here, Gordon, will you take charge? I know it's askin' a lot—but a lot's at stake!"

Gordon had seen the request coming. Up to a few hours before, it would have seemed incredible, but he was beginning to understand how Abe McKay's mind worked. In a physical sense, Abe was all but helpless, but his mind was unimpaired. He could still go to the heart of a matter, brushing aside all trivialities.

The habit of command was strong, not readily broken. Lomax gave a yelp of protest.

"Are you crazy, McKay," he demanded, "askin' *him* to take over as foreman, and Driscoll not yet in his grave?"

"I'm still owner here," McKay reminded him tartly. "And what I say goes. As for Driscoll—maybe he's where he can see clearer now. Given time, he'd have gotten sense. But leavin' him out of it—*you* got any good reason why I shouldn't hire Gordon?"

"Plenty of them," Lomax blazed. Resentment at his own demotion was inflamed by what seemed to him the monstrous choice of a man from Quirt.

"He'll be here—right along with Miss Mary. That's how the trouble started the other night, with him getting notions and tryin' to shine up to her. Driscoll warned him against that, ordered him to stay away from her! And now Driscoll's dead, and you do this—"

"Driscoll's dead because he was a fool!" McKay cut in implacably. "And he wasn't the only one! The whole crew of you acted like a pack of idiots, Driscoll most of all. He had the notion that because Slash Y runs a lot of cattle, that made him something special—so that anybody with McKay to their name was too good to associate with ordinary folks!" Abe snorted disgustedly. "Which is the biggest piece of foolishness of all!

"I built Slash Y—startin' from nothing. When I first picked this range for mine, all I had was a couple of scrawny cows and the shirt to my back! Some folks get the notion that havin' a bit of money makes them better than their neighbors, which is plain idiocy. Gordon, I'm askin' you to take on a tough job. You know how tough; you'll be turnin' against your former boss. He'll be fightin' mad and stop at nothing. But you're the only man that's tough enough to stop him. And you've a reason for doing it, after the way he treated you. And that's why I figure maybe you'll take it—because it is a tough job."

Gordon nodded.

"If you take the job, it'll be up to you," McKay went on. "What you say will go. Anybody who don't care to work under those conditions can draw their time. How about it?"

Startled, the truth was borne in upon Gordon. McKay had been looking straight at him, but he hadn't seen the nod. That explained why he'd stuck so close to home these past months, leaving the running of the ranch more and more to Driscoll and Lomax. It wasn't merely that his health was no longer good, his eye sight failing. Buoyed up by an unflinching will, he'd kept going, allowing everyone to assume that he was giving Driscoll a chance to prove himself.

Actually, Abe was blind. Probably the doctor had told him that nothing could be done for him, and he'd accepted the verdict, keeping his own counsel. Complete familiarity with the house, the buildings and paths around Slash Y, coupled with a keen sense of hearing and direction, had enabled him to move around without letting others guess the extent of his affliction.

Gordon did not allow his voice to betray his discovery.

"It sounds like a big order, but if you want me to try, I'll do my best."

"Fair enough. You're in charge." Finality was in McKay's pronouncement. "Lomax, you'll take your orders from him, and so will everyone else. What we have is a fight for existence, for life itself. Under those circumstances, there can't be any division of loyalty."

"That's right," Gordon confirmed. "As a better man once put it, either we hang together, or we'll hang separately. And in regard to that danger—from now on, when anybody rides, go two and two, not a single man alone, anywhere. And keep alert." He looked around. Gray was beginning to edge the eastern horizon, and it was too late for anyone to get any sleep that night.

"Let's have some breakfast as soon as possible," he added. "We'll have a busy day."

Somewhat to his surprise, there were no further protests, not even from Lomax. McKay had made his pronouncement, and McKay was still the boss. The disastrous consequences of even a small revolt had sobered them. Gordon turned to where Mary had listened from the background, looking lost and forlorn.

"I'm sorry matters turned out this way," he told her. "Mighty sorry."

Mary nodded uncertainly.

"Thank you," she replied. "I keep wondering if what has happened was my fault—if what I did the other evening caused this." She looked at him directly, and color flowed in a wave back into pale cheeks.

"Papa is pretty blunt sometimes—but he is a judge of men, and I want you to know that I approve his choice of you as foreman. Lomax wasn't big enough for the job, not the way it is now. As for what happened there in the restaurant, I'm afraid I was being foolish, too. I had no idea that you were from Quirt. I supposed of course that you were one of our own crew."

"I figured you did."

"If I had realized the situation, I would never have asked you to do something that would get you into trouble the way it did. I just wanted to show that I could be independent, that I had some rights, too. It wasn't that I wanted the beer. I loathe the stuff. But I thought that would show Driscoll."

Gordon was aware of a long-drawn breath of relief at the explanation. He'd judged her to be a spoiled brat, showing off after her years away at school, with habits which, in his lexicon, real women did not indulge in. Driscoll had felt the same way, and his manner had left her angry and resentful.

"I don't think you have any reason to blame yourself," Gordon reassured her. "Quirt had already made up its mind as to its course. O'Dion intends to smash Slash, to take over this whole range. He's been getting ready for a long while, biding his time, knowing that your father was failing. He decided that the time had come, and one of the first necessary steps was to get rid of Driscoll. Other things made no difference."

"Thank you." He understood that her appreciation was for the reassurance in regard to what had happened to her brother. "It—will things be bad—the war?"

Gordon nodded soberly. "Apt to be. O'Dion doesn't start on a venture as big as this unless he thinks he sees his way clear to winning. With Driscol out of the picture, he'll figure that he can do just about as he pleases."

He ran fingers wearily through his hair, suddenly conscious of his new responsibility.

"So I'd better start moving. They are apt to strike hard and fast, hoping to catch us all upset and off guard."

"O'Dion made one bad mistake," Mary breathed. "He didn't count on someone like you taking over for us at this juncture! That could turn out to be the worst mistake he ever made!"

6.

Gordon observed without surprise that the Slash was efficiently run. It was only a short while until the cook issued the call for breakfast. Having missed most of his meals the day before, Brick ate hungrily. The pace of events over the past thirty-six hours made him feel slightly dizzy, despite the dragging interval which he had spent in the bear pit. But he had his thoughts sorted out, a plan in mind, as he scraped back his chair and stood up.

"What has happened was all pretty sudden," he observed. "And it was just as big a surprise to me as to any of you. I'll say this: O'Dion told everybody on Quirt yesterday that there was going to be war with the Slash. I might have gone along with that, on a fair basis. But when he told us that Quirt was going to steal Slash Y blind, blotching brands as a part of the operation, I asked for my time. He wouldn't give it to me—I suppose he was afraid I'd betray his plans. He didn't aim to let me go."

The others were listening with interest, but he supplied no details as to how he had walked away despite the ban. They could guess at that.

"Right now, we're all in the same boat. O'Dion intends to fight dirty, and you know what that means. So we'll have to battle for existence. If any of you don't feel like staying, under such conditions, I won't blame you for pulling out now. But for those who stay, we'll go all the way."

He paused, but no one took advantage of the chance to quit. He'd known that they were a good crew, and loyal; loyal not to him, but to their outfit, to Abe McKay and Mary and the memory of Driscoll. That was as it should be; they'd follow his orders because that was Abe's decision.

"I'd like for you to take one man and go to town, Lomax," he went on. "Make whatever preparations are necessary for the funeral. Driscoll was your friend. Find out from Abe and Mary what they want. For the rest of you, remember what I said about riding in pairs —but don't be trigger-happy. And don't be caught with your guard down.

"Ride the border between Slash and Quirt, and turn back any of our stock which you find anywhere near the line. For the present, we don't want to take chances or lose cattle—especially calves. That's all."

By rights, he felt that he should confer with Abe,

but this was a poor time to bother him. Abe had picked him and told him to do the job.

Looking over the crew, he selected Drake to ride with him. He'd ridden double, behind Drake's saddle, during the night, and found the man likable as well as alert.

Both Quirt and Slash claimed a lot of territory as their respective ranges; between them they occupied the major part of the valley of the Bitter Sage. Bitter Sage Creek rose in the mountains to the west, rolling east and south, picking up tributaries and momentum as it went, until by the time it entered the Slash, it was already a sizable stream.

As a cowboy for Quirt, Gordon had become familiar with the long miles of border, as well as with most of the Slash Y. Across a couple of miles, a deep, almost sheer canyon divided the two outfits, and along that naturally peaceful stretch there had never been any question in regard to boundaries. But on either side of the canyon, for miles in both directions, there was only the creek, winding and twisting, and no firm agreement had ever been reached as to whose range it was.

Abe McKay had been watchful, a formidable opponent, demanding only his rights, but brooking no trespassing. There had never been trouble while Tom Landis was neighbor to Slash, but since the coming of O'Dion, an uneasy truce had prevailed. Now it had been broken.

With Drake jogging beside him, Gordon headed for the section known as the broken arrow. That was a section of low-lying ground, partially wooded, lush with grass, which jutted deep into nominal Quirt territory. The Bitter Sage twisted to the south, took a look at the hills looming as a barrier to its progress, then swung back. In the process it enveloped a thousand acres in the form of an arrow, blunted at the tip. Twice in as many years, O'Dion had protested that the land really belonged to Quirt. Twice he had been rebuffed, and the uneasy *status quo* had been maintained.

Only a couple of days before, Gordon had looked across the wide sprawling creek and observed large herds of Slash Y cattle in the peninsula section, chiefly cows and their calves. He had no doubt that O'Dion knew where every steer, calf or cow belonging to Slash Y was ranging, and he might be ready to take advantage of such an opportunity.

Swarms of tiny gnats clustered in the brush and swarmed around as they rode. The flies of the summer were gone; the tiny insects were a sign of the advancing season. Brush and trees were spending their gold with a lavish recklessness whenever a gust of wind shook them.

With the thick covering of leaves beginning to thin, it was easier to see the stock, or the place where they should have been. Today there was plenty of fresh sign, but nothing more. It took only a few minutes for him to realize that O'Dion had been ahead of them. Not a cow or calf was anywhere on the accustomed range.

There was no particular point in following the twistings and turnings of the creek in a search for sign. All along its length, the cattle were accustomed to drinking, frequently crossing to the other side, just as Quirt stock crossed in turn, mingling the herds. Twice each year at roundup time they were separated, to their manifest bewilderment.

Now, if the cows had been shoved across to Quirt territory, there would be no unusual sign to denote the movement. They might well have been moved the day before.

He explained his fears to Drake, then asked a question.

"Did any of you boys ride this territory yesterday?"

Drake shook his head. "Maybe Driscoll," he said. "All the rest of us were workin' the far end of our range. The only place they could have gone is over there, of course." He grinned, the smile somewhat strained. "Do we go over and look for them?"

Gordon shook his head. "Not today. If we did find them, chances are we'd end up being missing as well. We'll double-check to make sure they're really gone—then, when we cross, we'll go in force."

Drake nodded approval. "That's good sense."

"A day or so won't make much difference now. And we have to give Driscoll a proper burial. I'd prefer to hold off trouble till that's attended to—though I wouldn't count on doing so."

"Why not?"

"If I know O'Dion, he'll figure the time of the funeral is good to make another move."

They swung back to the home buildings, riding wide for a look at country where the cows might possibly have strayed. It was unlikely, but Gordon preferred to be sure of his ground before he acted.

The soft haze of Indian summer blanketed the valley in a deceptive calm. While hills and meadows flamed with color, the grass had turned drab. Streams ran softly, though along each one the sign showed an almost frantic flurry of activity among the rodents who called the waterways home. Beavers were putting finishing touches to dams, freshly barked sticks being thrust here and there among the seasoned wood. Willows and cottonwood saplings had been newly felled, towed away and sunk in deep pools to provide winter provender. Muskrats and minks were actuated by the same sense of urgency; their tracks were everywhere in the mud along the shores. In them was the knowledge that such perfect fall weather could not last much longer.

The rest of the crew returned when they did, and there was no good answer to Gordon's questions. The range had been peaceful, but no one had seen the missing cows. Nearly a thousand head had vanished.

The stock must have been rustled while Brick was in the bear pit, cut off from normal sources of information. It helped to explain what had happened to Driscoll. Probably he had sighted the rustlers at work, and had incautiously ventured across to protest. O'Dion was not a man to pass up such an opportunity.

Lomax had made preparations for the funeral, which would be held in town the next day, so that neighbors could attend. It was a last tribute, which would not be neglected and could not be by-passed. The trouble was that O'Dion would probably be ready to take advantage of the diversion, the absence of Slash's crew from their range. Gordon's conviction was so strong that it spoiled his appetite.

He crossed to the big house and found Abe sitting quietly in a chair in the echoing, empty-seeming kitchen. Abe listened to his conclusions, then nodded in agreement.

"Likely you're right," he conceded. "O'Dion has waited a long while for a favorable chance, and he thinks it's at hand. Now that he's started, he'll put everything on the board. It is his way."

Gordon agreed with that assessment. As a gambler,

O'Dion had patience and calculation. He'd waited a long while for the right moment. Now he'd go all out.

"You'll understand, then, why I won't be at the funeral tomorrow," he said.

"I'll understand," Abe agreed, "though some may not."

The hallway was dimly lit by a lamp near its far end. In these shadowy recesses, Gordon encountered Mary. She halted, looking at him questioningly, and he repeated what he had just told her father.

"I thought you should know," he said.

"That means you'll be off hunting trouble," Mary returned, "which you expect will be at hand."

"I'm afraid it may be. It would be a poor tribute to Driscoll to allow them to bury the rest of us at the same time."

Her eyes darkened. "Probably you're right," she agreed. "It's all rather terrible. I was so happy to come to the ranch, to be able at last to live here," she went on. "I had only visited it twice before in my life, each time for just a few weeks—weeks which never were long enough."

He listened, with increasing amazement and understanding, as she continued.

"Mother always hated the West, and while she lived, she was determined that I should be kept well away from it, shielded from what she termed its savagery. She lived with Dad for two years out here, and he endured one year back East with her. But neither of them could stand the other's country. Mother had imagination, but only the sort which thought of herself and what she wanted. It was terribly hard on Dad, who'd had big dreams and high hopes when he married her. He was the first to realize that neither of them could change, and he accepted it and didn't complain. And now—now I'm not sure whether I am more his daughter than my mother's, or not."

The revelation explained many things which had puzzled Gordon. The sudden savage turn of events, so soon after her dreamed-of return, must be hard on her.

"It's rough," he said, and there was a quality in his voice which made her look up swiftly, then look as quickly away. "But I don't think you need to worry—certainly not about yourself or how well you'll play your role, no matter how hard the going may become. And I'm sure that having you here is a great comfort to your father. He may not let on, but I know that it means a lot."

"Thank you," she murmured. "He's been disappointed and hurt too may times already. I promise you that he won't be again—not by me. And your confidence helps."

Gordon was asleep almost before he could crawl into his bunk, but not for long. Even the long ordeal of the bear pit, the sleepless night which had followed, and the tiring day could not keep him asleep long. The problems connected with his new responsibilities brought him awake, and a glance at the moon, shining through the window, told him that he'd slept no more than a couple of hours. Most of the night was still ahead.

He hesitated, hearing the sound of deep breathing or heavy snoring from the other men, mindful that they too had missed their rest the night before. Then, grimly, he reached and shook one man awake.

"Call the others," he instructed. "We've a job to do before the funeral tomorrow—one that O'Dion won't be expecting us to get at so soon—I hope!"

Only one man complained, when he realized the hour, and that work lay ahead.

"Couldn't this job have waited till tomorrow," he demanded, "after last night and all?"

"It might have," Gordon conceded. "But if I'm guessing right, O'Dion will aim to rid himself of the Slash once and for all. And one burial is plenty."

Sam Drake was tugging on his boots. "Unless it's a funeral for Quirt," he suggested.

"Yeah, unless it's Quirt that's to be buried," Gordon agreed. "Let's ride."

7.

Gordon led out at a brisk trot. He had a good idea as to where the missing cows and calves must have been driven, where they would be held. O'Dion would go ahead according to plans already made; it would hardly occur to him that they could be guessed because Brick Gordon would be with the Slash. He certainly would not expect him to be in charge. O'Dion would logically suppose that, having escaped, Gordon would make the most of his chance to get out of the country, beyond O'Dion's reach.

Well behind the point of the blunted arrow lay a section of Quirt so remote and rough that few even of Quirt's crew knew much about it. Gordon doubted if any outsider was familiar with that stretch. The hills appeared to have been dropped haphazardly, forming a maze. A few miles from the border between Quirt and Slash, there was a hidden meadow of half a hundred acres. It would be perfect for holding the cows and their calves.

The moon was growing old, and like a tired old man it was tardier in its rising, its light fading. They pushed through the broken arrow, hearing the warning slap of a beaver's tail on some remote pond, the rustle of a night bird disturbed by their passage. They were splashing across the Bitter Sage before the moon picked them out.

Shut in by higher hills, it was slow going, but they encountered no sentries. The absence of men on watch seemed a measure of O'Dion's confidence, his assurance that the steps he had already taken gave him control of the situation.

The hills appeared to close solidly, barring further progress. Gordon led the way into a patch of darkness so heavy that the fresh tracks of the missing herd vanished. But a path opened, narrow and twisting, widening suddenly near the meadow. Bathed in the pale glow of the moon, its expanse was dotted with tiny humps made by the sleeping cattle. It was almost bewildering to come upon so large a plot of grassland surrounded by mountains.

The two previous summers that he had worked for Quirt, a herd had always been pushed to this remote fastness, to get the benefit of the grass which otherwise would go uneaten. This year, the meadow had stood virgin, and O'Dion had offered no explanation. Now the reason for saving it was clear.

The faint smell of burnt wood, a lingering odor of scorched hair and hide assailed the nostrils. A blackened spot, with fragments of charred wood remaining, gave mute testimony that branding had taken place there within the last day or so.

"Let's have a look at them," Gordon said.

Riding among the stock, rousing them to stand and blink in sleepy astonishment at the sight of horsemen abroad at that hour, it did not take long to confirm his guess, or to see how O'Dion had already carried out his threat. The cows were all branded Slash Y. Once awakened, both they and their offspring seemed jittery and hostile. It was easy to guess that they had been slow to settle down for the night.

A considerable crew, probably composed of most of the men of Quirt, had been busy among them during the day. Most of the calves had been branded. Unlike their mothers, the blisteringly fresh scars on their skins showed the sign of the Quirt.

Though some of the Slash had expected something of the sort, the magnitude of the steal caused them to exclaim incredulously. The awakened calves huddled close to their mothers, but nothing could hide the new burns.

"Does that so and so think he can get away with this?" Drake demanded in astonishment. "Why, if the rest of the people—the men from the small outfits, and the town, saw what we're seein' now—"

"That's what we want them to see," Gordon observed grimly. "Quirt didn't count on anyone stumbling on them back in here. And after a few days, of course, the calves would be put off by themselves and the cows allowed to drift back to their own range. And then anybody could see the brands, but who could prove anything?"

The magnitude of the theft was breath-taking. This was most of the calf crop of Slash, whose loss could come close to ruining their owners. As O'Dion had intimated the other morning, he wasn't contenting himself with piecemeal rustling, which would merely invite trouble and bring no definite results. He was moving to destroy the Slash, deliberately taking a course which would cause retaliation and so furnish an excuse for further, totally crippling blows. The belief that he had gotten away with the first two moves— disposing of Driscoll McKay and now the calves—would embolden him.

"Round them up and get them moving," Gordon instructed. "We'll take them home."

The crew eyed him with new respect as they set to work. Some had resented being roused for night work so soon after hitting the hay, and following a sleepless night. Here was proof that he'd known what he was about. If they could get the herd back on Slash Y range, then bring in outsiders to view the evidence of misbranded calves still running with Slash mothers— O'Dion would be in an untenable position.

It would not be easy, for the cattle were as weary as the men, and disinclined to keep moving when they should be resting. The excitement and confusion of branding, of moving to a strange pasture, had kept them at an exhausting pitch. Now they looked upon every man with suspicious hostility.

Still they moved, and as the cows sensed that they were heading back for the home range, some of their reluctance vanished. It was off here, on alien ground, that trouble had come upon them. There was reassurance in the familiar.

Gordon had not made the same mistake as O'Dion by failing to post lookouts. It was unlikely that anyone would be around to see or hear, for the buildings on Quirt were a long way off, but he'd allowed himself to be caught off guard a couple of times, and he couldn't afford a third case of laxity. He'd posted a couple of watchers on high ground, and now one of them came spurring.

"Quirt's awake and on the move," he reported breathlessly. "The first thing I noticed was a light, then a lot of them, off at their place. Next thing I made out the crew, saddlin' up. The moon hits there, so I could see all right. It looked to me like the whole crew was on the move—and I reckon they'll be headin' to cut us off!"

The luck they'd had already had seemed too good to last. Apparently O'Dion must have had someone posted and on watch, after all. Instead of making the mistake of challenging them when they had appeared, the sentry had high-tailed it back with word of what was going on; that would give Quirt plenty of time to intercept them short of the line.

Gordon's scalp crawled. This was the sort of showdown he'd hoped to avoid, at least at this stage of the game. Now it appeared to be inevitable. Unless they deserted the herd and fled ignominiously, a pitched battle could result. Quirt, under such circumstances, could do nothing else.

In such a clash, many men on both sides would die. Since crews were fairly well matched in both size and ability, the battle might well end in a virtual draw. Both sides would be losers, writing one more bloody chapter in range warfare, with the final result still in doubt.

"You're sure they're out to stop us?" he demanded, and realized that the question sounded inane. What else could bring Quirt from their beds at that hour, to ride in force?

"They were just startin' away from the buildings

when I headed here to warn you," the sentry explained. "I don't know what else they'd have in mind."

It was a slender enough chance, yet the possibility that they might have some other purpose was worth exploring. O'Dion had been confident and complacent, and there had been no other sign of a sentry being posted to watch the cows. Gordon's notion became a hunch.

"Come along with me," he instructed the sentry. "The rest of you, keep the herd moving."

He rode fast, pushing his horse up the steepening incline which lay between them and the buildings, his hunch deepening almost to a conviction. Their purpose now might be something else; in fact, it almost had to be. Had someone been posted to keep an eye on the cattle, he could hardly have gotten back to the buildings and roused the sleepers so quickly. The only way in which they could have been warned at such speed would have been by firing a gun as a signal, and that had not been done.

Brush hindered and branches whipped at them as Gordon kept the horses at a headlong pace. Then they topped the rise, to the point where the lookout had been. The buildings at Quirt once more stood dark and remote, the lights all gone out. The band of riders, in close formation, were a mile away, moving steadily.

Studying them, Gordon's eyes lightened. His companion swore in bewilderment.

"Now what in tarnation are they up to?" he demanded. "That's a funny course they're takin'—if they're aimin' to cut us off."

"I doubt if they have any such idea in mind," Gordon returned. "Likely they don't suspect that we're here at all."

"Then what are they up to?"

The answer would have been highly useful, but Gordon could only speculate as to what O'Dion might have in mind, though he had a good hunch. The funeral was to be held in town, toward noon. Judging from the course which the crew of Quirt were now taking, they clearly were not heading for Long Rain.

"My guess is that they plan to finish Slash off while our back is turned," he explained. "If they keep on that way, they can be posted, say within a mile of our buildings, and be ready to move in as soon as our crew rides for town. That would give them a choice—either to burn us out, or to take over and stand us off when we get back. Either way, on top of all the rest, it would just about finish us."

Quinsell removed his hat to scratch his head, as though requiring some extra deep thinking.

"By golly, I'd say you've hit it," he conceded. "Only we won't be there to ride out, the way they expect." He replaced the hat, scowling as he pursued this line of thought. "But they'll see Abe and Miss Mary start off for town, as well as Jack and the cook—so they'll know we ain't there. Which'll suit them just as well, though it might give them some new ideas."

Quinsell's conclusion matched his own line of reasoning, and Gordon didn't like it. Quirt must be stopped short of their objective. How that could be managed, without having Quirt upon their own necks at the wrong time, was not so easy to determine.

A gunshot now would attract Quirt's attention, and it would bring not only an investigation but also an attack. Since a battle to a finish would be weighted in Quirt's favor, it had to be avoided, except as a last resort.

It would be possible to split his own crew, sending the majority of them back to the buildings. Several things were wrong with that idea, the main trouble being that it was already too late. Riding straight and fast, they might beat the invaders, but they would be seen, and again attack would follow. Should they circle to avoid being seen, they would arrive too late.

"That's a blasted dirty way to fight, if you ask me—" Quinsell said savagely—"to jump an outfit when they're buryin' a man!"

"What they're interested in is buryin' *us*," Gordon reminded him. "O'Dion didn't get where he is by playing nice."

Quinsell shrugged, eying him expectantly. He had considered the possibilities which were open to them, and had reached the same doubtful conclusions. The single reassuring factor was that Gordon was boss here, and making a decision was his responsibility. If he could come up with a workable plan, he'd be a genius.

Gordon's glance strayed back to the huddle of buildings, which now stood deserted and unguarded. O'Dion's thinking was perfectly logical. Because Driscoll McKay was the son of old Abe, it was natural that the whole crew should do him one final honor by attending his funeral. Thus their whereabouts could be accurately judged at any hour of the day. Most of Slash Y's neighbors would also attend. Thus it seemed perfectly safe to leave Quirt unguarded.

But there was a flaw in such reasoning, and if he could find a way to take advantage of it—

Gordon shook his head at the obvious. It would be easy to ride over there now and set fire to the buildings. The rising smoke would soon be seen, as daylight came, and duly interpreted by the riders of Quirt, before they were ready to make their own attack. Presumably, faced with such a situation, most of them would head back in a hurry in an effort to save what they could.

They would be too late, and such a loss would be a blow to Quirt, weakening but still not crippling them.

Moreover, that was the sort of fighting which Gordon hated. He'd asked for his time when O'Dion had announced his intention of going outside the law; practicing arson on such a scale would be equally criminal.

Worse, he doubted if burning the buildings would achieve its purpose. By the time the Quirt riders sighted the smoke, O'Dion might decide, from its magnitude, that his own buildings were already past saving. He might send some men back; but being a realist, he'd probably keep on with most of them, seizing the Slash Y and holding the buildings for living quarters. Such a plan would backfire.

Yet there might be a third course. It was a gambler's choice, but this clearly was a time for risks. Gordon outlined his plan, and Quinsell nodded.

"Watch for my signal; then help attract their attention," Gordon emphasized. "I'll do the rest." Swinging his horse, he headed for the vacant buildings on Quirt.

8.

The hour could be counted either late, or early, as
Gordon approached Quirt. The moon, having hovered
uncertainly in the Indian summer sky, had become
entangled among the spire-like mountains to the west.
There was a sharp chill to the air, and a coating of frost
was visible on both leaves and bare ground. The long
spell of fine weather still held, but he'd detected a
cloudy circle beyond the moon, one more indication
that winter might be expected at any time.

The waning of the moon might in itself be the signal for storms. A full moon frequently had the effect
of thinning clouds, holding back rain or snow. But
when it thinned in turn, they took their revenge. The
pattern seemed discouragingly similar to the contest
in the valley of the Bitter Sage.

It still lacked an hour to dawn, and any men who
might have been left behind would be sleeping more
soundly than ever, after being disturbed by the de-

parture of the others. The cook would probably be counting on the rare luxury of sleeping late, knowing that for once he wouldn't have to prepare breakfast.

Familiar as he was with everything about Quirt, Gordon was able to move without waste of time. He was tempted to go to the bunk house after some of his own things, but there was no time. The plan would be touch and go at best, timed desperately close.

The big house towered, shadowy and huge, above the other buildings, a vast pile of stone erected to the vanity of O'Dion. Gordon knew that it was more a monument to pride than a home in which to live; similar to the edifices which the rulers of ancient lands had caused to be built by enslaved multitudes. Fire might gut the house, but it wouldn't really burn.

Yet there was a way to destroy it, and it would hit O'Dion hard, right in his pride.

At the back of the house, almost lost in its shadow, stood another stone building. This was a storehouse, built originally as a root-house, also a part of O'Dion's dream. There had been a root-house on the farm when he was a boy, so he'd had to have one here. Not until it had been built had it occurred to him that it would be useless for that purpose, since no vegetables were grown on Quirt, nor were any cows milked; therefore there was no need to keep cream and butter in a cool place.

As a storehouse it was solid, the walls and roof a couple of feet in thickness. There was no window, and only one door, of heavy planks. O'Dion had built well, if foolishly.

The door was held shut by a stick thrust through a heavy iron hasp. Gordon removed the stick and pushed the door open. Inside, everything was as he remembered it, untouched since his last visit to the building, months before. At that time, since he possessed a skill unknown to most cowboys, he'd done some blasting for O'Dion, blowing down the side of a hill above a creek, thus building a dam and constructing a reservoir. The waters which until then had run to waste now formed a considerable lake. It was O'Dion's plan to irrigate a thousand normally dry acres.

Several hundred-pound cans of black blasting powder and a box, still crammed with sticks of dynamite, had been left over from these operations, stored back in this strong room. There was also a supply of caps and fuse.

Gordon worked swiftly, measuring a long length of fuse, able to judge from past experience. The heavy padlock, which had not been in the hasp, was on a table. The key, in a ring along with several others, hung from a peg, driven into a crack between the stones of the wall.

Disregarding the key, Gordon took the lock, then

lit the fuse. Outside, he fitted the lock in the hasp and snapped it shut. Now he had set in motion a chain of events which had to be timed right, or he'd have unloosed a demon which would really turn the sage bitter.

Remembering the agreed-upon signal, he lifted his revolver and sent two quick shots toward the fading stars.

Somewhere in the hills the echo came back, with a quavery, uncertain quality. Then, like a new and grimmer echo, two more shots disturbed the serenity of the night, from a greater distance. That would be Quinsell.

Gordon pushed his cayuse to its limit.

Even at that, he was barely in time, with nothing to spare, when he sighted the herd. They had halted when the guns sounded. Until then, his crew had kept them on the move, covering half the distance between the hidden meadow and the jut of Bitter Sage Creek which marked the uneasy boundary with Slash Y.

Here, the hills and timber which clothed that section of range had thinned, opening into a long valley. Night still clung relentlessly, the high stars giving a scant but sufficient light.

Hearing the shots, O'Dion's crew had reacted as he'd anticipated, swinging to investigate. Guns sounding in the dark of night were unusual, and with relations so troubled, they might be significant.

It hadn't taken them long to sight Quinsell; then, as he fled in apparent panic at being discovered, they had chased him, soon coming in sight of the herd. At that juncture it was natural to put two and two together. If they failed to add correctly, they could still be excused for believing the obvious, the evidence of their own eyes.

They were riding hard, startled, to stop the cows and their calves from returning to Slash Y. The tables had been partially turned, a surprise handed O'Dion, but he was ready to meet the challenge, even though it meant altering his own plan. It could be disastrous to allow such evidence on the hoof to get back for others to see. Now, if Slash wanted a showdown, this time and place suited him well enough.

Somewhat startled by the sudden appearance of the crew of Quirt, Lomax was gathering his own men for the expected clash. In Gordon's absence, he was in charge and ready to make a fight of it.

One of the men sighted the lone rider, and being more relieved than discreet, exclaimed loudly:

"Here comes Gordon!"

Not only did they hear, but in the stillness of the night, Quirt was close enough to hear, too. Momentarily, as though sensing an approaching climax, even the cows and their misused offspring had fallen silent; not a single forlorn bawl disturbed the night. To the east, a smudge of light was fumbling uncertainly at the curtain of blackness, trying to tear a hole in it.

Quirt was fairly close by now. Lomax had instructed his men to hold their fire, hoping to parley instead of shoot, though without much hope that talk would do any good. At this stage, neither side could afford to back down or even compromise, and the Slash had no intention of doing so. But neither outfit wanted to bear the onus of starting a shooting war, without at least an attempt at discussion. Blood would spill soon enough.

Both groups pulled up, not far apart, looking to Gordon as he came between them. He stopped, and the sobbing breath of his cayuse was the only sound for a moment. O'Dion leaned forward, peering in the uncertain light, and exclaimed in disbelief.

"Gordon! Now what the devil are you doing here?"

"That is a good question, which might work both ways," Gordon observed innocently. "But to save time, which is crowding us, and especially you, I'll tell you. I'm rodding Slash Y."

He saw the incredulity on his former employer's face give way to amusement, followed a moment later by a shout of laughter.

"What's that you're tellin' me, that you're roddin' the Slash? You! Tryin' to fill the boots of Abe McKay, to take the place of Driscoll, thinkin' now you'll have a clear field with the girl and win Slash Y for yourself! So that is it! Now, by all that's rich—"

"Shut up and listen." The incisiveness of Gordon's voice cut through the laughter, and despite himself, O'Dion listened. Gordon went on quickly.

"There's not a minute to lose, O'Dion, if you want to save your buildings. And you know that I know what I'm talking about in regard to explosives. When I saw what you were up to, I headed there and lit a fuse in the storehouse. There's more than enough dynamite and powder in that pile to blow your fine big house to sand, and the fire would take all the rest of the buildings."

Slowly, the dawn light was picking out objects, whitening the frost underfoot. In the brightness, O'Dion's face lost its ruddiness.

"Why, you—you—" he choked.

"Listen," Gordon insisted. "You'll have time to save your place, providing you get back there, fast, you and your whole crew. I used a long fuse, and timed it close, but I allowed enough. The door's padlocked—and the key is still inside, on its nail, out of reach!"

He gave O'Dion a moment in which to digest that, to come to a full understanding. O'Dion himself had selected that padlock, making sure that it was huge and solid. Even a volley of shots from a gun would have little effect on it.

Originally there had been two keys. But one of those

had been lost. Now, with the other locked inside the building—

"How the devil can I get to it, if you've left it inside?" O'Dion snarled.

"If you want to save your place, you'll have to work for it." Gordon shrugged. "Otherwise it would be too easy, and you might try to do too many other things also. Remember that big log lying near the barn? Use it as a battering ram. Carried by your whole crew, it will smash even that door in time for you to put out the fuse. But you'll have to ride fast, every man of you!"

O'Dion's face twisted thoughtfully as he understood. How it could have happened he was far from comprehending, just as it was incomprehensible that this man, whom he'd had thrown into the bear pit, could have escaped, and now be directing the opposition, with Slash Y following his leadership.

Yankus had reported the escape of Gordon, but O'Dion had been sure that Gordon, scared but thankful to be alive, would have left the country. He had been equally certain that Slash Y, with Driscoll McKay about to be buried, would be disorganized, virtually leaderless, and easy to take over. The shock of the discovery to the contrary was hard to take.

The other was equally bitter. His plan to seize control of the buildings on the Slash while the crew was absent was suddenly spoiled; worse, his own headquarters, including the house which he prized so much, was in danger of destruction. Knowing Gordon, he did not for a moment doubt that he was telling the truth.

Gordon's manner of hitting back, seizing control of the initiative, was equally unpleasant. There was no time left for argument or counter-action. Nor was the threat lost upon him or his pale-faced crew. If they were even a second tardy, the dynamite might blow up in their faces, enveloping them in the destruction.

Still worse, the showdown which he had been savoring would have to be postponed. The calves, tagging at their mothers' heels, with those damaging, damning brands on their flanks, would have to be permitted to cross back to Slash Y range, where an outraged public could see and judge. Such exposure might well spell the end to an inglorious adventure.

"You're a fine one!" O'Dion choked. "To hit at a man in such fashion—sneaking behind his back—"

"Now that's interesting, coming from you, O'Dion," Gordon taunted. "I wonder where you were riding just now, and what you might have had in mind!" O'Dion gulped, and he went on.

"The thing which amazes and shames me is that I worked for you so long! But I'm striving to make restitution, and I'm also giving you a chance to do the same, to save your house. I could just as easily have used a short fuse."

The truth of that was so manifest that O'Dion swallowed his pride and some of his rage, clapping spurs to his horse and leading his crew in a desperate race. The thunder of the blast, at such a juncture, would have accomplished what smoke alone could not have done, and sent him and his men scurrying back too late. In his present mood, he felt no gratitude for the chance which was offered.

As the dust settled behind the departing Quirt, Gordon lifted an arm, and the drive went on, into the face of the rising sun.

9.

By now, sensing the nearness of home, the cows stepped out briskly, anxious to be gone from this range which had been so full of trouble. Wearily, Gordon tried to plan his next move, but his mind, like his body, was too tired to respond well. It had been a long night, following another without sleep, but the results were worth it. The trouble was that endurance had a limit, and all of them were close to the breaking point.

Had he failed to follow his hunch, today would have marked the end for Slash Y, as well as for many of those who rode for it. O'Dion had come close to pulling it off.

He strained his ears, and it was not until they had crossed the creek onto Slash Y range that he could ease the breath in his lungs, certain that his gamble had not ended in a desperate holocaust. He'd tried to time everything right, but with so many factors involved, there had been room for error, human or otherwise. If O'Dion had arrived too late to save his house, but only in time to witness its destruction—

Or worse, if they had gotten there to be caught by the blast—

That, of course, would settle everything, assuring victory to Slash Y. Nor did he have any doubts that the public, the men on the other ranches and in town, would exonerate them once they heard the story and viewed the misbranded calves. The trouble would be that he'd never be able to free himself of the horror, the memory of men blasted and maimed because of what he'd done.

It was better this way, though the real war was just beginning. O'Dion was not a man to draw back in gratitude, because Brick had given him a chance to save his house. Instead, he'd dwell on the defeat he'd suffered, the humiliation of being forced to jump at Gordon's command, the risk they'd run while the flame along the fuse crept desperately close to the explosives. Had there been any doubt before, the night's events had removed it. It would be war now, war to a finish. Nothing else would salve the flayed pride of O'Dion.

It was day now, the day of the funeral, one scheduled to be set apart for mourning, for paying the last and proper respects to a man untimely and feloniously dead. Most of the neighbors could be counted on to take time off to attend, not so much out of liking or respect for the dead man himself as for his father. Abe McKay had been raised in a hard school, and he was blunt-spoken, short with sympathy for the foolish or the inept. He'd expressed the common sentiment when declaring that his son had acted like a fool.

But deep down, everyone knew that Abe McKay was a man who had suffered disillusion and a shattering of dreams when his wife had refused to live in a country which she termed barbaric, taking his tiny daughter and returning to the East to her folks. What attempts, beyond his own year in the East, Abe might have made to set matters right, no one knew or ever would. He was not one to talk about himself or his troubles. He had returned to the only life he knew, to the ranch he'd taken and was determined to hold; to the only place where he fitted. There, alone, he had raised his son the best way he knew.

Somewhere along the way he felt that he'd botched the job; or perhaps the fault had lain partly with Driscoll. In him had been the same unseemly pride, the same flaw of character that had manifested itself in his mother, a self-centeredness which took no account of others, either their wishes or their rights. Driscoll had been a disappointment, and when his father had needed him most, the son had derided him, making a grab for power.

Now it had brought him to his grave, and almost

everyone would attend the funeral, the gesture one of sympathy and understanding for the living; for Abe, and for Mary, who showed promise of being sturdy and unspoiled, despite her mother's training.

It would be natural for a raging O'Dion to use the day for his own purposes. So to take chances would be folly.

Brick asked Lomax to go with Abe and Mary to the funeral, "to make sure that nothing happens to them."

Lomax's astonishment showed in his face.

"You mean—you're leavin' it up to me to look out for them? I'd sort of supposed—"

"It's important, and I'll be busy with other things. I figure that Slash comes first, with both of us."

Lomax swallowed. He was grateful for this show of confidence, and his words came impulsively.

"Sure," he agreed. "That's right enough. And I'm glad that you're handlin' matters now, instead of me. That was a stroke of genius, the way you managed tonight."

A haze was spreading over the sky, beginning to blot away the early sun. Gordon scanned the horizon apprehensively, testing the feel of the air. Normally, a heavy frost was followed by a fine day, but after a prolonged spell of good weather, anything might be expected. The feverish activity of the wild seemed to be accounted for. A change was on the way, and when it struck, winter was apt to hit with full fury.

Breakfast over, he outlined the situation to the others.

"We can't risk leaving this place unguarded, especially when it would seem safe to do so. A third of the crew can represent the rest of us at the funeral. The rest of us will stay, taking turns at keeping watch and getting some sleep."

Lomax drove a two-seated buggy as the cortege set out for town. Abe McKay and Mary were on the rear seat, wrapped in a heavy buffalo robe. Even with gloves, fingers stiffened, and breath began to blow frostily from the nostrils of horses and men alike. The brief sun had vanished.

Despite the imminence of a storm, it seemed as though everyone for a wide radius had turned out for the funeral. As the casket was lowered into the ground, Lomax was surprised to see O'Dion at the edge of the crowd, head bared like the others, his face solemn. He was the only one from Quirt to be seen.

Standing beyond O'Dion was the sheriff, a blocky figure in a heavy bearskin coat. Lomax scowled, made his decision. As soon as the service ended, he moved to intercept Harder, steering him toward his employer.

"Abe wants a word with you, Harder," he explained.

Harder moved restively, as though guessing what that word might be. Then he followed, stumping along impatiently.

"I got a lot to do," he protested. "I took time off to come out here, but I'm a busy man."

"Likely," Lomax agreed laconically. "But Abe's got something for you in the line of business."

"Well?" Harder halted, spitting out the word truculently. "What is it, McKay?"

McKay's Scotch ancestry was evident in the dryness of his reply.

"It's a comfort, now, to have a man in your place who is as chary of wasting time as money. If you'll come to the ranch, we've something to show you. Evidence, fresh burned on many a calf's tender skin; brand blotching."

"What's this you're saying?" Harder sounded incredulous. "Has your brand been overlaid with another, or altered with a running iron?"

"Nothing like that. These are new brands on calves which had no burn before; calves still running with their mothers, who wear the Slash. So if you will come and see for yourself—"

The sheriff shied like a cayuse catching a whiff of grizzly.

"To make such a trip right now is out of the question," he said flatly. "I'm in the middle of another job. If you have such evidence as you say, it will keep."

"So will a rotten egg," Lomax cut in angrily. "Only it gets worse the longer it stays around."

Harder favored him with a stare of manifest dislike. "I run my job my way," he grunted, and stalked off.

"He'd been confabbin' with O'Dion just before I talked to him," Lomax explained to Gordon. By now, the clouds had pulled down tightly all around the horizon, the wind was whetting its edge across the broad wastes to the north, and a few flakes of snow were beginning to push like wary outriders of an advancing army. "Likely enough that was O'Dion's only reason for showin' up there."

Gordon nodded. O'Dion had made certain that he would have no trouble from the law before making his move. If there was evidence, Harder would find some pretext not to take a look, at least until it was too late to matter.

Gordon had slept for a couple of hours, and felt ready for whatever might come. He could go a long way without much rest. The rest of the crew were not so well off. Two sleepless nights in succession, along with the emotional strain, were taking a toll. Many of them were all but walking in their sleep.

That posed a dilemma. That O'Dion was also caught upon its horns was scant consolation, for he could be counted on to resort to desperate measures to get off. So many new-branded calves, running with cows of another brand, posed a serious threat. Even though the law refused to have a look, others would ride to view them as soon as the storm had blown itself out.

At the moment that was the big problem. Already the snow was choking the air, reducing visibility to a few dozen feet. It would be a bad night to be out.

Gordon would have liked to move both cows and calves to the home corrals, where they could be held and watched, during the day. But doing so had been out of the question. There were far too many to be held in the corrals, and they were too tired to drive any farther. They, too, would have to wait out the storm.

He could post guards, but in a black night, sentries would be useless and helpless. The worst part was that there was no one fit to send.

He crossed to the house and found Mary washing the supper dishes for her father and herself. She turned, wiping her hands on her apron. Outside, it was already dark. The beat of the storm was steady against the windows, the wind howling, moaning. She managed a tired smile.

"Jim told us how you checkmated O'Dion," she said. "He was proud of you—and so am I!"

"That was a lucky break, that dynamite being in the right place and needing only a match to the fuse," Gordon returned. "I had only to take advantage of it."

"Perhaps, but not everyone would have thought of such a thing, or known how to make use of the chance," she returned. "It won over all those who had been resentful or doubtful, even Lomax."

"It was luck," Gordon repeated. "It's tomorrow that I'm worried about."

"Tomorrow?" She gestured to the window, where the beat of flinty pellets made a steady rattle. "But you'll be ready to move if they do, after a good night's sleep. And you've certainly earned it."

"What I mean is, O'Dion may have something waiting for us by the time morning comes. He's desperate, and he's that sort of a man."

"But what can he do? Surely it's too black and bad a night for anyone to be abroad in—"

"It would seem so," Gordon acknowledged. "On the other hand, a night like this would be a perfect cover. He knows that our men are played out, that they must sleep tonight."

"But his men must be tired, too."

"They could have slept today," he pointed out. "Still, I'll not borrow trouble—that would be foolish, when there's plenty already. I just wanted to make sure that you and your father were all right."

"I'm all right," Mary assured him. "Papa's asleep already—this had been hard on him, though he doesn't let on. He feels that with you looking after things, matters will come out all right. I don't know how we'd manage without you."

"There's nothing for me to brag about—yet," he

protested, suddenly diffident. "I'm sorry that this has been so hard on you."

She turned, facing him directly, and he saw that in her face which stilled his words. There was something of the calmness of her father's expression.

"What happened to Driscoll was dreadful, of course," she told him. "I'm sorry, as we all are. But for the rest, we have to face up to life, and I learned long ago that it's no use to try to run from it. That was Mother's mistake, and by that attitude, she almost ruined a lot of lives, including her own. It's hard, many times, but we can do what has to be done. Besides, I feel just as Papa does. With you in charge, things will come out all right."

He scarcely felt the storm as he moved across to the bunk house, her words still sounding in his ears, her promise a soft gleam in her eyes. She had made a declaration of faith, faith in him rather than in the situation. Given such an incentive, a man could hardly fail.

10.

Daylight brought no indication of any let-up in the storm. During the night, it had become a full-fledged blizzard, despite the earliness of the season. Snow lay everywhere, and more was coming, buffeted and shifted by the wind. Drifts were already growing deep. Other sections, swept free of cover, seemed to shiver in the cold. The ground had turned frozen and unyielding.

Wild weather presented problems for cattlemen. The older stock would be all right for a while, but the cows with calves still at heel would need to be moved in closer, fed with hay from the stacks put up during the summer. Gordon was in the saddle as soon as it was light enough to see, with half the crew beside him.

Tired as he had been, he hadn't slept well; he'd dreamed and turned, haunted by a sense of impending disaster. He pushed his horse hard, anxious to learn the worst, hoping that his hunch was wrong. Reason was on his side, but some people had a way of doing the unreasonable.

Again, as on an earlier occasion, the vacancy of the broken arrow hit them as they crossed it. They clung to a faint hope, since the cows might be huddled in little bunches in the coulees and brush, waiting out the storm. Few creatures, even such hardy wanderers as coyotes, ventured abroad on such a day.

As though conjured up by the thought, they heard the sound of a coyote, the howl lifting wraith-like. In response, a cow bawled, then another. That should have been reassuring, for the cows were there. Instead, the sound was keyed to a troubled pitch, lost and mournful, different from the complaining note of the previous day.

Something moved, and Brick swung his horse that way. It was a coyote, slinking guiltily, after gnawing at something in the snow. Gordon bent to examine it, and Lomax came to join him.

"What the devil?" Lomax asked, staring in disbelief. He stirred the partly frozen mass with the toe of a boot, turning a blank face to Gordon. "It's not a cow—or a calf. But it looks like one had been gutted here."

"That's about what it is," Gordon agreed tightly, and swung back to the saddle, suspicion mounting to a dreadful certainty. The day was rawly cold, almost numbing after the mild weather which had prevailed until the previous evening. It would require at least a couple of days for men and animals to grow accustomed to the change.

Not far away, they found another similar mass of partly frozen remains. Then they came upon several cows, and by now the chorus of complaint sounded louder, rising from many throats. The cows, plastered with snow which cracked but clung when they moved, regarded them with hostility. Their udders hung full. Nowhere was there a sign of a calf.

Additional searching yielded further confirmation. It verged on the incredible, yet it was past doubting. There were no calves with brands which failed to match those of their mothers. But there were far too many piles of entrails, despite the feasting coyotes. The calves had been butchered, then the hides and meat hauled away.

This could spell catastrophe for Slash Y. Gordon stared glumly. He'd feared some sort of a counter-move by O'Dion, but nothing of this sort had occurred to him. He would have said that under the circumstances it was out of the question; there had been so many calves, so black a night with driving storm.

But O'Dion had matched his own impossible feat of the day before, simply by refusing to concede that it couldn't be done, then by making an all-out effort. He'd had two things going for him: the first being

the certainty that Slash Y would have to get some
sleep; the other the chance for his own men to sleep
the day before and ready themselves for a rough, hard
night.

His crew had responded to the challenge. Whatever
else they might be, Quirt's crew were loyal to their
boss, especially when faced with a danger which, unless remedied, could threaten their necks.

In one respect, the storm had been their ally. On open
range, cattle would drift with a storm, but here, where
there was shelter, cows and calves had huddled, almost
unmoving, reluctant even to stir. Also, the snow, added
to the night, would have afforded a cover in which the
gleam of lanterns would have been invisible except
close at hand.

Looking closer, it was possible to find additional sign,
where the snow had been whipped aside, or along the
creek, where in the brush it was barely ruffled by the
wind. Additional snowfall had partly covered the tracks
of wheels, but not entirely. Wagons, a lot of them, had
been brought in, loaded with the veal meat and
stripped, telltale hides, then moved out again, taking
the evidence with them.

Brutally efficient, the crew of Quirt, implemented by
extra hands whom O'Dion had hired in anticipation
of some emergency action, had moved among the
herd, some of them carrying lanterns. The stir and

bustle throughout much of the night had not been enough to stampede the cows. Men on horseback could check such attempts, turning back or holding any who tried to get away. Between darkness and daylight, they had been able to do a remarkably thorough job.

The calves, of course, had been slain in the quickest, simplest and quietest manner. They had been knocked on the head with an axe, then bleeded and gutted, after which the hides were quickly stripped off, meat and hides slung onto the waiting wagons.

Gordon could envision what a tremendous operation it had been. A big crew had worked hard, under adverse conditions. But the evidence showed that it had been done.

So far, they had failed to discover a single remaining calf with the telltale Quirt brand. The evidence of the sides was gone, along with the meat. The cold, with the temperature steadily dropping, had made the operation feasible. The frozen meat would keep until it could be taken to a market, thus making the night's work a financial success—something which always bulked large in O'Dion's planning. At the same time, though he had failed to acquire the calves to fatten the big herd on Quirt, they had been taken away from Slash, which had been his main objective.

To try and drive them back onto Quirt range would have been a hopeless task, besides, it would have been impossible to hide them from a search. Stragglers would have fallen out all along the line and not have been missed in the darkness.

This way, the evidence was gone. What remained—cows mourning for their calves, the refuse from butchered animals—was being buried by the storm, as well as eaten by wolves, coyotes, magpies and other scavengers. In any case, it was not proof which could be used against any one. No brands or marks of identification had been left behind.

The real reason for O'Dion's attendance at the funeral was explained. Using it as a cover, he'd been able to pass the word, marshaling his extra men, wagons, teams and whatever was required for the night's operation.

As the manner and extent of the catastrophe were understood, the other Slash riders were swearing, exclaiming in anger and incredulity.

"But they can't get away with it!" Lomax exclaimed. "We'll be able to come up with the wagons—and the evidence. They can't move fast enough to outrun us."

The same thought was in Gordon's mind. Laden wagons could be followed and overtaken. It would mean trouble when they caught up, the showdown which had been averted the day before. But it was no longer a matter of choice.

The others were all for instant pursuit, but Gordon

checked the rush for horses. If and when they caught up, they'd be faced with a strong, hostile force; inevitably, they'd need every man that it was possible to muster for such a contest.

On the other hand, O'Dion had schemed and planned for a long while, and last night, as the evidence indicated, he must have recruited a lot of additional men to his standard. Not only would they outnumber the Slash in an encounter, but he undoubtedly would have a force in reserve, ready to hit at the buildings on Slash if they were left unguarded. A second crippling blow, such as burning them out, with winter suddenly blasting the country, would just about finish them.

Gordon pointed this out. Lomax scowled, but agreed reluctantly.

"We'll have to leave those who are there to stay on guard," Gordon said. "As for the rest of us—when we catch up, we'll have to fight that much harder."

"Well, what of it?" Sam Drake growled. "Let's get at it!" The others nodded assent.

They rode, a grim and silent group, fully aware what might await them. Quirt's crew, guarding the wagons, would be riding those same wagons, sheltered under heavy buffalo robes, warm and ready for action. That would give them a tremendous advantage over men half-numb from long hours in the saddle, whose hands and feet had scarcely any feeling.

Yet time was of the essence. Unless they overtook them, and with the evidence, it would be too late.

The storm showed no let-up as the day wore on. It would probably last at least through the night, and the drivers of the wagons, taking advantage of its cover, would do their best to lose the pursuit. They were probably experiencing some uneasy moments at the thought of vengeance riding hard in their wake.

Despite wind and blowing snow, the tracks of several wagons could not be fully covered. The trail became easier to follow, though except for that trace of sign, and themselves, the road seemed deserted. They had come out upon a road, leaving Quirt behind, swinging off toward the south. A part of O'Dion's intention was becoming clear.

Beyond, deep in the mountains, a large construction camp was located, consisting of a combined logging and mining operation. It had been there, on a small scale, for more than a year. During the summer, the operators had made two important moves. One had consisted in bringing in and setting up a sawmill, to cut logs into rough lumber. Getting finished lumber out was far easier than transporting logs to a mill, where water was not available to run them.

The mining operation had also prospered, with the rich vein they had hoped for finally being located.

Now the camp had mushroomed, and would afford a ready and eager market for even several wagonloads of newly butchered meat. More to the point, they could be counted on to buy, and no questions asked.

O'Dion must have planned for most possible eventualities. With Slash Y forced to improvise against him, that left the odds increasingly on the side of Quirt.

It was midday when they finally sighted the wagons, a long line of them, crawling through the gloom of the storm, each wagon pulled by six horses, the triple wagon-boxes piled high under snow-blanketed tarps. Gordon counted a dozen wagons, and more might be ahead. He could see no escort of men on horseback.

There were at least two men on each wagon, however, and the total would add up to a formidable force.

Inevitably, the pursuers had been seen. At sight of them, sudden panic seemed to develop among the fugitives. The wagons had topped a long, easy rise. Now, ahead for as far as could be seen, the road dropped, gradually but surely. With that advantage, the drivers whipped up their horses, sending the lumbering wagons into a swaying, jolting race.

"They're scared!" Drake gritted from beside Gordon. "And they've a right to be!"

Only panic, or some similar emotion, could have persuaded the drivers that such an effort would be of any avail, though for the first half-mile, the teams, aided by the down-grade, maintained their distance. Then the riders on horseback commenced to narrow the gap, and after that it closed swiftly. Gordon lifted his gun and fired a couple of shots in the air as a signal to halt.

Reluctantly, the others obeyed, and the wagons were standing in a long, strung-out line as they came up, the heavy breath of the draft horses like fog upon the air. Somewhat to his surprise, Gordon did not recognize any of the drivers, nor were they making any show of resistance.

"What's all this about?" one demanded. "What you stoppin' us for?"

"You know very well what we're stoppin' you for!" Lomax snapped. "You with loads of stolen meat!"

The other man's eyebrows raised.

"Stolen meat? That's a serious charge to make—and you'd better be able to back it up, mister!"

"We'll back it up, all right," Lomax growled. "We're going to have a look under those tarps. And don't try to stop us!"

The driver shrugged.

"Looks like you can have your way, seeing the size of your crew," he conceded. "Have a look if you want. We've nothing to hide. This is Getchell's Freight—and we're hauling on contract."

Gordon knew about Getchell. He had commenced

hauling with a pair of run-down wagons and some equally worn-out horses, at the time when the camp had begun operations. As the camp had prospered, so had he, bringing in supplies and taking out ore. Now, apparently, he owned this whole string of wagons. The possibility that O'Dion might be the real owner of the freight outfit had not occurred to Gordon until then.

Such an established business was a good cover for the present job. Again he had the nagging feeling that they had been outwitted, outmatched, but there was nothing for it but to go through with what they'd started. Some of the crew were loosening ropes, throwing back the tarps.

In part, they saw what they had expected to see— the close-piled, frozen carcasses of butchered calves. Regarding that, there could be no question. There had been no time to cut them up, and they were impossible to disguise.

At that point the evidence faltered. Clearly O'Dion had foreseen the possibility of discovery. The calves had been skinned, and the telltale hides, with their incriminating brands, were no longer on them, nor were any to be seen.

The driver regarded them sardonically.

"Satisfied?" he asked. "You got any proof that those chunks of meat belong to you?"

"Take a look all along the line," Gordon instructed, disregarding him. But he knew, by the bland attitude of the transport men, that it was hopeless. That was soon confirmed. There were no hides in any of the wagons.

Again, the thing was unbelievable. They had followed closely after the wagons, yet somewhere along the way they had been spoofed, fooled. Without evidence they could do nothing, and they'd be a laughing-stock as well.

11.

So many hides, even those of calves, would take up a lot of room, filling more than one wagon. With such brands burned into the skin, they were tangible evidence, the sort which could not readily be disposed of. Had they been flung over the side, even among deep drifts, they would be found. The hungrily questing coyotes, with noses attuned to the smell of meat, would make sure of that. It was to make certain that such proof was not found that O'Dion was going to extreme lengths.

Gordon had the bitter conviction that he was being cleverly fooled. Somewhere along the line, they had overlooked something.

The answer hit him with the force of a blast of the blizzard, and he pulled his horse half-around, then checked the gesture. If he was right, there was no hurry. In this situation, he couldn't afford either to tip or overplay his hand.

"I'm putting in a claim before these men as witnesses," he announced. "All of this meat is from stolen cattle, and it belongs to Slash Y. Go ahead and deliver it if you like, but I warn you that in the end you'll have to pay for it."

The driver of the first wagon shrugged.

"Mister, you produce some proof to back up your words, and that'll be a different matter. Till you do, it's a case of put up or shut up! As for us, we're going on."

There was no way to stop them, short of a fight, and the taunting note in his voice, as well as the look on other faces, showed that they hoped for just that. They were playing for delay. Gordon remounted and turned back. After an uncertain moment, the other Slash riders followed.

"What now?" Lomax demanded. "You got a new notion?"

"I sure have," Gordon agreed. "They had a piece of luck, that we overtook them just where we did, though the chances are that they held back till they saw us coming, to make sure that we'd come up with them at that particular place—where they could act scared and make a show of running."

"You mean they wanted us to chase them?"

"What else? And they worked it so that we accommodated them, and ran right past a side-road that turns

off toward New Cheyenne. As I recall, the turn-off
is near the top of the hill."

Drake's uncertain face lightened.

"Sure, that must be it. The hide wagons were ahead
and made the turn—then the others waited to lure us
past, so that we wouldn't notice!"

"That just about has to be the way of it. We'll take
a short cut and catch up with the others."

"And when we do, they'll have to pay for that meat,
like you told them." Drake grinned. "I want to be in
on presentin' that bill!"

Wind and storm had all but obliterated the sign at
the turn-off, but a quarter of a mile farther along the
new route, where the wind brushed lightly, the trail
was clear and easy to follow. It was plain that the
wagons with the hides were well ahead, the drivers
pushing their teams at top speed to reach their destination.

"They'll likely take them straight to Barclay's,"
Gordon said.

Barclay's was a hide and fur house, whose reputation
had spread widely if not favorably. Barclay was not
adverse to dealing in honest produce, but it was an
open secret that he preferred questionable consign-
ments, which frequently offered greater opportunities
for profit.

New Cheyenne owed its existence largely to the

existence of the mining and lumbering camp, and was not much older. It had sprung up, toad-stool fashion, as a supply base for the camp. Since it served a real need, with a big spread of country on every side, its growth had been rapid. In the last year it had outdistanced the older community of Long Rain, which was also the county seat. Besides Barclay's it boasted several more or less solid businesses.

Gordon halted again, and the others grouped around him.

"A couple of us will go on," he explained. "Those wagons will reach New Cheyenne ahead of us, and if we all rode in, the whole town would turn out to stop us. So the best way will be to slip in, have a look around and discover the evidence, then act. The rest of you get back to the ranch and keep an eye on things. Sam and I will do the snooping."

Drake was grinning in anticipation as they went on.

"I suppose you know who Barclay is?" he suggested.

"All I know is what I've heard," Gordon confessed. "They say he'll accept a cargo of misbranded hides and no questions asked—if the price is right. But I've never been over this way before."

"Me neither—but I've heard aplenty. In this case, they'll fix the price between them—O'Dion, Lem Harder and Barclay. Barclay's half-brother to the sheriff."

That explained such points as had been obscure.

It explained why Barclay could go unmolested, despite his conducting of a shady business. It explained why O'Dion was sending the hides to him. Once they had been unloaded and stored inside the big warehouse, it would be difficult to get a look at them. They would then be shipped out, hidden among bundles of legitimate cargo.

Everyone knew what went on, but obtaining proof was something else. It was highly effective to have the weight of the law, or what passsed for law in that country, on your side.

"How we going to work it?" Drake asked. "I've heard about Barclay's. They say his warehouse is a long building, with iron bars on the windows and padlocks on the doors; not easy to get into or out of."

"And whoever's in charge would be suspicious of strangers," Gordon observed. "They'd probably ask for credentials."

"And ours wouldn't suit—'less they're stamped by Colonel Colt. But if that's what they require—" He shrugged and grinned again.

"We'll have to wait and see what comes up," Gordon responded. One way or another, he intended to have a look at the evidence. Properly presented, it might be enough to defeat O'Dion, without the need for a bloody showdown.

As the excitement of the new venture wore off, the

ld crept back, chilling them from head to foot. A
uple of times they dismounted, leading their horses,
warm themselves, but that made for slow going
ad helped only a little. Drake's voice was wistful.

"You think maybe we could risk getting a bite to
t when we get there?" he asked. "And can we have
chance to thaw out?"

"We'll sure enough take the chance," Gordon agreed.
e had an idea that the temperature had dropped
-low zero, and it was still plummeting. The day had
en long, and, hastened by clouds and the relentless
orm, night would come soon after they reached the
wn. They would have to eat and get warm. That
as a bare minimum for existence.

New Cheyenne was a long way from Long Rain, a
untry apart. Even so, some of its inhabitants might
cognize one or both of them, in which case their
nission would be easily guessed. The chance of success
ould be enhanced if such recognition could be
voided.

They could see only an outline of the town as they
pproached. Darkness was already at hand, with lights
pringing up here and there, like faint candles against
he vastness of the winter night. The snow swirled and
rifted.

The first building, set well apart from its neighbors,
was long and low, and a couple of big wagons stood

alongside. The teams had been unhitched, the cargo u
loaded. Despite the bitter cold, odors drifted out, ma
ing clear that this was the hide warehouse.

It was easy to make a circle, unobserved, with n
one around. The heavy door was padlocked.

The next building was a livery stable, and here
lantern gave a feeble glow. They turned in, the hors
stumbling with weariness. The stable boy, a lanky you
with unkempt hair whose hue matched the hay
forked, displayed no interest in them or the bran
on the horses.

He was in the midst of forking hay to them whe
a clamor sounded outside, and he dropped the fork an
rushed eagerly to the door. Voices exclaimed in reli
or complaint, some of them feminine. It was apparen
that the stage had arrived, delayed well beyond i
usual schedule by the difficult weather. At least thre
heavily bundled figures climbed stiffly down from th
box, while from inside was debouched a cargo of h
manity, which appeared to have been packed as tight
as hides, once they were bailed for shipment.

Watching from the background, Gordon and Drak
marveled that so many people had managed to crow
their way in. There were more than a dozen in all, an
one man explained that a second stage had broke
down, compelling them all to take the one. They were
theatrical company, a traveling road company wh

were scheduled to put on a show that same evening, at the opera house.

Those were magic words, testimony to the growth and affluence of New Cheyenne. It had had an opera house for almost a year. Because of that, O'Dion had gotten the notion of establishing a theatre in Long Rain, turning O'Rourke's Saloon into the Grand Theatre. This same road company would be going on to Long Rain after their engagement here.

The passengers lost no time in trooping off toward the main part of town, anxious to get supper and to refresh themselves before it was time to put on the play. Most of them were laden with baggage and stage props as the storm swallowed them.

The driver of the stage was pressed into service to help transport some of the gear, once a huge pile of it was unlashed and taken down from the rear of the stage. That left the stable-boy to handle the six horses alone.

Gordon and Drake moved to assist him. The stolid youngster was now eager and voluble. Here was a subject dear to his heart.

"Yeah, they're the thee-atrical company," he confirmed. "I was sure gettin' worried that they wouldn't make it tonight, and if they hadn't, a lot of folks would have been mighty disappointed. They're puttin' on a three-act play, 'Our American Cousin.'" That's the one President Lincoln was watchin' when he was shot."

He pointed to a poster tacked to the wall, visible in the light from a hanging lantern. The style was flamboyant, the post a yellow sheet which was already beginning to fade and discolor.

"Read it," the boy urged. "Ain't that something, now? Read it out loud," he added. "I sure like to hear it."

Rightly deducing that he was unable to read for himself, Gordon complied.

The Renowned
Great Lakes and Seaboard Players
Under the Direction of
Mr. Scott Glosson
Present
OUR AMERICAN COUSIN

Following was the cast, including such characters as Georgina Mountchessington, Captain DeBoots and Lord Dundreary. The boy repeated the names, rolling them off his tongue with gusto.

"I sure aim to see that," he asserted.

"You know, I wouldn't mind seein' it myself," Drake confessed, and sighed wistfully.

"It would be nice," Gordon agreed, though he knew that it would be out of the question. They went outside, conscious anew of the bite of cold, and set off in the tracks of the theatrical company. Drake stumbled, almost falling, then plucked from the snow the object against which he had stubbed his toe. It was a carpet-bag.

"I'll bet those folks dropped this," he observed. "They were so loaded down with stuff they wouldn't have noticed. Maybe we should give it to them."

"Let's have a look," Gordon suggested. The bag was partly open, some of the contents on the verge of spilling. Excitement gripped him as he looked closer. These were theatrical props—sets of false whiskers, as well as other articles about whose use he was uncertain.

"We'll leave the bag where they'll find it," he decided. "But let's follow the pattern of some others in this town and engage in a bit of petty larceny." He thrust a generous mustache into Drake's hand. "It seems to be ready to stick on, just by pressing it down. I'll take this set of whiskers."

The beard was full and black, and served pretty well to hide his face, completely altering his appearance. Drake stared, dumbfounded, in the faintly reflected light from a store window, then backed away.

"If I didn't know who you were, I'd sure be scared to meet you on a night like this," he asserted. "You look like a desperado."

"You're quite a character yourself, with that mustache," Gordon assured him. Again, faint light shone through a frosted window, and the sign as well as the fragrance indicated that this was a restaurant. The unmistakable voice of one of the actors reached them.

"Food, my good fellow, food is what we require. Sustenance for the bodily man, hot, and in plenitude. What it shall be we leave to you, only let it be your best."

Gordon placed the carpet bag on the steps.

"They'll find this, all right—and I hope our appropriations won't leave them short. We'll have to pick some other place to eat, for they might recognize our whiskers."

They found another restaurant across the street; it was virtually deserted. Everyone who could was clustering in the other, if not to patronize it, then to gaze in awe-struck admiration at these beings from another world, who were bringing not only entertainment but culture to the community. Some might be perfectly willing to share in the profits from such mundane enterprises as the hide house, but for this evening at least, they were anxious to forget such things.

"Sure a piece of luck, them hittin' town and putting on the show tonight," Drake observed. "Nobody'll have any time or interest for anything else."

As though his words had summoned them, another

pair of customers entered, seating themselves at another table. They gave only a cursory glance at the two already there, then began to confer, low-toned. It was as he was starting on his pie that Gordon caught a phrase:

"—couldn't be better, a night like this, with everybody headin' for that playhouse. I'll show you what we've got in the warehouse. Mighty fine shipment came in today."

12

Gordon paid for the meal, taking time to engage the waiter in conversation, to inquire about obtaining tickets for the show. Having implanted the idea that the theatre was their destination, they went back outside. It was full dark now, as unpleasant a night as could well be imagined.

Farther up the street, a lantern burned fitfully, buffeted but not quite blown out by the gusts of wind. It marked the path to the opera house. Despite the inclement weather, people were already streaming in, making certain of a place to view this opening performance of the season.

"They tell me that the play is quite a show, an excellent comedy," Gordon commented, "though in everyone's mind now it is associated with tragedy. Too bad we can't see it."

"Yeah, but for a choice, I'd rather see the inside of that hide house," Drake grunted. "Here they come."

The other two diners emerged, then set off toward the warehouse and were immediately swallowed in the darkness. Following, it was unnecessary to take precautions, just as it was impossible to see those who went before. But they had only to follow the beaten road to reach the hide house.

The big padlock hung open, and they pushed open

the door and let themselves in. Halfway down the length of the long room, a lantern bobbed, the two men moving between hides stacked higher than their heads. Some were dry, already baled, ready for shipping out. Others, clearly the calfskins, were frozen together in great piles.

The two were discussing these. It appeared that the one man was a hide buyer, representing some outside company. The man who was showing him around was Barclay.

"Those fresh brands are bad business," the buyer protested. "If anybody was to get a look at them, they're evidence. And the condition they're in, the brands make for a lot of wastage. Every one will have to be cut out, and that chunk of skin burned."

"Which I'm taking into account," Barclay reminded him somewhat sharply. "I'm making you a mighty good price on the lot."

"Not good enough, considering. I don't mind a few bad hides scattered here and there among a lot of bales. That's normal. But all these—I've never seen anything like it. Somebody was takin' a mighty big chance."

"If it's taking a chance that worries you, forget it Getchell's wagons hauled them here, and Getchell will haul them on to Salt Lake and turn them over to you there."

"Well, if I take delivery there, that's different.

But Getchell must be crazy to take such chances."

"I tell you he takes none. The sheriff is my half-brother; Getchell is my cousin. And it's Curt O'Dion who is selling these skins. O'Dion owns half this country—and it won't be long till he has the rest of it."

"Includin' the men in it, and the law, eh? Well, that puts a different face on the matter. I'll take delivery at Salt Lake, and pay on delivery."

Barclay's head-shake caused the lantern to bob.

"Not good enough. You'll pay half down, now, same as on other deals, same as we agreed on. If you don't trust me, I don't trust you that far, either—not with a cargo like this."

The conversation was highly interesting, but this seemed a good time to take over. The pair stared with widening eyes as the other diners stepped from the gloom, with guns aimed.

"Sorry to interrupt such a high-minded deal as you're cooking up," Gordon observed blandly. "But you do engage in a chancy business. Get their guns, Sam."

The hide buyer was quaking, and he offered no resistance. Barclay sought to bluster, mouthing threats, and when those had no effect, he sought to bribe them. Drake worked silently, disarming them; then, using a piece of rope which was conveniently at hand, he sliced it into lengths and tied them hand and foot.

Such grim precision, all in silence, was having its

effect. Barclay was as jittery as his companion.

"What you going to do?" he demanded. "You can't just leave us here—that's murder. We'll freeze."

"Hardly that." Gordon shrugged. "But lie on the floor, and we'll throw some skins over you, to keep you warm." As they were half-shoved, half-eased into place by Drake, he selected a dry cowhide and spread it over them.

They took a couple of the calfskins with the fresh Quirt brands, forced to pull and pry to get them loose, for the green, frozen hides were hard to handle. Then, deaf to the pleas of their captives, they went out, snapping the padlock in place.

"They'll work loose, but they'll probably have to spend the night there," Gordon observed. "With everybody at the opera house, and the storm on top of that, I doubt that they can make themselves heard."

Except for horses, the stable was empty. The stable boy had slipped away as planned. They selected a fresh pair of horses from those in the stalls, and Gordon scribbled a note on the back of the theatre poster, tearing it loose for the purpose. He explained that they were leaving their own animals as evidence of good faith and would return the others within a few days.

"Perhaps they won't like it, but like us, they won't have much choice," he granted, and turned his cayuse into the storm.

It was a punishing ride. Keeping to the road was largely a matter of instinct on the part of the horses, who went reluctantly. Like himself, Drake possessed an instinct for going straight even under adverse conditions. Both of them were reasonably confident that they were keeping in the right direction.

At intervals they walked, leading the horses, warming themselves and giving the animals a breather. Finally, almost numb with cold, Gordon risked a swing, leaving the road, and Drake roused from a long silence to grunt a question.

"What's up?" Where we headin'?"

"Slash," Gordon explained. "The house ought to be off there about a mile."

Drake sighed in relief.

"That close? I thought we'd keep on to Long Rain."

"I doubt if we could make it," Gordon said frankly. "I'm about at the end of my rope, and so are the horses. We'll get some rest and food before we go on."

"Sure suits me. I didn't think I could keep going," Drake confessed. "But if you kept moving, I figured I'd tag along."

Absently, Gordon fingered the icicles which had formed on mustache and whiskers from his icy breath. He sensed that the storm was finally slackening, the snow ebbing, the wind dying. There was a lightening in the cloud wrack overhead, and in that faint illumination he made out the dark cluster of ranch buildings.

They got the horses into the barn, tugging off saddles by feel and instinct, their fingers too numb to strike a match or make a light. Keeping together, they stumbled across to the bunk house and tugged open the door. Gordon crashed against some obstacle, and a startled voice demanded to know who was there.

"Us—Drake and Gordon," he mumbled, and drew in a long breath of the warmer, but still chill air. There was another grunt of surprise; then others of the crew came tumbling from their bunks, to light a lamp, then to build a fire in the stove, at the same time exclaiming in pity and disbelief.

"But you ain't Gordon," one man protested. "You cain't be—even if you do sound like him."

Gordon caught a glimpse of himself in the mirror on the wall, and stared incredulously. He had forgotten all about the heavy set of false whiskers, too preoccupied with other matters to remember. They were still in place, probably having shielded his face from some of the bitter cold during the ride. They accounted for the clustering icicles on mustache and beard.

He clawed these loose as they commenced to loosen in the warmth of the room, sending them rattling to the floor, then pulled off the whiskers. He accepted a drink from a proffered bottle, a long, deep potion which barely warmed his throat. One man was tugging off his boots, while another performed the same service for Drake. He'd intended to ask questions as to what had taken place during their absence, but the next thing he knew he was in his bunk and tumbling into sweet oblivion.

It was daylight when he awoke, to discover that he had slept the clock around. Outside, the clouds still shut away the sun, the world looking white and cheerless. His discovery that it was past noon shocked him fully awake. He'd had no intention of sleeping so long.

At the ranch itself there had been no trouble. But the other members of the crew, who had ridden with him the day before, and who had been sent back under Lomax, had not been seen.

He wondered about them uneasily, though it was probable that they had tired of the ride in such bitter weather, and had sought shelter, also sleeping late.

By now, the veal meat would be on the tables at the construction camp, and the branded hides might be on their way to Salt Lake, consigned along with other skins, with a faked bill of sale. Thus the evidence would soon vanish.

Drake roused, blinked and yawned as Gordon shook him, then tumbled reluctantly from the bunk.

"Man, I never slept like that before in my life,"

he confessed, and eyed the blankets wistfully. "And I wouldn't mind crawlin' back in for another round of the same!"

"It sounds like a grand idea," Gordon conceded. "But how about something to eat? Then we still have to finish our ride."

"Now you mention food, I believe I could do with a bite or so—about the size bites a starvin' grizzly would grab off." Drake grinned. They ate; then Gordon took time to shave. Feeling halfway himself again, he crossed to the house.

Mary McKay was frankly glad to see him. Her face betrayed the anxiety she had felt.

"I was certainly relieved this morning when I heard that you were back, though they said that you were just about all in when you returned late last night. We all worried, of course, with such bad weather on top of all the rest."

"I'm going to take that worry as being more or less personal," Gordon observed. "Which gives me a chance to ask a question that I've been wondering about. The more I've thought it over, the more it seems to me that that meeting at Selway's Restaurant the other evening must have been set up by somebody—planned to stir up trouble. What do you know about it?"

"Not much, but I think you're probably right," Mary agreed. A trace of color flowed in her pale cheeks and forehead. "I never did get it quite straight, but Driscoll dropped some remarks which make me think you are right. Someone had been taunting him, and others of our crew, about being afraid of Quirt, and standing aside for them on certain days, as though Quirt had any better right to a place to eat than the Slash. Of course such talk was foolish, and only designed to cause trouble—but it worked."

"It sure did. I knew there must have been some reason why Slash would violate the truce the way it did."

"Well, a part of the reason—" Her color was higher now, but she met his eyes steadily. "Part was talk, that you had been seeing me on the sly—that you were interested in a girl who would inherit a big slice of a big ranch. I got that much out of Driscoll afterward. Of course there was no truth in any of it, but it served its purpose. He was always hot-headed and impulsive."

The explanation cleared up certain points, and definitely proved that the whole scheme had been contrived, carefully planned. As far as Slash Y was concerned, the purpose was readily understandable. But why had he been picked as the goat? The nagging question was still unanswered, but somehow it had a big part in the total sum of events. For he had been sent into town by O'Dion himself, on what had turned out to be a completely trifling errand; sent in alone, to get into trouble, perhaps to die.

13

Riding toward Long Rain, Gordon was preoccupied. Sam Drake offered a tentative remark or so concerning the improving weather, then, finding that he re- ing the imphoving weather, then, finding that he received no answer, lapsed into silence. The pair of calf- skins were tied behind Drake's saddle, evidence which could be shown to the law. But Abe McKay's eye- brows had lifted skeptically, and Gordon, viewing mat- ters in the cold light of day, felt almost as skeptical. Where would be the profit in forcing evidence upon a man who was determined not to look at it?

Even so, it had to be tried. The law must be given a chance to handle the situation if it would. Not until legal recourse had been attempted could he justify turn- ing to Judge Colt for a decision, with the writing in red.

The short winter day was waning as they reached the town. There would be time enough to visit the sheriff's office and show the evidence, and that was about all. By now, Gordon's mood was almost as stark as the day. Maybe it had been a fatal mistake to play the game as he had. A showdown, however heavy the odds, would still have given them a fighting chance. But with a law which abetted and protected the lawless—

A shrill voice, almost piping, roused him from his reverie. Someone had called from the snow-packed sidewalk. Eli Jenkins, postmaster, bulked formidably, clad in a heavy cap and buffalo coat, barely recognized as the slight, meek little man who usually hovered behind his cubbyhole and peered timidly out through the wicket. Gordon pulled up.

"Did you want to see me, Mr. Jenkins?" he asked.

"I fear so, sir—indeed, I believe so. Could I have a few words with you, Mr. Gordon?"

"No reason why not," Gordon agreed, surprised. When it town, he usually called at the post office for Quirt mail, and so was casually acquainted with the postmaster. Rarely, if ever, had they exchanged more than the time of day, just as there was seldom any mail for himself.

"Look after the horses," he instructed Drake. "I'll join you at the stable." He dismounted to join the bundled figure on the sidewalk. "What is it?"

"Let's step inside the post office," Jenkins suggested. "It'll be warmer there."

Gordon followed willingly. The warmth was welcome after the ride into town. A cherry-red heater gulped hungrily at a split log; then Jenkins divested himself of the heavy coat, tugged off the fur cap, and became again his usual meek self. He peered uncertainly, as if disliking the question he had to ask.

"I—something set me to wondering," he confessed. "Perhaps a chain of incidents. But you—I presume that you received your letter all right, the other day?"

"Letter? What letter?" Gordon asked. "I haven't had a letter, or any piece of mail, for going on a year now. I never write, and nobody writes to me."

Jenkins made a small clucking noise. "Dear me," he protested. "Are you telling me that your employer, Mr. O'Dion, failed to give you the registered letter which came for you? He signed for it—and since he was your employer, to say nothing of being Mr. O'Dion, I assumed—quite naturally—that there would be no question as to its delivery. Of course, I should have had you sign for it yourself. Oh, dear me!"

"When was this?" Gordon asked. "I've had no letter, or any word about one."

"Incredible. I can't understand such forgetfulness on the part of Mr. O'Dion. It was ten days, possibly a couple of weeks ago, that a letter came, addressed to you. I remember quite distinctly that it was from Kentucky—a registered letter. I assumed—mistakenly, it now appears—"

"Kentucky? You wouldn't remember the return address, or the town it was from?"

"Yes, I recall the point of mailing quite well. It was Frankfort. Also, the envelope had been torn in transit. The enclosure was not too well protected, as I pointed out to Mr. O'Dion—"

"I used to have an uncle who lived in Frankfort," Gordon commented thoughtfully. "I never saw him but once in my life, and then I was too small to remember. I'd supposed he must have died years ago."

"As to that, of course, I cannot say, but I blame myself—most severely—for carelessness, for dereliction of duty, in regard to your letter. It must have been important; else it would not have been registered. And I—it has come to my ears that you are no longer employed at the Quirt—"

"No, I'm not," Gordon agreed. On the face of it, he couldn't see how the receipt of such a letter could be very important, though the timing and the fact that O'Dion had not turned it over to him, or mentioned it in any way, might be significant. If the envelope had been torn, O'Dion might have had a look at what it contained. Meanwhile, the day was running out, and so was time.

The door opened, letting in a swirl of air which gusted frostily across the room, and a bundled figure thrust a small package toward the postmaster.

"Here's the mail," he explained. "That's all there was this time. Not a single letter or paper—that must have got held up somewhere and missed the stage. Just this one package. Registered mail. Sign for it, will you?"

Jenkins did so, moving mechanically, peering somewhat nearsightedly at the package. His head jerked violently and he looked again. Then, as the door closed behind the messenger, he thrust it at Gordon.

"This is for you," he said heavily. "From the same place—Frankfort, Kentucky. You sign this time, and I'm putting it into your own hands."

Surprised, but agreeable, Gordon signed, studying the packet a moment. He thrust it into a pocket, and with Jenkins' apologies for the earlier error still sounding in his ears, returned to the street.

Drake was waiting at the livery stable. There, in the shelter of a stall, Gordon ripped open the package, then stared in increasing astonishment, along with a glimmer of understanding.

The package contained a thick sheaf of money. There were hundred-dollar bills, gleaming with newness, carefully wrapped. A hasty count indicated the amount to be twenty thousand dollars. Drake blinked in astonishment.

"What's going on?" he asked. "Have you fallen

heir to a fortune or something?"

"It looks like that—or something, sure enough," Gordon agreed. The letter had probably contained an explanation and necessary information; he could begin to fit certain obvious facts into an answer.

As far as he knew, his uncle had been his only living relative, so, by the same token, he was probably his uncle's sole heir. He'd never known or even wondered as to whether or not this relative had any property, or thought of himself in connection with it. It was surprising that an uncle who had never written should have kept track of a nephew sufficiently to know his whereabouts.

Yet he must have done so, and now the estate, in cash, had been sent to him. Thinking back, he recalled that his uncle had been mentioned as a man of strong opinions and prejudices, one of which had been his great distrust of banks. He had never kept any money in them. It would have been natural for him to instruct whoever was delegated the task of settling up his estate to send the money in cash.

Ironically, the administrator must have secured new money from a bank!

Quite clearly, the letter, which had arrived ahead of the money, must have explained these details and said that the cash was coming. When O'Dion had learned that one of his crew was to receive such a sum of money, he'd kept the information to himself, then set about scheming to get hold of it. In view of his other activities, that was not surprising. Twenty thousands dollars would be a juicy windfall.

It might well be that that particular piece of information had helped trigger other events, including the timing of the attack against Slash. There had been those stories carefully planted in the ears of Driscoll McKay and others of the Slash Y; the sending him to town, alone, on that particular day. Events were clear enough now. He was not called Brick for nothing; he had red hair and a temper to match. If his propensity for trouble should lead him into more of it than he could handle, on the eve of the arrival of the money, O'Dion, as his employer, would know to handle all that.

The scheme hadn't worked entirely according to plan, especially since the money had been turned over to him now. But it explained a lot, all of which fitted into the larger ambitions of O'Dion.

Gordon hesitated, then shoved the package into his saddle-bags. Drake had the other package containing the frozen hides.

"Don't mention anything about this money to anybody," Gordon cautioned. "Let's go make our call on the sheriff."

Drake shrugged, but contained his curiosity as they

swung down the street. The clouds were showing signs of breaking, and it would probably be a colder night than ever, but with sunshine on the morrow. Now, early though the hour was, dusk was closing over the town.

The stone pile of the two-story courthouse was off at one side, a few pale blobs of light gleaming murkily through windows heavy with frost. They headed for the sheriff's office, connected with the jail a block away. A light there betokened that someone was still around.

There another red-hot stove made the room over-warm. Lem Harder was seated, boots on his desk, chin on his chest. His chin jerked and the boots made a thump on the floor as he swung guiltily at the opening of the door. His face went blank as he recognized Gordon, then smoothed to its usual, faintly oily composure, though he checked his start toward rising.

"You want something?" he asked gruffly.

"We've something to show you," Drake explained and, cutting the cord which held the rolled-up skins in position, struggled to unroll them. Holding them close to the stove, he gradually succeeded, as the heat thawed the ice. The sheriff was on his feet now, watching sharply, his face still expressionless. Drake spread the evidence on the floor.

"We thought you should see this, Gordon explained. "Quirt stole the entire calf crop of Slash Y the other day—ran off cows and their calves alike, then branded the calves with the Quirt. We went across there, Slash Y's whole crew, and found them with their mothers, all Slash Y cows. Ye got them back, but Quirt was alarmed by then, and that night they moved in, butchered the calves, and shipped out the meat and the skins. We found the meat enroute to the big construction camp, and the hides in Barclay's hide house at New Cheyenne. We brought a couple of them to show you."

The sheriff listened, with varying shades of expression, then shook his head unbelievingly.

"Do you expect me to believe a wild yarn like that," he asked, "or any part of it?"

"Here's proof," Gordon pointed out grimly. "And we've plenty of witnesses—the whole Slash Y crew."

Challenged by such a solid argument, Harder veered to a new tack. "I'd heard that you'd turned renegade from Quirt," he observed bitingly. "But I didn't suppose that anyone would go quite this far."

"Let's leave your opinions and suppositions out of it," Gordon suggested. "You're the sheriff, so we've come to you. We represent Slash Y, and this is a case of rustling on a wholesale scale. We want you to do something about it."

"You say you found those skins in the hide warehouse at New Cheyenne? How did you get hold of them?"

"We went in, had a look around, then helped ourselves to some of the evidence, to show you. The whole calf crop of Slash was there, all branded with the Quirt."

Harder shrugged.

"You mean you found hides branded with Quirt. That is no proof that the rustling wasn't against Quirt—though that's what the evidence would seem to indicate."

"We told you where they came from. We followed the hide wagons all the way from where the calves were butchered on Slash Y, and we have plenty of witnesses."

"Witnesses?" The sheriff was shaken, searching for a way out of this dilemma. The last thing that he wanted to do was to enforce the law against his real employer, O'Dion, or against his cousin or brother-in-law, all of whom were so deeply involved. Yet as sheriff, he had obligations not readily shrugged aside.

"If you expect me to believe any part of so wild a story, you'll have to make it credible," he said carefully. "I've been in Barclay's hide house, so I know what it's like. He keeps it locked, except for people who have legitimate business there. I don't for a minute believe that he'd have let you in, under the circumstances—or that he'd let you out again, with evidence such as' that, if what you say is true. In that case, such evidence could land him in trouble up to his neck."

"We got in," Gordon reminded, "and had our look. And we've brought the evidence. Now, this isn't a matter for you to please yourself about. We're speaking as citizens, as representatives of Slash Y. What I've told you, we make as a charge against Quirt—stealing Slash cows and calves, misbranding them, then slaughtering the calves. We want action, and fast, to stop those skins from being shipped out of the country. We want the evidence impounded for a jury to look at."

Harder hesitated, chewing his lip. He was fairly caught, and he knew it. If he refused, and the story got abroad, then was confirmed, he'd be through as sheriff; worse than that, he'd be lucky to get out of the county without being tarred and feathered.

On the other hand, he owed his job to O'Dion, and some of his relatives were implicated; Gordon suspected that Harder also had a share in the business, so he had to protect them in every way possible, even to further subversion of the law—which was the reason he had been put in as sheriff in the first place.

He swung in sudden decision, nodding.

"Maybe you've got a case," he acknowledged. "I never heard a crazier-sounding story in my life, but if you take the necessary legal steps, I'll do my part.

What you want is for me to go to New Cheyenne and impound those hides?"

"That's a first step."

"That's the second step," the sheriff contradicted. "The first is for you to go to the judge and get a warrant to search that warehouse, one which will authorize me to seize and impound the evidence if found. I can't do such a thing merely on your say-so. Get that; then I'll ride."

"We'll get it." Gordon was shrugging back into his heavy coat. Drake gathered up the hides. "Get ready to ride!"

14.

For all his show of confidence, Gordon was far from certain if they would get far. Night was closing over the town as they headed for the courthouse, though it was not yet so dark but what their breath steamed about their faces, while boots crunched like sled runners in the snow. Harder would go only as far and fast as he was compelled.

The hides might already be beyond reach; suddenly it seemed like a hopeless task. But they were too deeply involved for any other course. This must be played to the end.

The courthouse corridors were dimly lit, dank and echoing. A clerk appeared suddenly from the shadows to halt them short of the judge's chambers. He listened doubtfully to their request to see the judge at once.

"Well, I don't know about that," he hedged. "It's closing time, and past. You'd better come back tomorrow."

"Tomorrow will be too late," Gordon protested. "This is urgent business, and we want to see him now— at once!"

"Well, I'll tell him that you're here," the clerk agreed, and withdrew. He was gone a long while, during which they could only wait and fume. Finally he returned, to announce that the judge would see them.

Judge Uland was tall and thin, and his habit of dressing always in black, coupled with a beak of a nose under eyebrows like miniature mustaches, gave him the appearance of a bird of prey. Before his elevation to the bench, he had enjoyed a dubious reputation as a lawyer, so much so that even the backing of Quirt had barely gotten him elected. Like the sheriff, he did not forget to whom he owed his elevation. He peered forbiddingly from behind his desk, scowling at the hides outspread on the floor.

"You tell a somewhat incredible story," he pronounced. "However, for the moment, the matter of credibility is secondary. Just exactly how did you get hold of these—of this evidence?"

Not giving time for a reply, he leaned across his desk to waggle a finger in their faces, then altered the gesture to a snap of the fingers. At that manifest signal, the rear door to the office opened and the sheriff entered.

"On that point you have been evasive, both with me and with Sheriff Harder," Uland thundered. "That attitude is easily understandable, since the truth would implicate you. It is clearly evident that you obtained these skins by breaking and entering, with felonious intent. Need I remind you that such conduct is a crime of a most serious order? Accordingly, I hereby instruct the sheriff to place you under arrest and to hold you in close custody, while this affair is sifted and investigated and the truth arrived at."

He should have expected something of the sort. Gorddon realized bitterly. He'd forced Quirt and its henchmen into a position where their backs were against the wall. In that situation, they would go to any lengths.

When he attempted to protest, the judge overrode him with a roar.

"This court will permit no quibbling," he thundered, "particularly in view of the stories which have come to my ear concerning the murder of Driscoll McKay—above whose dead body you were discovered! Lock them up, Sheriff."

It was a bitter moment as the sheriff thrust them triumphantly into a cell, not troubling to hide his elation. Clearly he had scuttled across to the courtroom by the back way, beating them there, gaining the ear of the judge and apprising him of the seriousness of the situation. While they had been kept waiting, the two had planned a course of action.

Beyond question, their intent was to keep him locked up, at least long enough for the evidence to be transported out of the territory, and until O'Dion had tidied up his affairs. It would require only a little more to place Slash in a position where it could no longer fight back and, deprived of leadership, O'Dion would move ruthlessly against the ranch. His blunder had lain in trying to fight back within the law, seeking to avoid a bloody range war. These men didn't play by such rules.

To his demand that they be allowed to see a lawyer, Harder shrugged. Clearly, he would find reasons for not getting word to a lawyer that evening.

Both prisoners were doubly surprised when, within half an hour, Larry Vick came into the jail, accompanied by a grumpy sheriff. Vick was comparatively new in the territory, still a tenderfoot by most standards. But he was a lawyer, and already he had demonstrated that he was not only competent but hard to bluff. He explained why he was there.

"It appears that Miss McKay and her father were rather dubious as to how you might make out, so they followed you right to town," he said. "They got here just in time to find that you had been arrested, so they have hired me to look after your interests. Let's hear your story; then I'll go to the judge and try to arrange for bail."

He listened, with no appearance of surprise, asking a few clarifying questions, then set out as promised. Hopefully they waited, and when he returned, the look on his face told that the news was bad.

"Sure, he agreed to grant bail," Vick reported bitterly. "Ten thousand dollars, cash money, for Drake—and as much more for you, Gordon, on the charge of breaking and entering, with an added fifteen thousand in your case, on suspicion of murder. I attempted to persuade him to adopt a more reasonable attitude—" He smiled wryly. "In fact, I'm afraid I almost lost my temper. His Honor—I use the term loosely—soaked me with a fifty-dollar fine for contempt of court—which amount, confidentially, doesn't nearly begin to express my real feelings in regard to the gentleman! The upshot, however, is that you'll have to languish where you are, at least for a while."

Though disappointed, Gordon was not surprised. O'Dion had the upper hand now, and he intended to keep it, regardless. Should the law be bent and twisted in the process, that was his conception of its purpose.

Supper was brought them, but if any visitors requested admission, they saw no sign of them. Harder had a sound respect for his prisoners, and he did not intend to take any chances.

Gordon sat on the edge of his bunk and pondered, to no good effect. He'd never had much experience with

jails, but this one seemed reasonably clean. Beyond
that, he could find no good point in its favor. It was
solidly built, and escape appeared to be out of the question. They would hold him, on one technicality or another, until it was too late to matter.

Meanwhile, all that he had tried to do would go for
naught, and O'Dion would hasten toward a final roundup. Driscoll McKay was dead. He was in jail. Abe Mc-
Kay was blind. Lomax, again acting foreman in his
absence, would be helpless in such an emergency; as
helpless as himself, because he'd again underestimated
the opposition.

Drake was in the adjoining cell. They discussed the
situation, unable to find anything hopeful; then Drake
stretched on his own bunk and was soon snoring. Gordon listened, his anger as tight as his clenched fists.
It was too dark to see, since no light had been left burning. Except for themselves, the jail and the adjoining
sheriff's office were empty. It could be a long night, and
he'd do well to follow Drake's example, so as to be
fresh should any opportunity develop. There was no
profit in worrying or in blaming himself.

The trouble with such advice was that it was easier
to propound than to follow. He was tired, but not at
all sleepy. Even the barred window was invisible, and
when he stood on tiptoe and strove to see out, the town
was equally dark. The citizens retired early, after the

manner of hibernating animals.

With the town asleep on a wintry night, there was no sound, not even a dog, to answer a coyote on a distant hill. The stillness was as intense as the blackness.

Then he heard a key, turned softly in a lock.

Tensely Gordon listened, sounds coming like muted whispers. Someone was out there, moving in that stygian blackness without a light. Whoever it was seemed to know his way by instinct, to go surely and without difficulty.

Shoes made a soft, shuffling noise; then there was a faint scraping as keys were tried and rejected, until one fitted the lock, this one the lock to his cell. A voice whispered his name.

"Brick—you awake?"

"I'm awake, Abe," Gordon confirmed, and allowed pent-up breath to dribble from his lungs.

"Then we'd best be moving." The observation was matter-of-fact. "Come on; I'll guide you. Put your hand on my arm. Where is Drake?"

"In the cell right next to mine."

Drake was awake then, disturbed by their voices, but he refrained from asking questions. More fumbling was required before the right key was found to open his door. Then the three of them moved along the corridor.

"I don't quite get this," Drake protested. His voice

was both doubtful and amazed. "You do about as well as if you could see where you're going, Mr. McKay."

Abe's chuckle was amused. "Better, most likely," he returned. "Since I can't see at all, any time, I'm used to moving in darkness. As for this place, I was actin' sheriff here for a few months, a few years ago, so I got to know my way around. Everything's still kept the same, includin' the keys. Which reminds me. You boys will feel better-dressed with guns on."

He turned toward the jail office. Gordon heard a desk drawer opened, then soft clicks as the chamber of a revolver was twirled, while sensitive fingers made certain that it was filled with loaded shells. Then the gun was handed to him, another to Drake.

"The sheriff has a way of takin' guns away from people, then forgettin' to return them," Abe explained. "So there's always a few in here."

Here, where he had neither looked for nor expected a break, was extraordinary luck. No one but a blind man could have managed what Abe was doing. Even the sheriff would have required a light to move around in the darkness, to unlock doors and guide them, simply because, like most others, he was accustomed to light. Only a man who no longer depended on vision could manage in blackness.

Anyone working with a light would run the risk of it being seen and investigated. On the other hand, no one would even suspect that the jail could be prowled in such darkness.

"Lucky for me Harder didn't lock the outside door," Abe added casually. "Mary was plumb upset about them throwin' you into jail. Larry Vick, he's still working, trying to think of some way to help, but I doubt he's having much luck. He told me what our pillars of the law are up to—aimin' to hold court, first thing in the morning, and to throw the book at you. You've giving O'Dion a bad time, and they don't aim to take no chances."

Such news was not surprising, but the casual manner in which he had gone about rescuing them was revealing. It explained, at least in part, why O'Dion had restrained his ambitions as long as Abe McKay was actively rodding the Slash. Only when he had been certain that Abe was helpless, and when Driscoll McKay was marked for assassination, had he felt safe in making his play.

"I've sure bungled things, bad," Gordon gritted.

The fingers which rested lightly on his arm tightened in a reassuring squeeze.

"In a fight, a man usually gets hit just about as many times as he lands a blow," Abe observed. "It's the last lick that counts. I like the way you've handled this fight, Brick. You've set Quirt back on their heels, hard. I'd have done things just about the same, if I could have planned it. We at Slash ain't never stood for being pushed around; but we try to live and let live."

His words were warming, so that the sudden bite of the outer air hardly mattered. The outer door was closing behind them. Long Rain was silent, with no light showing, the hitch rails deserted. High stars gave a faint illumination, which was enhanced by the blanketing snow.

"I'll join Mary and be getting back to the ranch," Abe explained. "You'll have plans, I reckon."

He was gone, fading into the gloom, offering no suggestions for future movements. That was the sort of boss who commanded loyalty, who gave his trust and then backed a man to the hilt. Gordon wished fleetingly that Abe had volunteered some word of advice. But this was his job, and the old man knew, from his own experience, that he was more conversant with the situation than anyone else.

"Gee!" Drake breathed, as they moved ahead. His head-shake expressed both bewilderment and admiration. "You know, I never guessed that he was really blind—but he's better than most men with eyes!"

15

Gordon would have been glad to share Abe's confidence in his ability. Showdown could not much longer be delayed, but except for that certainty, he had no clear idea as to what his next move should be. It might be morning before the jail break was discovered; when that occurred, the pattern to follow could be readily guessed. He would not merely be branded an outlaw; they would also charge him with the murder of Driscoll McKay. Vick had relayed the word to Abe that they intended to do that, hurrying through a mockery of a trial, then hanging him. Cheated in that, they would offer a heavy reward for him, dead or alive.

Having branded him as fair game, Quirt could join in the hunt, along with the sheriff. Daylight would heavily increase the odds.

The fact that Abe McKay had considered it necessary to set them loose showed how serious he considered the matter. Giving him his freedom, even at the price of outlawry, had been the lesser evil.

Gordon's jaw set, his fingers closing instinctively around his gun butt. As Abe had pointed out, Slash preferred to live in peace, but it didn't stand for being pushed around.

Drake opened the stable door, and they slipped inside, closing it after them. The vague rustlings and stirrings of horses came to their ears; then another sound, this one unexpected: a familiar but aggravated voice.

"Blast it, Curt, we need a light. Nobody's awake anywhere to notice—and what would it matter if someone did?"

"We can't run that risk, not right now," O'Dion retorted. "Jenkins is a snoop, and when I asked him if that package had arrived, and he told me he'd turned it over to Gordon, he acted mighty suspicious. Right now, he hasn't much to go on except his own notions. But if he got really stirred up, he's just the sort who'd send in a full report about the whole affair to his boss. And I don't want any nosy inspectors from the post office snooping around. I can handle local law, but the federals could be nasty."

"Sure, I know that. But we could say that we were in here after our horses. How are we going to find anything in the dark? And for that matter, wouldn't Gordon have kept whatever it was right on him?"

"Harder searched him when he locked him up," O'Dion returned impatiently. "He didn't have it, so he must have left it somewhere, and this is the most likely place. That letter said that a package would follow in a few days, containing hard cash."

In the stress of other events, Gordon had temporarily forgotten about the money. But O'Dion had not; it was very much on his mind. He had apparently been summoned to town after Gordon had been arrested, and he'd risked asking the postmaster about the expected package. Eagerness had caused him to take that chance, since he had been fairly certain that Jenkins would be unaware of recent developments.

Gordon grinned. This was a break he hadn't expected. Still, luck had a way of being impartial. If you were alert and ready to take advantage when the chance came, you were called lucky. When a man failed to do so, he was termed unlucky. Quite often it was as simple as that.

Drake nudged him as a signal, then slipped away in the gloom. Gordon drew his revolver and carefully eared back the hammer, then took a couple of steps and jammed the barrel against a shadowy figure.

"Reach!" he instructed, while with his other hand he helped himself to the holstered weapon of his prisoner.

Drake was working in unison, surprising Yankus at the same instant. Both men from Quirt were taken without difficulty.

"Now what do we do with such a pair of thieves?" Drake asked. "We've caught 'em red-handed in the act!"

"Well, I suppose we could take them to the nearest patch of trees and hang them," Gordon observed, "seeing that they planned that sort of a welcome to the new day for me."

O'Dion stumbled into the trap.

"You can't do that, Gordon," he protested. "You were to have a fair trial before you were hung." He started to say more, then stopped, aware that he had betrayed his knowledge of the plan.

"You'd be surprised," Gordon assured him grimly. "And after what you've just said, as well as the way you've been carrying on, I'm running out of patience."

Drake scratched a match and touched the flame to a lantern wick. Rope was conveniently at hand, and he tied their prisoners' hands, then held them under guard while Gordon checked his saddle-bags, making sure that the package of money was intact. Growing desperation was upon the face of O'Dion as well as on Yankus'.

"You can't get away with this," the latter burst out. "Our crew's outside—and this time they'll hang you!"

The bluff was so manifest that Gordon did not bother to answer it. Two saddled horses from Quirt had been brought in, and they made the prisoners mount, then ran thongs from their bound wrists to the saddle-horns, leaving them helpless.

"Now we ride," Gordon said.

There was no sign of anyone else from Quirt, and the remainder of the crew were probably asleep. Being sure of himself, O'Dion had risked a quick trip in to town after receiving a report that Gordon was behind bars. He would keep in the background, while pushing for a swift trial in the morning, making sure that neither his sheriff nor judge failed to hang this rebel before most people even knew what was going on. Once that was done, the war as well as the battle would be won.

Even with fresh horses between their legs, this had the markings of another long night, though it would be more comfortable as far as temperature was concerned. There was a feel of change in the air as they left the town behind, a quality as intangible as a woman's mood, yet definite. Already it had warmed a few degrees, the arctic bite blunted by a returning softness which might have been left over from the summer.

Two courses of action were open. They could return to the Slash, or keep straight on toward New Cheyenne. Despite their having O'Dion as a hostage, either method would bristle with hazards. Striking for the distant town was riskier, but the increasing odds might be balanced by greater rewards. To hole up at the ranch meant a certain clash at arms, and as far as the law and the record went, they'd be in the wrong all the way. The longer course might still avoid a murderous battle of the crews, and that had been his objective from the first. If it was inconsistent that hired hands should die to decide an issue for O'Dion, it was equally so where he was concerned.

O'Dion grunted in surprise when they failed to make the turn to the ranch. Clearly, he had expected nothing else.

"Are you heading for Barclay's?" he demanded. "Or do you want just to get out of the country? *That* would be sensible."

"Well, we could keep riding," Gordon conceded. "We should come up with the wagons, sooner or later."

O'Dion gave a snort of laughter.

"If ever you do, you'll be too late, as you've been from the beginning."

"In that case, what are you worrying about?"

O'Dion shrugged. "No worry for me. It's merely that I'm reminded that the wicked flee when nobody pursues. It's just that I hate to see you knock yourself out for nothing, Brick. You should have stuck where you belonged, with Quirt—and it's not too late to change."

Gordon imitated the shrug. "With *me* paying you for the privilege—to the tune of thousands? There's a sour note to that."

The reminder that he knew all about the money left O'Dion without an answer. They moved at a steady pace, putting miles between themselves and the county seat. They were penetrating into enemy country, but it was clear that O'Dion's apprehension was mounting faster than his own. His manifest nervousness reassured Gordon that he was doing the right thing.

It continued to grow warmer, and now a chinook wind was blowing down from the mountains. Rawly cold at sundown, the change became striking. Gordon unbuttoned his heavy coat, noting that Drake was doing the same. The snow underfoot no longer squeaked

and rattled with an icy brittleness. It was assuming a
soft, almost clinging quality about the hoofs of the
horses. No longer did breaths rise and swirl like fog.

So swift a change in the weather seemed like an
omen. Gordon had seen the temperatures alter swiftly,
though seldom to such an extent. When conditions
were right, the thermometer could climb or drop a
degree a minute, and tonight it was shifting from below zero to above the freezing point. Occasional small
puddles appeared in the road, and tiny streams struggled to cut courses for themselves among the snow-
banks.

O'Dion finally raised his voice in protest and suppli-
cation.

"Have a heart," he begged. "We're cooking, but-
toned up in these heavy coats. Either loosen our hands
so we can do it ourselves, or help us shuck out of them."

The request was too reasonable to refuse, though
Gordon recalled how uncomfortable he had been while
imprisoned in the bear pit. Both men were sweating,
their faces beaded with moisture. Gordon rode alongside O'Dion and reached with his free hand to loosen
the buttons of the overcoat.

"That helps," O'Dion muttered, and turned his face
to the moon, which until then had been obscured by a
haze of cloud.

"Ain't it pretty, now?" O'Dion's mood seemed to
have softened, like the air. "I'll make a guess that you'd

rather be ridin' with a certain lady for company, a night like this. Suit me better, too, if you were." His chuckle covered the sudden convulsive twist of his body as he swung a foot free from the stirrup, reaching, lifting. The rowel of the spur caught at Gordon's gun-belt, and instantly the Quirt boss gave a savage, lunging kick downward.

Frightened, Gordon's horse veered away, and in that moment, O'Dion came close to accomplishing his purpose. The needle-pointed spur had been aimed to puncture like a knife, to tear a wound in Gordon's side. It failed as the horse jerked away, partly deflected by heavy shirt and underwear. Then the slashing bark raked downward along Brick's thigh, tearing cloth and flesh alike, while blood spurted and pain lanced.

The next instant, O'Dion was roweling his horse with both spurred boots, sending it into a wild gallop; Yankus was quick to emulate his boss. That was the moment chosen by the moon to duck back under the cloud.

Desperation lay in such a try at escape, but for a few moments it seemed as though by its very recklessness it might succeed. Both prisoners were shackled by their wrists to saddle-horns, but they still held the bridle reins in their fingers and so were able to control their horses.

Here the valley widened, flattening out, spotted with a scattering of pines and cottonwoods. Among these, much of the snow had been swept clear by the wind, leaving the ground bare, providing easy running for a horse.

With the moon gone, the darkness seemed thicker than before. Once lost among scores of acres of trees, a fugitive would be hopeless to find.

Gordon pursued, pain lancing along his thigh, his fury mounting with the agony. His gun was in his hand and clear of leather before he could check the wild impulse to use it. The longer reach it would give to his arm would check escape, but the trouble was that he couldn't shoot a man in the back, even an escaping prisoner; particularly not when the man was unable to fight back.

Nor could he blame O'Dion too much for the trick, or the manner in which he'd worked it. Tonight, it was more than Quirt or Slash which was on the board. Their lives topped the gamble, and when the stakes were the sky, all limits were off.

His anger had become brittle as he overtook O'Dion, his horse sweeping alongside. He leaned to grab at the bridle, and again O'Dion spurred, driving his cayuse to a frenzy, sending it rearing, almost breaking loose. Allowing his own horse its head, Gordon grabbed his gun again. Twisting, about, he smashed hard with the barrel.

The clubbed steel caught O'Dion on the skull, raking down along his cheek, leaving a livid track. O'Dion slumped, the fight gone out of him. Drake pulled to a halt to stare.

"You killed him?" he asked.

"I wouldn't much mind if I had," Gordon growled. The pain along his thigh was subsiding to short and savage jolts, but the leg would remain sore for days to come. By the time they returned to the road, O'Dion was able to hold himself erect, riding in sullen silence. When he broke it, his words were baleful.

"They that take the sword shall perish by the sword. So it is written. This now has become a personal matter between us."

Gordon did not bother to reply. He was listening to a new sound, faint but increasing. The others caught it also, and Drake's face showed concern.

Other riders were abroad, despite the hour—many of them, judging from the muted jingle of bridle bits and the soft thud of hoofs. Men were coming up the road from the south, about to top the slope, and would be upon them almost without warning.

Drake's face smoothed with sudden relief. "Luck's with us!" he breathed. "It's our missing crew! That was Lomax's voice!"

16

There was no mistaking the voice. A grating quality set it apart from most others, as though rust had crept into the vocal cords, rust which might be improved by a drop of oil. The tone and words matched.

"When it comes to that, I cut my eyeteeth on the trail from Texas to Arizona, and I was weaned on Chisum's road. I can ride to hell and back if I have to—which is not to say that I like to."

Drake's face was relaxing, widening to a grin. It hung, wide and vacuous with dismay, as the others topped the rise and were suddenly all around them. This was a big crew who rode by night—twice too many for the missing bunch from Slash.

Lomax was one of them, and the others who had journeyed with him were there. On that count there was no mistake. But they rode as prisoners, and the men who watched the captives were on horses branded with the Quirt.

There was no chance to resist, none to make a break. Within a matter of moments, Gordon and Drake had been added to the list of captives. Almost as quickly, O'Dion and Yankus were cut loose.

O'Dion blinked, then slid from his horse, shaking himself like a dog emerging from water. He looked about, savoring the feel of freedom. Then he strode across to where Gordon was standing, suddenly helpless with his arms twisted behind his back and his wrists already pinioned with a tightly drawn rawhide thong.

"The way of the transgressor—" O'Dion spat, and drove his fist into Gordon's face.

The blow was venom-packed, savage with pent-up hate. Gordon pitched on his back, making a muddy splash into a pool of melting snow. With the same calculated deliberation, O'Dion drove the toe of his boot against Gordon's side. He twisted at that moment, so that his arm deflected part of the force; otherwise several ribs might have been cracked. While he lay, gasping and half-numb with pain, O'Dion set a foot on his chest and held him, staring heavy-lidded.

"That's what you get for hitting *me*," he observed, then turned away.

Yankus was no less vindictive, rubbing his own chafed wrists. "Why don't we string the pair of them up and be done with it?" he demanded.

"It may be that we will do just that," O'Dion returned thoughtfully. "We shall see whether or not that is as effective as certain other methods. In any case, we should await the proper time. There is a tradition that it comes harder to die at sunrise."

Sunrise would not be far off. The haze of clouds which had returned when the chinook began to blow were dissipating again, and it would be a fine fall day.

"How did you get hold of them?" O'Dion questioned, indicating the Slash crew with a wave of his hand.

"We had a bit of luck," Yuma admitted. "We came upon them where they'd camped for the night. It having turned warm and they being tired, they were so sound asleep that we had them before they realized what was going on."

O'Dion's mood was abruptly jovial. "They have the look of small boys caught in mischief," he observed. "But when a prodigal journeys into a far country, he gets took."

Chuckling at his own wit, he ordered Gordon lifted from the mud and onto a horse. Gordon had been wondering about the crew and their predicament. With Lomax in charge, they had turned back toward the Slash, while he and Drake had continued on to New Cheyenne. Apparently Lomax had taken it upon himself to swing again toward either the camp or the town. The reason no longer made a difference.

Soaked, mud-encrusted, his face battered and bloody, Gordon made a sorry figure as they again turned about, heading once more for the country of the Bitter Sage. Never had it seemed more aptly named.

It did no good to review the mistakes along the way; some, such as the last, had been impossible to foresee and as difficult to avoid. The total added up to disaster, leaving O'Dion in full control. Some of the Slash riders were still at the ranch, but it would not be hard to surprise them.

Immediate matters had temporarily driven other things from the mind of O'Dion. Now, taking a review of events, memory gave him a pleasant reminder, and he pushed his horse alongside Gordon's. Dawn was spreading, a sudden lightening of the heavier blackness which had closed briefly, as if to help hide the shame of Slash.

"I was almost forgetting something," O'Dion observed, "so much has happened this night. But the philosopher observed that joy cometh in the morning." He made clear his meaning. "There is the matter of that package sent out from the East."

At his order, the man who led Gordon's horse halted it. O'Dion himself dismounted to delve eagerly into the saddle-bags. Finding them empty, he scowled in angry disbelief.

"Where is it?" he demanded. "Now what the devil have you done with it?"

"Done? With what?" Gordon countered. "Should I be a mind-reader, now?"

"You know what I mean," O'Dion growled. "Where's the money?"

"Do you mean the money that was sent me, as an inheritance—by registered mail, as Eli Jenkins will testify—"

O'Dion hit him again, his fist smashing hard against Gordon's mouth, so that he reeled in the saddle, then spat out blood. O'Dion stood a moment, breathing hard, but he did not pursue his questioning. The answers, with men from both crews listening, were worse than embarrassing. They might even prove incriminating.

Again with a change of mood, O'Dion swung to view the horizon, which was beginning to flame in vivid hues as the sun gave notice of its coming.

"I smell the dawn," O'Dion murmured. "Dawn—and sunrise. But I might be inclined to make a trade—and if I was in your boots, I would consider any sort of a deal to my advantage."

Gordon shrugged.

"You've already made sure that I haven't got an advantage," he pointed out. "Also, dead men reveal no secrets!"

He thought O'Dion was going to hit him again, but the boss of Quirt restrained himself, conscious of the battery of watching eyes. Disapproval was in the faces even of his own men. Scowling, he climbed back on his own horse. For the moment, it was checkmate. There would be no profit in hanging Gordon, if afterward the money should prove so securely hidden that he could never find it.

A new notion occurred to him. Gordon might well have cached the package somewhere along the line of the night's ride. There had been chances enough.

"It's a long chance you're taking," O'Dion warned balefully, "especially while there are higher stakes on the board. And my temper is growing short."

Knowing that to be more truth than bluff, Gordon made no reply. For the time being the money was an ace, and O'Dion was too greedy to risk its loss merely to satisfy a personal grudge.

Yankus pushed alongside O'Dion with a suggestion, and a halt was called. Wood was gathered, cook fires kindled. It was still a long ride back to Quirt; moreover, the crew of Quirt were equipped with all necessary provisions, in packs tied behind saddles. They had been on the go through most of the night, as well as the previous day. Tired and hungry as they were, there was no need for haste.

The aroma of frying bacon and boiling coffee soon spilled tantalizing fragrances on the air. The captives were untied, with a single exception. Gordon was left with his hands still fastened behind his back, to stand against a tree and watch hungrily while the others ate.

"You have but to say the word, to enjoy breakfast with the rest of us; then you can get on your horse and ride out," O'Dion observed. "The choice is for you to make."

"The price of such a meal would come too high," Gordon replied.

"Were my own neck in the balance, I should count the cost as cheap," O'Dion contradicted him, but let it go at that. Gordon was boosted back to the saddle and the ride resumed, the other prisoners tied again. O'Dion was not inclined to take any chances which could be avoided.

"A man's errors may be pardoned seven times," he commented. "But there comes a limit both to patience and good-nature."

"Did you never hear of seventy times seven?" Gordon wondered, and O'Dion scowled and swung away.

It was full daylight, and the untrammeled sun seemed intent on making up for its aloofness of the past couple of days. It was not long before the horses' hoofs were churning the snow to slush. Here and there, tiny rivulets moved to form small streams, and puddles were becoming ponds. Bare spots of ground began to appear, lending the hillsides the speckled appearance of a turkey egg.

So peaceful a ride could not last long. Inevitably they would meet others who were using the roads, and with one crew riding disarmed and under guard, questions would be asked and, sooner or later, a challenge raised. Yet the chance of any serious challenge diminished with each accession of power to the Quirt.

Gordon, bound hands tied behind his back, dried blood and bruises marring his face, took note of the eager watchfulness in O'Dion's eyes as they rode. He was like a ferret, his eyes questing, darting back and forth, calculating, weighing, ever hopeful. The snow was a vast blanket, largely unmarred except for the trail made by the four of them as they had headed the other way. It was that which O'Dion watched, hopeful for any sign which might indicate where the package of bills had been hastily cached during the ride.

Several times the Quirt boss drew off, once to turn over a large flat rock, again to thrust his arm into the hollow of a tree, once to search above an outthrusting branch on another tree. There the snow had been disturbed, a large chunk falling. O'Dion's failure to find what he sought did nothing to improve his temper.

It was mid-morning when they sighted another group of horsemen, heading their way. They continued to come on, with no change in pace, and O'Dion in turn gave no sign or order to slow down. The gap narrowed, vanished, and both sides pulled up by common consent.

Here was Slash, or what remained of the crew; they had been riding to meet them. Having heard of Gordon's escape from jail, they had waited for him to return to the ranch. When neither he nor Drake had showed up, it had been easy to guess where they must have headed, and why.

By the same token, they were likely to need help. The rest of the crew had set out to try to give it.

Now, faced by a crew twice their own number, they were standing their ground. The trouble was that the odds verged on the hopeless; not only were they outnumbered and outgunned, but Quirt had the advantage of hostages.

As though even that had not been enough, another group of riders were coming into sight, further to over-balance the scales. At their head rode Sheriff Lem Harder.

17.

Harder came on without a pause, cutting across open range, the horses leaving a sloppy pattern in their wake. The sheriff was no poker player, and an expression of triumph fitted itself to his face like a misshapen mask as he took in the situation, the overwhelming weight of the odds, and the hostages which Quirt held. His glance turned baleful as it fastened on Gordon.

He swung to join with Quirt, pulling up only when his men had become a part of the larger group.

"Good morning, Mr. O'Dion," he greeted. "From the look of things, you have done a good day's work already. I was looking for some of them," he added grimly. "So I'll be pleased to take Gordon off your hands. The judge is anxious to see him in court."

O'Dion was savoring his triumph, as a cow savors its cud.

"It will be a pleasure to turn the man over to you, Sheriff," he agreed. "I was taking him to town for that purpose."

Then, the formalities having been observed, O'Dion's patience, never long, grew suddenly thin. He swung in the saddle to scowl upon the remaining crew of Slash.

"Well?" he challenged. "What do you men want? You wouldn't be looking for trouble, now—or riding with the intention of aiding and abetting known outlaws?" His head thrust forward. "You're through, on this range—finished—you as well as your outfit. Throw down your guns and ride out, and you have my word that no one will interfere with you. But if you don't—"

He paused, staring challengingly at their leader. A new man filled that role today, one who had suffered frustration the day before and found its flavor bitter in the mouth. Larry Vick was leaving his law books behind for a while, shifting his trust to Judge Colt, because of his contempt for the man who had been shoved into a judge's robes. Somehow, he looked more at home in the saddle than in an office, though he still wore his rusty frock coat. But under its long skirts nestled a holstered gun.

He lounged in the saddle, looking from one group to the other, assessing the odds, studying the situation. Then, surprisingly, he smiled.

"I had thought that the storm was over, but there is still a strong wind blowing," he observed. "And while it's words we're bandying, I'll offer a bit of advice, O'Dion. Down Texas way they have a saying that it's a long rope which has no hangman's knot at its end!"

At the implication, O'Dion's face reddened. No one could mistake the lawyer's meaning.

"You may be right," he barked. "And some such ropes might well be put to use! Am I to take it, Vick, that you think of yourself as a fighting man? For your own sake, you'd better prove a better one than you managed to be with your law books."

"If it comes to fighting, I've learned to know one end of a gun from the other." Vick shrugged. "However, before anyone resorts to such drastic measures, I've a word for you. It should be enough. It has to do with tampering with the United States mail!"

O'Dion's face went from ruddy to pale and back again. Victory and triumph had seemed complete, and he'd temporarily forgotten about the theft, yet this was the one factor which left him uneasy. Now it was apparent that Eli Jenkins had been wagging his tongue. In effect, Vick was telling him that the postmaster had sent word to some higher-up in the department, and that the federal law was too big even for O'Dion.

As well it might be, O'Dion conceded. But the fool was overlooking one thing. A dead lawyer could push no charges, and once Quirt was in undisputed control of the range, Jenkins would know better than to voice even his suspicions.

In one way, it was not too bad. For days now they had played a grim game, in which Brick Gordon had striven to checkmate him without recourse to force, hoping to avoid a clash in which many would die. On that point, O'Dion had been willing to go along.

There was a saying that circumstances altered cases, and he was ready to accept that. Even a week before, he'd been eager to show his power, at whatever cost. All at once, he stood on a pinnacle of which he'd not even dared dream when coming to the valley of the Sage, the threshold of absolute dominance. From the heights the view was not only wider but different.

As overlord of the range, he'd be somewhat in the position of a country squire, and such a title carried respect—or should do so. The additional spilling of blood was a blot to be avoided if at all possible.

But if the choice was rule or ruin, faced with hotheads like Vick—then his course was clear. Whichever way had to be taken, he couldn't lose.

"You're a fool, Vick," O'Dion said cuttingly. "Did you never hear of the prodigal who wasted his inheritance? You should never leave your books in favor of a gun. But that you have done, asking for a showdown, so it's up to you. If you are eager to lead these hotheads to their death, it's your choice."

Harder cut in urgently. Affairs seemed to be building to the sort of climax which made him squeamish.

"As sheriff, I call upon you, all of you, to throw down your guns in the name of the law!"

Vick's face had lost color until it almost matched the melting snow, but his voice held as steady as if in a courtroom.

"Go to hell!" he returned.

This was it, and tension was poised at hair-trigger balance. Every man sat poised and ready, and the nervousness or over-eagerness of anyone on either side might precipitate a crisis.

It came whence none had looked for it, sudden and sharp. There was a rapped order in Brick Gordon's voice.

"Reach, O'Dion," he instructed. "And think hard, man!"

His hands were no longer behind his back or hidden under the skirts of his long coat. With attention centered on Vick and O'Dion, no one had noticed as he withdrew his hands, shaking the left arm briefly to free it of the loosened thong, nudging his horse another step with his knees, bringing it alongside O'Dion's.

Gordon's wrists were red and swollen, bruised and chafed, but it had been easy enough to close his fingers about the butt of O'Dion's holstered gun, to draw and jab the muzzle against O'Dion's back.

"Should I squeeze on the trigger, it could be a short,

quick journey to where Vick has consigned you," Gordon added, and the pressure of the gun muzzle was unrelenting.

Dismay and surprise battled in O'Dion's face. He twisted about to stare in disbelief, and met Gordon's grim smile in return.

"It was yourself did it, if that's any comfort to you," Gordon answered his unspoken question. "Rawhide draws mighty tight and holds as grimly as the jaws of a bulldog. But rawhide stretches when wet. It was your pleasure to knock me flat on my back, then to shove me deeper in the mud with your boot! But while you held me there, my hands and the rawhide were in a pool of water, where it soaked and stretched!"

It seemed as though no man breathed, and rage flamed higher in O'Dion's face as he understood. His own hand was poised, neither lifting in a token of surrender nor stabbing toward a gun which, he realized with a shock, was no longer waiting to be grasped.

He tried to calculate coolly, for either way lay ruin. Would it be more satisfying to go out in a blaze of gunfire, and not alone? Men who drew their pay gave loyalty to their outfit in return, and these men would follow him even on the long ride. They could turn the day to devastation—

"Here comes Eli Jenkins," Gordon added. "And someone's with him—a stranger by his looks."

O'Dion's gaze shifted as others were doing. No one had seen the little postmaster on a horse for at least a dozen years, yet now he rode, jerkily but determinedly. The other man seemed as little at home in the saddle but equally determined.

Jenkins looked around, taking in the position and condition of the rival crews, and understanding came into his face. Always pale, it was even whiter now, but he kept straight on to a position between the two groups before pulling up.

"You've lost already, O'Dion," he greeted. "Give up. Luck runs both ways, and you've had a lot of the breaks. Mr. Gordon's side got one when Mr. Struthers came to town this morning. He's an inspector for the post office, and he's here to arrest you for tamperin' with the United States mail."

"That is correct." Struthers' face was flat and as devoid of expression as his voice. "I will take him off your hands, sir," he added to Gordon, "with your leave." A pair of handcuffs flashed in the sun, clicking shut like a conjuring trick. O'Dion stared blankly at the manacles in which his hands were encased.

The fight went out of Quirt at the sight. There was much which they did not understand, but two things were clear. O'Dion had lost his gamble, and you did not fight federal law.

In any case, Gordon was in control.

The newly arrived riders from Slash were already at work, cutting loose their fellows. The men from Quirt, making use of their opportunity, began drifting away.

Lomax pushed alongside Gordon, his face showing anxiety as well as relief.

"Are you all right, man?" he demanded. "You look hard-used. But you made all the difference. If you hadn't moved as you did, everything would have gone up in smoke."

He was probably right. Gordon, in the moment of reaction, was suddenly very tired, and it came to him that the victory was far from complete. As though reading his thought, Lomax grinned.

"Relax, man," he said. "Everything's working out fine—better than we'd a right to expect. We've an air-tight case, even to the hides."

Gordon was beginning to understand. "So that's what you've been about, eh?"

Lomax nodded, not unpleased with himself.

"I got to thinking, right after we left you," he admitted. "You and Drake were going on, risking your necks. Why should the rest of us head back, just to get warm and take it easy? So I took it upon myself to turn about again. We ate some of that veal at the camp—and very good meat it was. Also, we got some sworn statements as to where they had gotten hold of the meat in the first place!

"Then," he added modestly, "we swung off and over took a couple of wagons loaded with hides, not far or from New Cheyenne but headin' off toward Salt Lake and danged if those hides weren't calfskins, with fres Quirt burns on them!"

Gordon grinned, too, beginning to catch the con tagion of Lomax's mood. Any way you looked at i these men of Slash would do to ride with.

"What happened to the wagons?"

We sent them toward Long Rain, but by the lowe road," Lomax explained. "It's a full day longer, bu we figured it might be safer. They should be showin up in town sometime today."

Not knowing of the transfer of the hide wagon: the crew from Quirt had remained ignorant that thei ace had already been trumped. With the hides, the cas would be complete, with no loopholes. Not that it wa especially necessary, except that Quirt, and whoeve assumed its management, would be required to mak full restitution.

"Let's get back to the ranch and have somethin to eat," Gordon suggested. "I'm hungry."

"You do have a hungry look," Lomax agreed. "Tha ain't to be wondered at, after missin' your breakfas the way you did. But if I ain't presumin' too mucl in suggestin' it—I'd say that you have other reason just as strong as your stomach, or maybe more so

or getting there. Like tellin' the good news to Miss
Mary—and Abe, of course."

Rewarded by a wave of color which flowed across
Gordon's unshaven face, Lomax chuckled and forebore
to pursue the subject. Drake, however, had a question.

"If I ain't being too curious," he said, "I'd like to
know what you did with that package, there at the
table. You fooled me as well as O'Dion on that."

"You mean the money?" Gordon roused from a
pleased reverie. He crossed to where the inspector was
preparing to ride with his prisoner and delved into
O'Dion's saddle-bags, pulling out the packet before
O'Dion's widening eyes. "It seemed like a good place to
put it for safekeeping," Gordon observed.

CHEYENNE

JUDD COLE

Born Indian, raised white, Touch the Sky swears he'll die a free man. Don't miss one exciting adventure as the young brave searches for a world he can call his own.

#1: Arrow Keeper.
__3312-7 $3.50 US/$4.50 CAN

#2: Death Chant.
__3337-2 $3.50 US/$4.50 CAN

#3: Renegade Justice.
__3385-2 $3.50 US/$4.50 CAN

#4: Vision Quest.
__3411-5 $3.50 US/$4.50 CAN

Two Classic Westerns
In One Rip-roaring Volume!
A $7.00 Value For Only 4.50!

"These Westerns are written by the hand of a master!"
—New York *Times*

LAST TRAIN FROM GUN HILL/THE BORDER GUIDON
__3361-5 $4.50

BARRANCA/JACK OF SPADES
__3384-4 $4.50

BRASADA/BLOOD JUSTICE
__3410-7 $4.50